Wicked Wives

# WICKED WIVES

*by*
*Gustine J. Pelagatti*

**Published by Mill City Press**

Mill City Press, Inc.
212 3rd Avenue North, Suite 570
Minneapolis, MN 55401
612.455.2294
www.millcitypress.net

ISBN - 978-1-934937-16-7
ISBN - 1-934937-16-9
LCCN - 2008929774

Cover Design by Andrea Horne
Cover Art by Betty Jane Devereaux
Typeset by Phillippe Duguesnoy

Printed in the United States of America

*Dedicated to my wife, Rita*

# FOREWORD

Beginning on October 24, 1929, stock prices on the New York Stock Exchange plummeted for a full month, beginning a decade-long depression that crippled the nation. By 1930, industrial stocks had lost 80 percent of their 1929 value. Forty percent of all banks failed, and millions of depositors lost lifelong savings. National unemployment rose to 25 percent.

By 1938, prices were drastically reduced; a new three-bedroom, stone house cost $4,500 a Ford sold for $500, a can of coffee was just 30 cents, and a loaf of bread cost a nickel.

Desperation permeated the air, and even wealthy families found themselves falling on hard times. The NYSE did not return to pre-1929 levels until 1954, and in the years following the crash, every dollar was coveted.

Desperate for money, a group of Philadelphia housewives found a way to get some of those coveted dollars. All it took was a willingness to kill.

# Chapter One

*Philadelphia, 1937*

"Lillian Stoner doesn't have female friends," Fern Rogers told Edith Adams at a society fund-raiser for Children's Hospital. At a cocktail party, I saw her get tipsy and then use her body language to mentally seduce another woman's husband. When his wife objected, she got a bigger kick out of humiliating the homely wife with a tongue lashing."

Edith nodded. "Face it. The phony blonde bitch is more attractive, articulate, and quick-witted than most 30-year-old girls and she knows it." Lillian is also irresistibly charming when she finds it necessary; married men are instantly overawed by her, making their wives Lillian's instant enemies.

Fern shook her head. "I envied her. At fourteen, Lillian was besieged by an army of guys who wanted to date her. She could afford to be fussy."

Edith laughed. "You're right. I remember her older brother, Billy, telling me that she accepted Danny Dilworth's invitation to his Haverford School junior prom. 'So?' I replied. Billy looked puzzled and said he couldn't figure it out. Danny was a skinny kid with bad breath and a face peppered with pimples. Lillian found him physically repulsive and Billy knew it. But I laughed at him.

'Billy,' I said, 'you don't even know your own sister. Danny's a member of the city's fading group of aristocrats. Lillian loves those WASPs and their way of life. That's why she let Danny feel her up in his father's car, and that's why she's going to the prom with him.'"

At twenty-one, Lillian found a key to the Aristocrats' clubhouse door by eloping with 30-year-old Reginald Stoner III. He boasted to her, "Our members pride themselves on privileges of birth. My forefathers came from England, Scotland and Wales." He smiled and winked. "We've ruled Philly since 1670."

Lillian grew up accustomed to luxury. Her deceased father, Adolph Steinhoff, had been a devout German Catholic immigrant who'd made a fortune as a beer baron. Upon learning of his daughter's elopement, he was upset.

"You were born and raised Catholic! He shouted. "How the hell do you piss that away in a fifteen-minute marriage ceremony to a WASP?"

Lillian replied. "You taught me to think and act independently. Now, because I choose to marry a Protestant and live his lifestyle, you have objections?"

Adolph shook his head. "Who the hell are you kiddin'? You're not in love with that WASP Stoner. You're rejecting your heritage cause you're a white Anglo-Saxon wannabe. For some reason, you think those people are superior to us. The fact is, they were criminals who arrived on the damned Mayflower after being kicked out of England."

Initially, Lillian loved her house and the neighborhood she lived in. Chestnut Hill had its sprawling, WASP-owned mansions and its corresponding lifestyle. It was truly the jewel of Philadelphia. She was secure in maintaining her affluent lifestyle and bragged to her brother, "Reggie's family is a charter member of the town's elite."

Although Reggie owned a lucrative family insurance brokerage and a cement company, the newlyweds were not prepared for the economic consequences of the times. Depression had hit Reggie's businesses hard, and Lillian had been forced to take a mortgage on her home. Unable to save his businesses, even with the extra monies from the mortgage, they sold many of her prized family heirlooms. The Stoners now dined on cheap dinnerware.

On Lillian's birthdays, Reggie normally took her to dinner at the Ritz Carlton Hotel, the scene of their first date. But, this year's birthday celebration was strained. Sitting at their usual table, they sipped their gin martinis and stared at each other. She thought, *After nine years, I'm bored and he's anxious.*

Reggie planned on using the occasion to try and ease some of the tension between them.

"You know, when I met you, your lifestyle was so affluent: maids, servants, gardeners and a chauffeur," he said.

"I was the belle of the ball," she said, looking into his eyes. "Young society beaus became breathless, whenever I came near. Heads turned on any street I set foot on."

She paused.

"And then, I married you."

The insult hurt, but Reggie nodded. He promised himself he wouldn't lose his cool. *I've got to avoid an exchange of bitter barbs with her. She's becoming increasingly nasty as our fortune dwindles.*

"I admit our marriage hasn't been a happy one thus far," he said. "I'd like to turn it around." He looked at her with pleading eyes, but she ignored him.

"I remember bragging to my brother," she said, 'I've eloped with Reginald Stoner, a 30-year-old who controls an insurance brokerage business.' My brother objected. He claimed you were too old for me. Then I made the worst mistake of my life: I told him I didn't need Daddy's money anymore."

"I know. I know," he whispered.

When Lillian's father had died, he was still bitter. He left her only $30,000, and her brother the bulk of the estate, estimated at a million dollars. She had used her inheritance to buy their home and Reggie's cement business in an effort to increase their assets. But her decision backfired. People weren't building or renovating houses in the middle of the Depression.

And there was the infidelity.

Ten months before her birthday dinner, Reggie's mother found Lillian naked in a bathtub with an old high school boyfriend; they were both high on opium.

Reggie had demurred when his mother insisted he divorce Lillian. "For a marriage to survive, a husband and wife must forgive one another on occasion," he said. His mother wasn't as sure.

Several weeks after their trip to the Ritz Carlton, Lillian Stoner climbed the curved marble staircase of her stately Chestnut Hill home, her hands shaking, clutching a glass of brandy. As she approached the master suite, she could hear her husband's relentless coughing from inside. She shook her head in disgust. *When will this be over?* With a deep sigh she pushed open the cherrywood doors to the suite, careful not to spill the brandy, and entered the room.

Sitting up with his head propped on two pillows in a king-sized bed, Reggie Stoner looked like death. His once tanned skin was jaundiced and his athletic body was now reduced to the skin and bones of a prisoner of war. The Stoner's family physician, Dr. Masters, had been to the house the day before. His prognosis was grim. Reggie had one of the most persistent cases of pneumonia the doctor had seen in years, yet he refused to be admitted to Chestnut Hill Hospital. He told his doctor, "If I die, it'll be in the privacy of my home."

Though pneumonia was a vicious killer in Depression-era Philadelphia, Masters was baffled by the course Reggie's illness had taken. Accompanied by bouts of weakness and numbness in his extremities, Reggie's pneumonia sapped his strength rapidly during his illness. Some days it seemed he would pull through, when he acted more alert and the symptoms subsided. But tonight his coughing was worse than ever and he appeared alarmingly weak.

"I brought you your brandy," Lillian said.

"I can't...I can't drink...any more," Reggie's voice was halting and weak.

"It will help you sleep and Dr. Masters said it'll relax your muscles."

Lillian sat down on the bed beside her husband. As Reggie struggled to lift his head off the pillow, she reached over and helped prop him up as she placed the glass to his lips. It seemed to take all his effort as he swallowed from the glass. As Reggie lay back down, his breathing became slower. Lillian placed her hand on his chest and felt Reggie's heartbeat becoming erratic. She watched his eyes roll toward the back of his head.

"My legs...are cold," he said.

"I know," she said. "The brandy will warm you up."

Suddenly Reggie's body shook violently as he gasped for air. Lillian held his arms down so he wouldn't harm her or break any of the medicine bottles on his nightstand. Her own breathing was now faster as she waited for the fit to pass.

Reggie's body was now still. He had nothing left.

Lillian placed her hand on his neck and felt for a pulse as she had done every night for weeks on end. There was nothing. She leaned in toward his face and listened for any signs of breathing. Again, there was no movement from Reggie's tortured body.

Lillian slumped to the floor and cried. But her tears were not for Reggie and they weren't tears of sadness. They were the release of the relentless stress and fear she had been harboring for months. She gazed at Reggie's corpse and smiled. *You fought the good fight Reggie. But as always, you lost the war.*

Lillian rose and walked back down the carpeted steps of her home to her stately living room where a handsome dark-skinned man was waiting for her, puffing on a cigar.

"Finally. It's done," she said. "First thing tomorrow morning, I'll call the doctor."

He smiled, nodded and then looked at his watch. "I gotta get goin'. It's past midnight."

Lillian wrapped her arms around her lover. Now confident, she laughed with a release that surprised even her. Her mind filled with thoughts of a brighter and happier future.

# Chapter Two

Dr. Masters and Reggie's mother, Nancy Stoner, were engaged in polite debate in the bedroom. Reggie's sheet-covered corpse still lay in bed as an impatient undertaker stood by, awaiting approval to remove the body.

Masters quietly lectured Nancy.

"I've been Reggie's family physician and your physician for years. Trust me. I have full confidence that your son died of pneumonia. He had the classic symptoms. As a matter of fact, as we speak, a pneumonia epidemic is plaguing our city. If I had even a small inkling that this was a suspicious death, I wouldn't be willing to sign the death certificate."

The torment and anxiety that Nancy had undergone during her son's illness was reflected in her face. Bags hung under the eyes of the attractive 65-year-old.

"I see no harm if an autopsy is conducted on my son. In the last several weeks he complained that his alcohol tasted funny and that he was losing feeling in his legs." She let out a sigh of disgust. "His gutter snipe of a wife was cheating on my Reggie. I know. I caught the scheming drug addict red-handed."

Masters shook his head. "Nancy. I know you're distraught and bitter right now. But demanding an autopsy will unnecessarily delay burial and create emotional trauma and bad press for the family."

"Doctor. My decision's final. Only an autopsy will bring this matter to closure in my mind." Nancy turned and began her exit from the bedroom.

As Masters and Nancy made their way down the stairway, Lillian and her uncle, powerful Deputy Mayor Bill Evans, were waiting at the bottom to greet them. The deputy, a large man, generated a commanding presence with his booming voice.

"Nancy. Please accept my condolences. I know you've gone through hell coping with Reggie's illness. This pneumonia business is getting out of control in our town."

Masters broke the news to Lillian and Evans.

"Unfortunately, although I will sign the death certificate attributing death to pneumonia, Nancy Stoner, either rightfully or wrongly, is insisting on an autopsy. This death has now become a legal issue.

Upon hearing the news, Lillian quietly sobbed into a handkerchief and placed her head on the deputy's shoulder.

Evans did not hide his anger or disappointment.

"That's incredible!" he shouted at Nancy. "Why is my niece being subjected to the humiliating delay of a funeral and burial when the family doctor is willing to corroborate pneumonia as the cause of death?"

Nancy Stoner found it difficult to control her anger.

"Bill! Your shouting won't make me change my mind. My son died under very suspicious circumstances."

Evans shook his head. "First of all, mere suspicion is not the standard justifying an autopsy. Secondly, I'm sure a thorough homicide investigation will negate your alleged suspicions. And lastly, I won't allow the city corner's physician to perform an autopsy on my niece's husband based on your mere suspicion."

Nancy folded her arms and leered at Evans. "Everyone, including my personal friend, Mel Green, the publisher of the *Globe*, knows that you control the police department in this town and the homicide squad in particular. In addition, it's no secret that Lillian is your niece. Mel has assured me that if you don't allow the district attorney's office to conduct an independent investigation into the cause of my son's death, he call for the D.A. to conduct a grand jury investigation of you and your influence in the police department."

Evans shuddered at the thought of such an investigation. "Nancy, we'll play this your way. Then we'll see who wins this battle." With that, the deputy stormed from the house.


Tom Rossi smiled at the woman he loved, as she lay asleep beside him.

*Hope looks so beautiful and serene,* he thought.

A tall man with dark, classic Roman features, Tom struck an imposing figure. As first assistant district attorney, he was respected by his peers and trusted by his superiors. Today, though, his tired-looking eyes and slumped body belied his exhaustion.

He was about to playfully tickle the back of Hope's neck with his tongue
when the jingle of the phone shattered his moment.

*Damn*! *Who the hell's calling me at 8 a.m. on a Saturday?*

He quickly picked up the phone to avoid disturbing Hope.

"Rossi here."

"Tom, I need you to get down to the office as soon as you can."

It was the district attorney, Pat Connors.

"What's going on, Pat?"

"I'll fill you in when you get here," Connors said before hanging up.

Tom forced himself from bed and grabbed a pair of slacks, a shirt and a sweater. He blew a kiss at Hope, and then walked out into the morning sun.

Thirty minutes after leaving his apartment, Tom found Pat Connors seated at his desk with an annoyed look on his face.

Seated across from Pat was Mike Fine, chief of county detectives. Mike puffed on his pipe and nodded towards Tom as he sat in the vacant leather chair beside Mike.

"You ever meet a guy named Reggie Stoner, Tom?" Pat asked.

"Sure," Tom replied. "I've met him and his wife, Lillian, at parties here and there. Why?"

"He's dead. His mother called me this morning. She said he wouldn't wake up. Apparently he'd been fighting pneumonia for some time. By the way, Reggie's mother is a personal friend of the publisher of the Globe.

"I'm assuming I'm here because we believe differently?" asked Tom.

Pat nodded. "We're not sure, but we think there may be some foul play involved. Reggie's mother is convinced Lillian killed Reggie and she wants our office and not Homicide to investigate."

"Why? What's her reasoning?"

"She knows that Deputy Mayor Evans controls the police department. In addition, he's Lillian Stoner's uncle," replied Connors.

Mike nodded. "I spoke to Reggie's mother after Pat did. She caught the wife cheating last year. She also suspects that Lillian is having an affair with another guy."

"And that makes her a murderer?" Tom asked.

"No, but it's enough to ask for an autopsy," Mike said.

"Well, then we do the autopsy and figure it out."

"Evans says he won't allow it," Mike said.

Bill Evans's political clout meant that few things happened in the city that he didn't approve of. He butted heads with Connors whenever an investigation was getting too close to his personal interests and without his say it would be difficult for Connors and his team to get an autopsy. Besides, Connors needed Evans political cal backing if he decided to run for re-election.

"What's the hold up on an autopsy?" Tom asked.

Mike scratched his head and gave Tom a tired look.

"The deputy says it's too much for Lillian to take. The family doc says its pneumonia and that's enough for Evans."

Tom frowned. Evans was a bastard to work with unless you had something to offer him.

"Well, let's at least go look at the body," Tom said.

Reggie's corpse lay on a gurney in Room C of the city morgue. Tom and Mike arrived to find Evans and Lillian already standing near the sheet-covered body. Lillian stood beside Evans on the other side of her dead husband. She was sobbing and frequently held a handkerchief to her eyes. Across from them stood Dr. Masters and Dr. Summers, the city coroner's physician.

"Tom, this is Dr. Masters," Evans said, pointing to the elderly physician.

Tom nodded to Masters and approached Reggie's body.

"It's unfortunate to meet again under these circumstances, Tom," Lillian said.

"Yes, Mrs. Stoner, it is," he replied, too busy studying Reggie's face to look her in the eye. "Please accept my condolences."

Masters turned to Tom. "Pneumonia caused Stoner's death. I'd been treating him for it for the past few weeks."

"Pneumonia and the booze," Evans said, referring to Reggie Stoner's penchant for heavy drinking. "Don't waste your time, Tom. An autopsy would be an ordeal for Lillian. She wants to move on. Reggie deserves a proper burial."

"Mrs. Stoner, is that what you want?" Tom said.

"I just don't want him to suffer anymore," Lillian said. "He went through so much and he's at peace now. Please, just let him go."

Tom looked at Lillian. She was dressed in black and carried a veil with her.

"Mrs. Stoner, I appreciate your coming down here. I'd like to ask you a few questions about Reggie in the next few days. For now, I don't see any reason you have to stay down here today. We'll be in touch with you soon to let you know our decision."

Lillian looked at Evans. He nodded and the pair headed for the door with Dr. Masters.

Evans smiled at Tom as he headed for the door.

"Tom, our party is considering you to replace D.A. Connors."

"I appreciate that, Bill." Tom could only say it half-heartedly. He hated Evans and despised his affiliation with the political machines in Philadelphia.

Tom had been pegged by Connors as his de facto successor. Connors was set to retire in the following year and Tom knew that he would likely have to overcome a hand-picked candidate supported by Evans and his cronies. Evans would never support Tom, given Tom's status as a first-generation American. Evans was part of the old-money set with the Stoners and Rossi wasn't a name they saw as part of their circle.

Tom's parents had emigrated from Chieti in Italy's Abruzzi province in 1905, when Tom was five- years. An only child, Tom was the son of Julia, a former grammar school teacher in Chieti, and Raimando, a carpenter who found work doing day labor for local Italian-owned businesses.

Mike took a puff from his freshly packed pipe.

"I guess when Evans tells you Stoner died of pneumonia…he died of pneumonia," he said.

Tom ignored Mike and turned to Dr. Summers.

"Doctor, would you excuse us for a moment?"

Summers nodded and left the room. Tom and Mike both moved closer to the body.

"Look at Reggie's color, Mike. Hell! He was jaundiced and, according to you, his mother told you he had no feeling in his legs in the days before he died."

"So?"

"I've tried enough poison cases, Mike. Jaundice and paralysis are signs of poisoning, not bacterial pneumonia."

Mike shook his head. "Can you prove it?"

"An autopsy can."

"Look, I don't know if Lillian's old man got poisoned, but even Pat would rather not have an autopsy unless it's absolutely necessary. Why make waves?"

"I'm not about to abort a homicide investigation because Evans' feelings might get bruised."

Mike looked at Tom. "You have a helluva shot at becoming the D.A. of the third largest city in America. Play around with a powerful guy like Evans and you'll get screwed."

"Evans is a ruthless bastard, Mike."

"And you're a stubborn Italian."

"With guys like Evans, you take a stand or end up on your knees," Tom said.

Tom called Dr. Summers back into the examination room.

"Dr. Summers, did Dr. Masters mention anything unusual in his report on Reggie Stoner?" Tom said.

"Well, it seems pneumonia was certainly a factor in his death, but some of the symptoms Dr. Masters reported seem out of the ordinary."

"Like what?" Mike asked.

"For one thing, he reported that Reggie complained of numbness in his legs, and cold feet. Dr. Masters also said he was weaker than most pneumonia patients."

"You're not saying what I think you're saying, are you?" Tom asked.

"Well, I don't know that it's a poisoning," said Dr. Summers, "but I could test for some of the more common poisons like arsenic using a Marsh test."

The Marsh test, the doctor explained, was introduced by British chemist James Marsh in 1932, and would prove arsenic poisoning, even with only trace amounts left in the body.

"Can you do it without an autopsy?" Tom asked.

"No. I need access to his stomach."

"Well, then we're going to have to get a court order," Tom said, "with or without Evans' approval."

Evans re-entered the room alone. He nodded to Dr. Summers and Mike. "Gentlemen. If you don't mind, I'd like to have a private word with Tom."

The doctor and detective left the room.

Evans smiled at Tom while lighting a cigar.

"Counselor, my niece, Lillian, is the only person in the world I care about. Play your cards right. Agree not to recommend an autopsy. The coroner's physician and the family **doctor** will attribute death to pneumonia without the need for autopsy. And I'll guarantee you anything you want in this town from a legal standpoint.

Tom was shocked.

"Mister Deputy Mayor. Did you just offer me a bribe?"

Evans let out one of his famous belly laughs.

"A bribe? Certainly not. As head of the Republican Party in this town, I've a duty to see that our party nominates the most qualified candidate for D.A. I'll guarantee your future. You're a very bright lawyer. If you want to be the next D.A., it's yours. Or maybe you have ambitions of being appointed a common pleas judge, that's no problem. As a matter of fact, if you want to enter the private practice of law, I'll guarantee you receive lucrative city work."

Tom was angry.

"I'm not a gambler. So I wouldn't know how to play my cards right!" Especially if your niece has committed murder."

Evans scowled at Tom.

"During my political career I've tangled with many stubborn assholes. As always … I win out in the end. Think about that … Wop … before you commit economic suicide in this town."

Tom gritted his teeth and clenched his fists, but Evans smugly smiled, puffed his cigar and walked out of the room. It was obvious that Tom and Evans had declared war on each another.

# Chapter Three

Four days after Reggie's death, Lillian still hadn't heard from Tom Rossi and the district attorney's office. Reggie's body still lay in the city morgue and his mother wasn't speaking to her. Estranged from her own family, Lillian had holed up in her Chestnut Hill home, trying to keep out of the public spotlight.

Reggie's death and the delay in his funeral proceedings was drawing attention from a press corps hungry for any smell of scandal from Philadelphia's society families. Lillian feared the possibility of any unwanted attention. The last thing she needed was a reporter snoopin g around. But Lillian couldn't stay home forever. She had needs, and those needs pulled her from her seclusion and out into the Philadelphia night.

During the last year of their marriage, as Reggie's businesses failed, Lillian began a desperate search for money. The Stoners' monthly income had dwindled to nearly nothing, and as the money from their mortgage began to disappear, Lillian became frantic. She found a helping hand in an unlikely place and it was to this hand she went tonight.

At 8 p.m., Lillian climbed out of a cab outside City Hall. Careful to keep a low profile, she avoided driving to her appointments with Deputy Mayor Bill Evans. There was a good chance someone she or Reggie knew might recognize her 1935 convertible Ford roadster. The old, stone building was abandoned this late at night, save for a few lit offices sending light into the dark night. Lillian  stepped from her cab and  looked up at the statue of Philadelphia's founder, William Penn. Clothed in the traditional laced trim of the Quakers and standing on a pedestal at the north side of the Hall, he rose 540 feet into the sky. He was a constant reminder of his influence over the city's founding. Lillian looked away and headed up the front steps, trying to stay inconspicuous. *Why do I still do this*, she wondered.

Lillian didn't have to knock on the door of Room 224, the room from which Evans ruled over the city. She had a key. She opened the door and stared into the large space. Evans' office had paneled walls specked with photos of the city's most powerful men. An American flag stood guard in the far corner, a sentinel watching over the red leather furniture. A box of Havanas and a bottle of brandy sat on his massive desk.

Evans was not in his office when Lillian entered. She crossed the office and entered the washroom where she changed from her conservative, ankle-length mourning dress into a black set of lingerie. Her bosom tucked tightly into a lace bra, she slipped into black panties and knee-high leather boots. Her hands shook as she laced up the boots. She covered herself with a hooded, satin cloak and waited for Evans' entrance. Her breathing was heavy as she prepared to whore herself to her deceased husband's uncle. Their encounters made her sick, but Evans was flush with money and he'd refused to aid her until he had something in return. Reggie knew nothing of their meetings. He was too proud to ask his family members for help while he was alive. Lillian had no such reservations.

After Lillian had waited for what seemed like an hour, Evans returned to his office, sweat dripping from his neck, his face flushed red. Lillian had the distinction of being one of Evans' playmates. In return, he afforded her a healthy dose of cash. Tonight, though, Lillian offered up her body in the hopes that Evans would give her more than cash.

"Hi. How's my big bad wolfie," she said, her voice just a whisper.

"Hello, hello," Evans said.

"Is my wolfie gonna keep me safe tonight?"

"You know I am," said Evans, his hands rubbing his belly as though a meal were about to begin.

"You know my heart is broken, baby," Lillian said, "I just want to be left alone. Can't you do something about Tom for me?"

Evans paused. "I just came from his office," he said.

Lillian's smile disappeared. "And?"

"Don't worry, my dear, he's not gonna get anywhere. And the more you keep me happy, the more your interests become mine."

As Evans approached, Lillian watched for his reaction to her outfit. It was his favorite, and he licked his lips. Lillian may well have been a ham or a piece of cake.

*God*, she thought. *He's like a villain in a silent movie…a grotesquely fat, mustachioed, bald-headed villain.* Lillian found it hard to let the subject of Reggie's death go.

"Wolfie, slow down," she said. "Why won't they just let me put my husband to rest?"

"Let's not worry about that now," he said.

"But, Wolfie, I can't please my big man if I don't know he can protect me."

She slipped off her cloak and touched her breasts while Evans stared at the motion of her hands.

"Don't worry, baby, nobody's going anywhere near your hubby. They're on a wild goose chase. For some reason, they think you offed poor Reggie," Evans said.

Lillian stared at him. Did he know something or was he probing for a reaction?

"You know I couldn't do such a thing."

"Of course, baby," he said, "but they may need to be convinced, and that's going to cost me some political capital. I need to be taken care of, too."

Lillian smiled and pushed Evans toward the couch by the office door. She straddled his lap and began undressing him. Once she had him stripped to his boxers, she stood and playfully nudged his crotch with her perilously pointy boot.

"I insist you wear the little, black riding hood costume when we do it, honey," he said. "It prepares my fire engine to burn rubber as it leaves the firehouse."

Lillian stepped away and walked across the office, swaying her hips to put on a show for the deputy mayor. To help her do what she knew must be done, she filled a glass with champagne and drank it down quickly.

"You look like an overstuffed seal anticipating a fish for dinner," she said.

He reacted to her attempt at humor with a sheepish smile. His face dripping with perspiration, he stared up at her with the pleading eyes of a pet dog.

She walked back across the office and pulled down the deputy's underwear. "Let's see if this ol' engine still has some fuel left in its tank," she said as she went down on him.

When Evans was finally satisfied, he rose from the couch and lit a cigar from the box on his desk. He took his time with the buttons on his freshly starched shirt. "Lily," he said as he poured himself a generous snifter of brandy, "you always know what's good for your bad wolfie." He gulped down the brandy like water and stared at her thighs as she dressed, her skirt covering her narrow waist.

"You're still irresistible," she said. Lillian forced a grin as she reapplied her lipstick in the mirror Evans used to check his appearance before meetings and speaking engagements.

Lillian was somber. She dropped her lipstick in her purse and clicked it closed.

"Thank God you help pay my mortgage," she said.

Evans pressed a hundred-dollar bill into her palm and gave her the kind of grin a father gives a daughter down in the dumps.

"Keep your chin up, kid. I'll do my part," he said with a wink, "as long as you do yours."

She clutched the bill. Lillian had endured humiliation to earn it. It would cover the monthly mortgage payment and provide for food and expenses for a month. She could trust the deputy to keep quiet as long as she serviced him.

Before she left the office, Lillian decided to throw caution to the wind. She glared at her uncle.

"Billie. Let's understand each other. You promised me that my husband would be buried by today. You failed me. If you don't have enough power to protect me from the likes of Tom Rossi, then I'll have to find another playmate." Lillian raised an eyebrow. "One with more influence, who'll guarantee results."

Evans, stunned by her sudden declaration, was too shocked to respond.

Lillian exited the office. At this point, all she wanted was to get back into the arms of her real love. She yearned for the embrace of her dark man, her Giorgio.

After leaving Evans' office, she hailed another taxi and fled to him.

# Chapter Four

An hour after servicing Evans, Lillian's cab took her to South Philly and stopped a few feet down from the tailoring shop of Giorgio DiSipio.

The Avenue, as Passyunk Avenue was known, contained rows of Jewish and Italian-owned businesses and Giorgio had owned a clothier there for several years. Lillian wore her black mourning dress and nylons and she had her hair in a bun. She exited her car and walked to Giorgio's shop door where she entered to the sound of a bell. The shop was small and a bit rundown. The front was a congested work area, complete with a sewing machine, boxed cutting board, and a presser. Jagged strips of cloth and half-used rolls of colorful fabric littered the floor. A sign made of peeling, yellow paint adorned the wall and declared: "Clothes make the man."

Giorgio greeted Lillian at the shop's door.

"Hi, gangster," she winked.

"How's my 'merican society girl?" he said as he grabbed her by the waist. Giorgio was fond of calling Lillian "'merican," a term Italian-Americans of the era used to refer to anyone other than Italians or Latins.

At 40, Giorgio was a Rudolph Valentino look-alike with black, straight, slicked-back hair. He had a well-earned reputation as a ladies' man and a small-time hood. The stage for most of his extramarital escapades was the couch at the rear of his shop. Even before Giorgio's wife, Maria, became disabled, Giorgio was hell-bent on bedding as many women as possible. He had a special interest in married women, especially those with strained marriages. It was women like Lillian that were now funding much of Giorgio's lifestyle.

Giorgio met Lillian through a broker who had helped her sell some of her more expensive heirlooms. Always conscious of an opportunity, Giorgio had contacted the broker, posing as a potential customer. Dressed in his finest pinstriped suit, he drew Lillian's attention immediately when he entered her foyer. After telling her he could supply her opium, she began visiting him at his shop.

Minutes after Lillian arrived, she and Giorgio stood at the rear of the shop and sipped wine from goblets.

Lillian smiled at him.

"I'm in mourning," she said.

"Poor Reggie," Giorgio smiled. "A wife wins a few and loses the loser." His smile disappeared. "I don't trust this Tom Rossi, though," he said. "I hear he's the type of jerk who lets his ego prevent him from gettin' ahead."

"Uncle Billie told me not to worry," Lillian said, raising an eyebrow. "If Tom Rossi starts trouble, he'll handle him. Rossi wants to be the next D.A."

Lillian looked around the room, trying to put off what she would say next.

"I need some medicine, baby," she said.

"Come here, Lily," Giorgio said, motioning for her to sit on his lap. "I got some real good stuff, fresh from the craftiest Chinaman since Charlie Chan."

Lillian opened the drawer of Giorgio's desk and removed a bong and a bag. Desperate for an opium fix, she packed the drug into the pipe head. Her hands shook as she attempted to light the burner, but it kept going out. "Giorgio!" she said. "These damn matches don't work!"

He snatched the box of matches from her and easily got the burner aflame. As she inhaled several times in quick succession, a sweet scent permeated the room.

"Christ," Giorgio said. "I don't know why the hell you got hooked on this shit in the first place."

"Neither do I," she said. She leaned back into the couch, turned and looked away from Giorgio. The opium felt good. Lillian hadn't felt good without the help of opium in a long time. She was introduced to the drug by a fellow society woman who had recommended its use to relieve tension.

Giorgio shook his head. "What's going to happen to Reggie's businesses now?" he asked.

"Who cares?" she said. "His concrete business will go bankrupt soon. I may lose the house and God knows what else."

"Well, when am I going to get my cut of his insurance money?" he scowled. "Baby, without me, you wouldn't have anything coming to you. It's not easy to get someone insured without them knowing about it."

"Don't worry about it." As the effects of the opium started to kick in, Lillian became more relaxed in the face of Giorgio's anxiety.

"Yeah, well, how come you ain't come to see me since he kicked it?" Giorgio said.

"I'm a society girl," she said. "There are certain protocols I have to follow."

Giorgio scratched his head, confused. "Yeah? Like what?"

She smiled, knowing her explanation amounted to Greek to him. "Women must marry eligible gentlemen to be accepted. But if either a male or female becomes divorced or is embroiled in public scandal... you're ostracized."

Giorgio stared at Lillian. He didn't like when she used words he couldn't understand. "What the hell does 'ostracize' mean?"

"It means kicked out."

Giorgio smirked. "Maybe I'll do yaa favor and ostracize this guy tom Rossi."

Lillian's dress rose above her knees as she lay on the couch, revealing thighs decorated with a garter belt and stockings. As Giorgio stared at her flesh, his interests wandered away from the words he didn't understand. He smiled.

"All right, society bitch, enough small talk," he said. He pushed her onto the couch.

Lillian, serene and sleepy, began to peel out of her expensive robes. As Giorgio made love to Lillian, his mind drifted to the only woman with a stronger lust for sex than his.

# Chapter Five

Eva Bell Fitzpatrick was trouble in more ways than one. She loved sex, gambling and danger, and each in good measure. To Giorgio, she presented a challenge, and a good dose of worry. It was dangerous for Giorgio to be involved with her. She was married to Dennis Fitzpatrick, the man in charge of Philadelphia's richest sports book. Worse yet, Eva had a gambling problem that brought her to other bookies—bookies that wouldn't forgive her debts like Dennis did. It was a violation of Dennis' cardinal rule for their relationship.

When she met Dennis, Eva found the handsome 40-year-old Irishman all the more attractive because he had run the fastest growing of Micky Duffy's sports books. Eva took his hand in marriage in the hopes he would ward off her debtors. She liked men with money.

Eva met Dennis at a bar in a popular Center City club, The Golden Dawn.

"I like action," she said to him over their first drink: a Manhattan he had paid for. "Horses, cards, numbers, I like anything with a big payoff. I'm a thoroughbred, sir. Can you tame one of those?"

Dennis didn't flinch.

"Who knows?" he said. "With me as your trainer, we might even win the Triple Crown."

In March of '33, at 34-years-old, Eva married Dennis. Giorgio had broken her heart when he told her he wouldn't leave his wife to be with her. He had traits Dennis lacked and Eva longed for him. He was strong and passionate and, at times, downright terrifying. But Eva loved her tailor. Giorgio's fiery disposition excited her. She married Dennis in part to make him jealous, hoping it would convince him to leave his bedridden wife. But luck never smiled on her.

Dennis placed only one condition on their union: "If you have to gamble, place your bets with me and only me," he told her. "I don't want everybody in South Philly to know what you're doing."

"No problem," she said, flashing him a smile. "I would never disobey my hubby."

Eva couldn't stand to have Dennis know the degree of her gambling problem. In February 1937, Seabiscuit's entry in the Santa Anita Handicap in Aradia, California got the nation excited. Eva, swept up in the excitement, told Nicky "Fits" Grande a mob bookie and loan shark, "I want fifteen hundred on Biscuit to win."

Nicky refused at first, afraid of taking action from Dennis Fitzpatrick's wife.

"Ya nuts or somethin'?" he asked. "If ya lose, ya gotta sell your row house to pay off the debt. And your husband ain't gonna like it."

Eva had her mind set on laying it all down and Nicky couldn't pass on the action.

"Don't worry about it," she said. "Book it."

A few hours after she placed the bet, Eva found herself biting her fingernails in her kitchen as she listened intently to what the radio announcer described as "a very close race."

Afraid of what might happen if she lost, she gulped down two glasses of wine between the race's start and finish.

"The horses are in the stretch," the announcer said, his voice crackling over the airwaves. "Seabiscuit and Rosemont are neck and neck. Seabiscuit is pulling ahead slightly as they charge the finish line! And the winner is ... hold your tickets ... it's a photo finish!"

Then, with Eva sweating out the wine, the results were in. "Ladies and gentlemen," shouted the announcer, "Rosemont has been declared the winner."

"Shit! Shit! Shit," Eva screamed.

A rumbling sounded in the pit of her belly. Eva vomited in the kitchen sink. Desperate to hide her mistake, she turned to Giorgio for help. It was then that Giorgio saw an opportunity to solve two problems in one. He could rid Eva of Nicky, and rid himself of Dennis Fitzpatrick. His mind raced as he thought through the possibilities to solve their problems, while enriching them both.

Two weeks after Seabiscuit's shocking loss, Eva studied her features in the bedroom mirror. Happy with what she saw, she thought to herself, *I'm still a red-hot bitch. I just have to use a little more blush and lipstick—maybe go heavy on the powder.*

Combing through her hair, she managed to discover a few streaks of gray.

*The lines around the corners of my eyes will soon be crows' feet,* she thought. As a woman who enjoyed her body as well as the bodies of others, she had to take her aging in stride. She said to herself: *Heck, men still turn their heads for a second look when they see me. As long as I can still excite them and they still make me wet, who the hell cares about wrinkles?*

That night, Eva was getting ready for an early dinner date with Giorgio at a small restaurant in Center City and the low-cut orange polka dot dress she wore said volumes about what she had on her mind, as did her tiny, elephant tusk necklace. The pendant was carved from basalt and capped in gold. Other than her wedding ring, it represented the only piece of jewelry she ever wore. It was a 100-year-old family heirloom. Her mother had given Eva the necklace to ward off attacks from "the evil eye" and to bring good luck. But the good luck part hadn't been too effective. She knew Fits would turn up looking for his money soon. And she knew from word on the street he had no problems hurting a lady, especially considering her large debt.

Giorgio had an intense hatred for Nicky. He was in good with the Lenzetti mob, and Giorgio's past with the mob was filled with the resentment surrounding his father's death at the hands of the

Mafia, and his own failure at becoming anything more than a low-level hood.

The doorbell rang. Eva went to answer it, and as she pulled the door back from the frame she saw the last face she wanted to see: "Fits" Grande. He dressed in a typically gangster motif: pinstriped suit, shirt, fedora, pointy shoes and a diamond stick pin in his tie. She tried to close the door, but he forced his way through. He grabbed her by the breasts, squeezed and then pushed her to the floor. Nicky slammed the door shut behind him, and locked it.

"Nicky!" she cried, "I called."

"Ya took fifteen hundred bucks in credit to bet on Biscuit," he began, his voice booming over hers. "Now ya owe me big time, Eva."

Her mind raced faster than the horses that had gotten her to this point. Eva knew men like Fits. She knew what he was capable of. Eva believed men had a weakness, and for most of them it was the same. She moved her eyes toward his crotch and forced a grin. Her hand began to reach for his fly as she tested the waters.

"Look, I can get the money, but I figured…"

With one hand, Nicky grabbed her wrist before she could get to his crotch. He used his other hand to snatch the back of her hair and then pulled Eva onto her knees. "Better broads got worse for trying the same shit," he said.

He reached behind him and pulled out a long-barreled .38 caliber pistol.

"Open your mouth, whore."

Eva's jaw trembled as Nicky slid the steel between her teeth. As he placed the pistol in her mouth, he snatched the tusk necklace off her neck with his free hand. As he threw it across the room, Eva could see the bullets in the revolving chamber of his pistol.

*Jesus, this fucker's going to kill me*, she thought. Without warning, Eva felt her own urine running down her left thigh.

"You're a stupid broad, ya know that?" Fits said. "This tusk ain't gonna bring ya no luck. You got one week to get the dough or I'm gonna make you look so bad your husband will have to put ya in the Philly Zoo with the rest of the animals." He removed the barrel from her mouth and punched her hard in the face. Blood poured from her nose.

Nicky saw the pool of piss forming beneath her and grinned.

"I guess I put the fear of God in you, Eva," he said. "Get me my money."

Nicky opened the door and left.

Eva lay on the floor sobbing. Her nose throbbed as she saw a myriad of flashing colored lights. A few moments later, she was able to stand and made her way to the closest mirror. She flinched at the damage. The orbit of her right eye was red and swollen.

"Nicky! You bastard! When I'm finished with you, they won't be able to put you in a damn zoo…they'll put you in a fuckin' coffin."

Eva got a piece of steak from her icebox and pressed it against her eye, then tilted her head back until the nosebleed stopped. After five minutes, she rushed upstairs to her bedroom to change into something clean. She wondered if she'd still be able to meet Giorgio. As she stared into the mirror, though, she realized it would be impossible. No amount of make-up could possibly begin to cover the purple, puffy sack of skin covering her eye. She placed more ice in a washcloth, placed it over her eye and lay in bed, crying herself to sleep.

# Chapter Six

The evening after Eva's run-in with Nicky, Dennis Fitzpatrick sat at the kitchen table in their row house. Fitzpatrick had spent the night and the following day working and hadn't yet seen the damage to his wife's eye. He called up to Eva, "Come down here, babe. I got something important to talk about."

Eva was anxious as she dressed to go out with Dennis. She hadn't figured a way to hide the swelling from her husband, and she was sure he would ask questions.

She called back to her husband, "Be ready in five minutes." Dennis wanted to ask his wife for something special for they went clubbing. He knew she loved the nightlife—restaurants, nightclubs, the theater, movies and boxing matches. He didn't even like going to sporting events, an unusual character trait for one of South Philadelphia's biggest bookies. He considered most events to be a waste of time unless they were making him money. Dennis liked to eat at home, read a good book, or listen to his favorite radio shows at night: "Amos and Andy" and "The Hit Parade."

Eva put on her best smile for Dennis as she descended the stairs. She wore her red polka dot dress. Actually, she'd chosen one of his favorites, though she hadn't remembered when she grabbed it off of the rack.

"Sorry I took so long," she said. "I wanted to look extra nice for you tonight."

After three years of marriage Dennis still found himself in awe of the woman he'd married. He adored her and she knew it.

In spite of the country's economic depression, Dennis earned an incredible four-hundred dollars a week with his sports gambling book, a book he wrote and banked himself following the recent murder of his boss by the Lenzetti brothers. Refusing to work for the Lenzettis, he'd struck out on his own, always remembering to stay armed. But the danger he feared from the outside world was a distraction that made him overlook the danger his wife had placed him in. His wife had debts to pay, and her debtors would look to collect from anyone they could.

"All you have to do is show me your smile and I melt," he said. "What the hell happened to your eye?" Dennis grabbed Eva's cheek and turned her face so he could see her swollen eye. He was furious.

She ran a playful finger over his lips.

"I walked into the banister," she said, quickly changing the subject. "Tonight, mamma's giving hubby some of her special honey from the beehive."

He leaned close to her and kissed her lips, not believing a word she said to him. But Dennis knew not to push Eva for answers. She still had secrets and he had learned to find out what he needed to know from other sources. That night he would have his men pound the pavement to find out who hit his wife and why. Despite his breath reeking of whisky and smoke, Eva sucked on his lower lip, letting her eyelashes caress the roughness of his cheeks. She whispered, "I love you, hubby."

"Ditto, baby," he replied, looking into her gray eyes. "But I don't want to pull out anymore. We've been married three years and, well...my Irish Catholic friends wonder if... if I'm queer...'cause we don't have kids."

Eva had refused Dennis' push for kids since day one.

"Like I said," she whispered, "mamma's going to give her hubby everything he deserves."

"Really?"

"Really," she replied, grinning seductively.

"I don't understand," he said. "You always told me keeping your figure meant more to you than having babies."

"I've changed my mind. My hubby gets what he wants."

Dennis's face came alive. Then he pulled his woman into a tight embrace and kissed her. "I'm giving you triplets tonight!"

She smiled and blew him a kiss. "I forgot my necklace. Go start the car and I'll be out in a few seconds."

They exchanged smiles as he opened the front door and left. Dennis was still smiling as he walked to his car, parked only a few houses down.

Upstairs, Eva admired her heirloom necklace, the one Dennis swore he would flush down a toilet the first time he got the chance. He didn't believe in trinkets, only the virtues of hard work and perseverance. "Hard work's why I'm only one of three families on the block who can afford an automobile in 1937," he told her. "Hell, my Chrysler Imperial 80 is a sign of my success."

Dennis couldn't wait to tell Mom and the guys. Eva had agreed to have a baby. Just as he turned the ignition, he noticed a smudge on the driver-side mirror. He thought of taking a handkerchief to wipe it clean. It was the last thought he ever had. His car exploded.

Eva stood safely in her bedroom to shield herself from any loose shrapnel and flying window glass. She stared at the burning fragments of her husband's corpse sitting behind the wheel of a blazing inferno. "Like I said, mamma's going to give hubby everything he deserves. Die, you boring bastard!"

As she mixed herself a gin martini, she smiled to herself. *Act One is over*, she thought. *Now for the finale.*

News of the murder would spread quickly through the city, reaching Tom Rossi just before he joined his own lover for dinner.

# Chapter Seven

A sign above the bar read, "VENICE LOUNGE." As usual, the place was half empty during the evening. During lunch and cocktail hours, anyone from City Hall who thought himself important patronized the Italian restaurant and bar, located two blocks east of City Hall. Judges, lawyers, politicians, cops, and City Hall workers all competed to be seen.

Tom, now aware of Dennis Fitzpatrick's death, sat at a table with Hope Daniels, an attractive brunette with Latino features and deep-set green eyes. A registered nurse, Hope had a well-paying job as one of the head nurses in the maternity ward of the city-owned Philadelphia General Hospital. She was beautiful, whip-smart, and spoke fluent Italian. Having grown up in Philadelphia's South Central neighborhoods, Hope was a tough woman. She was slow to let anyone past her guard, but Tom had been able to reach her.

She held up a snifter of Napoleon brandy to Tom, who complied by raising his Dewars. As a toast, he said, "Happy birthday, baby."

Hope laughed. "Happy anniversary, honey."

They clinked glasses and sipped their drinks. Tom leaned closer to her.

"Are you wearing that Chinese perfume? It drives me crazy."

She winked and pulled him into a kiss.

Just as Tom and Hope were beginning the evening together, Bill Evans entered the lounge with two tall goons—a pair of "assistants" who only assisted in persuading Evans' enemies to see things his way. The deputy spotted Tom and Hope and approached their table.

"What a surprise," Evans said, startling both of them. "How is our future district attorney?"

Tom knew the game, and played it well. "We're well, thanks," he said. "We appreciate your optimism."

Evans suddenly appeared somber, his voice reflecting disappointment.

"I've heard disturbing news," he said to Tom. "Is it true you're still seeking an autopsy authorization from Judge Miller for Reggie Stoner?"

"We have several more factors to consider before a decision is made," Tom said as diplomatically as possible. "We don't want to make any decisions that would upset Mrs. Stoner without cause."

Evans bent down without warning, smirked at Hope, and whispered in Tom's ear, "I see you're dating niggers."

Tom jumped to his feet and stood face-to-face with Evans, fists clenched, but the goons got between them.

Evans shook his head as a sign for his men to step back.

"If you're going to play politics, Tom, you'd better get a thicker coat of skin," he said, "especially when you're dealing with the man who has your future in his big, fat hands."

"Bill, you can't intimidate me. I hope you understand that."

"And you still don't understand the game, boy," Evans said. His face flushed red. "Cut Reggie Stoner open and you'll see how bad things can get." Evans started toward the exit, his goons behind him.

"God, what did he say to you?" Hope asked.

Tom threw a five-dollar bill on the table. "Let's get the hell out of here before I get arrested for assault and battery. I'll tell you about it later."

South Central Philadelphia had been a pocket for black residents since the post-Civil War era. Prejudice among whites living in neighborhoods that bordered the black neighborhoods motivated frequent neighborhood incidents of violence. Hope had grown up in these neighborhoods—a light-skinned black that sometimes passed for white. Her family had been victim to the hostility that existed between whites and blacks fighting for real estate. In October 1849, a group of young white ruffians objected to a mulatto man who married a white woman. They ransacked his hotel. The *Globe* headline read: "Race Riot Causes Death of Three Whites, One Colored; Twenty-Five Hospitalized."

That mulatto happened to be Hope Daniels' grandfather. Born in the city in 1908, Hope was the only child of Ben and Sarah Daniels. Her father, one-fourth black, met her white mother at West Philadelphia High School, where both were English teachers. They purchased a modest home in a white, West Philadelphia neighborhood and became active in a local, white, Baptist church. No one ever knew of Ben's background and Hope's parents made sure no one knew of her African roots.

Roy Daniels, leader of South Central Philadelphia's 30th ward, was Hope's uncle. His colored constituents were mostly Lincoln Republicans; their forefathers voted that way since the Emancipation Proclamation.

Hope owed her position at the hospital to her Uncle Roy. In 1930, Roy sat in Evans' office with Hope and made a request.

Evans had already received word: Roy wanted a position at PGH for one of his constituents. The deputy gave Hope the once over and thought to himself, *Now why would such an attractive white girl rely on the likes of a nigger to get her a menial job at the hospital?*

Roy scratched his gray head. He nodded at Hope. "Mister Deputy, this lady is my niece, and I want a job for her."

Evans couldn't hide the shock on his face. "Er…you mean she's colored?"

"She's also educated," responded Roy. "She graduated Jefferson Nursing School. I want ya to fix her a job as a nurse at PGH."

Evans still found the request incredible. "A nurse at PGH?" he said. "Hell, Roy, we don't even have colored doctors at PGH. If I gave her a job, my white ward leaders would mutiny."

Roy nodded after hearing Evans' response. "Ya been givin' me and my people crumbs, Evans, crumbs which done fell off the political plate for years and years. Let me tell ya how it's going to be. The coloreds in my ward—and a half dozen other wards—change their party registration to Democrat startin' tomorrow unless two things happen: One, Hope's a nurse at PGH, and two, she gets to be a supervisor in a month or so."

Uncle Roy and his niece left the office. Two days later, Hope started work as a nurse in the maternity ward of PGH. But Evans remembered her face when he saw her with Tom. It was going to be the ace in his sleeve if Tom ever gave him trouble.


Tom couldn't have known Evans' plan as he drove with Hope to her house. They had planned to spend the night together there. She blew smoke out the car window as she gazed at pedestrians along South Broad Street. Unbeknownst to Tom, she had heard Evans' insulting remark. She had been living a lie all her life. No one in her social or professional circle suspected she had colored blood. She had considered leveling with everyone, including Tom, but the timing had never seemed right. She thought of the old cliché: The truth shall set you free.

She looked at Tom and cringed. His firm arms, his strength, his jaw—they all made Hope want him. But in Tom's strength Hope saw a terrible power. Early in life, she had learned that men are stronger than women and she bore a scar above her left eye to prove it.

Suddenly she felt anxious about how Tom would react to the news. She felt sure Evans would use the information against him during the run up to the election.

*That fucker Evans is no good*, she thought.

Hope had been treated poorly by men her whole life and now she worried Tom would abandon her.

Once inside Hope's house, Tom waited for her to return with drinks from the kitchen. He sat on the couch and tried to push Evans out of his mind. Tom's love of antiques made him take inventory of Hope's antique grandfather clock. It had been an heirloom in her mother's family since 1790.

The clock reminded Tom of their second date. They had gone to her house after a late movie. He looked at the antique as she poured expensive Napoleon cognac into snifters.

"Ever been seduced by a girl with green eyes, mister first assistant D.A.?" she said.

"Only in my dreams," Tom said. The prospect of sleeping with such a beautiful woman excited him.

Hope put a Satchmo record on the turntable and handed Tom a cognac as they began to dance in the living room, sipping their drinks while swaying to the rhythm.

"My philosophy of life is simple," she had told Tom that evening. "Heaven and Hell exist right here on earth. So, I grab happiness whenever I can. Speaking of happiness, let's see if I can get you to forget your homicide cases long enough for you to live a little."

Tom learned how aggressive Hope could be. She went on the attack, wrapping her arms around him. She ran her tongue over his lips and began to suck on his bottom lip. He smiled and pretended to resist, but she backed him into the living room wall. Both their glasses fell to the floor and shattered.

When she ran her hand along his crotch, Tom's heart began to thump in his chest as his cock swelled and lengthened.

"What are you doing to me?" he panted.

"I think you'll survive," she said as she dropped to her knees to unbutton his trousers. She reached inside and found the object of her search.

But that night was a long time ago and tonight Tom was distracted by Evans' comment.

Hope finally entered the living room with cognac in two snifters from the new set she'd bought. "So, I can't stand the suspense. What did the deputy mayor say to get you so angry?"

"He called you a nigger," Tom said as he lit a cigarette.

"I've been called worse," she smiled. "Socrates, my favorite philosopher, would say, 'You can't teach virtue to an ignoramus like Evans.'"

Her lack of reaction surprised him.

"Wasn't Socrates forced to end his life by drinking a poison?" he asked.

"Yes. They made him drink from hemlock."

"Where the hell does Evans get off?" he said.

"It's not as much of an insult as you might think," Hope replied, struggling to maintain her calm. "My paternal grandfather had half-colored blood. He and my grandmother were involved in a mixed marriage. Evans knew my father's half-brother, Roy Daniels, through Republican politics. Uncle Roy had the distinction of being the only colored ward leader in the city. Unlike my father, he had colored features. As a matter of fact, he used his clout to convince Evans to give me a job as a head nurse at Philadelphia General."

"It's ironic," Tom said. "A bigot like Evans does your colored uncle a favor. Christ! Politics does make strange bedfellows."

"You ask where Evans gets the temerity to insult me?" Hope asked. "I guess because Uncle Roy is dead and the deputy got me my job, he believes he has a license to humiliate me. Plus, he's going to use it against you."

"Why didn't you tell me you had colored blood?" Tom asked.

Hope felt uneasy. "I ... I didn't think it mattered," she said, stuttering slightly. "Does it matter?"

Tom hesitated for a few seconds. "I didn't mean it the way it sounded," he said. "My God, certainly not. I love you and you know it."

His answer didn't satisfy her.

"I wonder how you'll feel tomorrow, or the next day. How will you react when people learn you're sleeping with a colored girl? How would you feel if we were married and nobody would support you for D.A. and—"

He placed a finger on her lips and with his other hand pulled a gift-wrapped box from his jacket pocket. "A long time ago a guy named Molière said, 'Take love away from life ... and you take away life's pleasures.'" He gave her the box. "Happy birthday, Hope."

She ripped away at the wrapping and opened the box. Inside was a gold locket on a gold chain. Hope found an inscription on the back: "Love is life's pleasure." The locket contained a photo of Hope and Tom together.

He took her in his arms. "You're the only pleasure in my life," he said.

Hope kissed her man. She knew she loved him. But she also knew there would be a time when love might not be enough.

As Tom embraced Hope, he couldn't help but think about how her revelation would affect his chances for office. It was something he had wanted for years. Now, given his conflict with Evans over Reggie Stoner's body, things were bound to get worse.

# Chapter Eight

Chief of County Detectives Mike Fine looked tall, lean and mean. The gray-haired, bespectacled, 55-year-old had developed a cynical attitude growing up poor in a South Philadelphia ghetto. His Eighth Street and Snyder Avenue neighborhood consisted mostly of Russian-Jewish immigrants, who had migrated to America in 1900.

Years of oppression left these immigrants insecure, uneducated, and unskilled. They kept to themselves and rarely ventured out. When harassed by neighborhood street bullies in South Philly, they avoided confrontation by ignoring taunts and insults, just as they had in their native country. But Mike refused to be a typical South Philly Jew. He never backed down from a fight, leaving more than a few bloody tormentors in his wake. His friends tagged him "Angry Mike" at an early age.

Between 1880 and 1920, Jews were denied admission to clubs and hotels. Banks, law firms and corporations denied them employment. Skilled and unskilled Jews saw signs reading "Christians Only" outside factories. So Mike understood why after his 26 years on the police force, his anti-Semitic superiors had passed him over for promotion six times. When a would-be bank robber ignored his warning to drop a revolver aimed at the head of a hostage, Mike shot him. His police captain denied him a promotion for the "alleged use of excessive force."

As part of the Stoner investigation, Tom asked Mike to have his detectives do an background check on Lillian and her late husband, and they were now both eager to learn what the probe had revealed. Tom had asked Mike and his men to his office the day after Evans' revelation about Hope. He leaned back in the chair behind his desk and waited.

Mike strolled into Tom's office with his detectives Joe Horner and Sam Whittaker. Joe, the only black detective in the police department, had been a patrolman for 15 years before finally being promoted. Sam, Joe's former partner and a close friend of Mike's, owed his detective's shield to Mike's endorsement.

"Lillian Stoner is a society girl," Sam began, reading from his notes. "She underwent the whole bit: a lavish coming-out party on her eighteenth birthday at the Ritz Carlton, then pissed off her father, Adolph Steinhoff, the beer baron. Then, the old man died in '32 and willed his son, Herman, the lion's share of his estate. She only got about twenty grand—"

"But Stoner had money, right?" Tom interjected.

Sam nodded. "Reggie Stoner and his family were Philly aristocrats, but he ended up with zilch after his businesses went under."

Joe Horner began reading from his notes.

"Upon receiving her inheritance, Lilly bought their house in Chestnut Hill. Then, she bought Reggie a cement company. She drives a convertible Ford roadster, but he got around in a company truck. To his credit, Reggie made a decent profit from his business at first," Joe said. "Now, the story gets interesting. Reggie's mother told me her son loved Lillian. He allowed her to spend lavishly, but managed to pay his bills. They didn't even have a mortgage for a long while. A year ago Reggie's mother comes home one day and finds Lillian screwing some guy in the bathtub. They'd been smoking opium."

Mike quipped, "A pleasant way for bluebloods to spend an afternoon."

Joe added. "The mother wanted her son to divorce Lillian, but he refused."

"Is Lillian Stoner still on opium?" Tom asked.

"We don't know," Joe said.

"After discovering Lillian's infidelity," Joe continued, "Reggie became depressed. His businesses went downhill, the losses getting worse with the economy. That's when his drinking got worse."

"I'm more convinced than ever he didn't die of pneumonia," Tom asserted.

Joe smiled. "Lillian's hocked almost every piece of jewelry she ever owned, as well as most of her antiques, paintings and furniture. She also took out a big mortgage on the house. We think she and her husband were living on this loan for the past couple years."

"How have they been able to pay their mortgage?" Tom asked.

"Every month Lillian deposits close to 200 bucks, in cash, into her checking account. We don't know where she gets the dough, but she uses it to pay the mortgage and the other essentials."

"She's selling something," Tom said.

The men laughed, but Tom had a serious look on his face.

"My instincts tell me there's foul play, maybe poison. I also suspect the motive for murder is insurance. Starting tomorrow, Mike, have your men scour every insurance company in the city. Find out if someone insured Reggie Stoner and, if so, the particulars of his policy."

"Even if I use my full staff," Mike said, "it'll take weeks for us to complete an insurance investigation."

"I don't give a damn if it takes months," Tom declared. "By the way, Mike, when you guys investigated Lillian, did you assign someone to interview her neighbors?"

"Our staff has been so damn busy I didn't get around to it. But I'll put someone on it right away."

"No, I'd like to do it personally," said Tom. "I want to know what her neighbors think of our society girl."

# Chapter Nine

The morning after Tom made plans to visit Lillian's neighborhood, a black 1936 Buick pulled in front of Giorgio's shop. The driver, an attractive brunette, stepped out of the auto, but left the motor running. She dressed in black, signifying a woman in mourning. The veil of her black hat concealed her face. The potted plant in her hands stood about 12-inches high, and resembled white parsley on purple-spotted stems.

A man in his mid-50s, dressed in a hat and suit, sat in the passenger seat of her car. He looked very tall with gray, curly hair and mustache.

The brunette knocked once on Giorgio's shop door and waited. He appeared almost immediately. Giorgio took the plant from the woman, nodded to her, and waved to her passenger. He acknowledged Giorgio with a similar wave as the brunette got back in the car and drove off.

An hour later, Eva Bell stood outside Giorgio's shop. Although her husband had perished recently, she refused to dress in mourning. She wore a bright orange, low-cut polka-dot dress with matching pumps. Eva peered through the shop window and saw the place was empty. *He's probably in the back room, sleeping on the couch*, she thought.

She tapped the glass door three times and waited. No response. Eva scowled, and tapped harder.

It took another minute for Giorgio to appear, unshaven, in a wrinkled pair of trousers and an undershirt.

"Christ, Eva. What the hell you doin' here so early?"

Eva marched past him, heading straight toward the rear of the shop, disrobing on her way. She smiled at Giorgio.

"What the hell do you think I'm doing here?" she said. "I want to be with you as soon as I hear the roosters." Eva looked at the clock. *6:01 a.m. I'm going to play 601 with the bookie today.*

Giorgio let out a sigh. *She used to come at night when her husband met with his bookies. Now that she's free, there's no tellin' when she'll appear.* He pulled the rear curtains closed and put a Caruso recording of "*La donna è mobile*" on the Victrola. By now, Eva had shed her clothes. She stood, grasping the back of Giorgio's heavy captain's chair, and stared at the wall.

The look on Giorgio's face changed from indifference to fury.

"*Putana!*" Giorgio hissed as the sound of his belt thrashing her bare bottom echoed off the walls. "Dennis ain't dead twenty-four hours, and you're here lookin' for sex. Eva, you're a broad who ain't nothin' but a"—Giorgio's belt cracked again—"*putana!*"

She continued to stand, still clinging to the back of the chair. Red welts began to appear on her quivering buttocks. "Again, Giorgio," she gasped, "hit me again."

Giorgio obliged her. "You're a slut!"

Giorgio's belt thrashed Eva's bloody, naked bottom even harder. She bit her lip to keep herself from screaming, as her eyes became misty.

Giorgio dropped his pants, grasped Eva's hips, and entered her from behind, forcing himself into her.

Eva let out a loud sigh and spread herself open farther with each thrust as Giorgio's nails buried into the flesh of her hips. Eva frantically thrust her ass into Giorgio's belly.

She could no longer control herself.

"My God, Giorgio—oh, my God!" Eva shouted, her shrill voice vibrating off the walls.

Giorgio, fearing neighbors would hear her, stuffed a towel into her mouth.

Eva was the only woman Giorgio knew with the same instinct for survival as his. It was a trait he had developed as a young man in the sun-bleached countryside of Italy.

On a blazing hot day in 1908, Giorgio's father, Pasquale, was forced to put his life in the hands of the local Mafia boss, who rightly accused him of cooperating with the police. He stood in the blinding heat at the center of the town square, his head bowed in shame. Mafia soldiers surrounded the tailor on all sides. Pasquale had gone to the police in the hopes his information would get him a government job.

Don Vito Cascio Ferro, the local mafioso, conducted the hearing to determine Pasquale's fate. Don Vito stared at Pasquale, who wept, his hands tied behind his back.

In a voice spoken loud enough for all to hear, the Don taunted him.

"Only a fool bites the hand that feeds him!"

Pasquale begged: "Mercy, Don Vito, mercy! I have a 10-year-old son whose mother died at childbirth. I'm all he has left."

The Don glanced over at Giorgio, who clutched the hand of his Uncle Mathew, 30 feet away. Giorgio was not looking at his father. He stared at the ground. The Don didn't like doling out punishment. But he didn't have a choice. He had to set an example for all to see.

What happened next would shape Giorgio's life, instilling him with a deep sense of cynicism, and robbing him of his humanity.

The Don nodded to two men, who lifted the wailing Pasquale off the ground and tied him down in the back of a horse-drawn wagon. The wagon master tied a bandana around Pasquale's eyes and then drove off.

The next morning, Giorgio awoke to find his father hanging from a fig tree outside his home. A wine cork was stuffed in Pasquale's mouth and his head was riddled with bullets.

Giorgio never forgot what his uncle said on the day they buried his father. "Tonight, we'll flee for America. We can no longer live here because of your father's *infamita*." Giorgio was ashamed of his father and angry that he was stupid enough to get himself killed when Giorgio was already without one parent.

From the time he arrived in America, Giorgio was on the offensive. His goal was to get *his*, without any thought for the effects it may have on others.

Giorgio's upbringing was a polar opposite to the immigrant experience Tom Rossi shared with his family. The two men came from the same country, but their paths in life were starkly different.

The Rossis had determined that Tom would live the American dream, and they drove him to succeed where few Italian-Americans had. The Rossis insisted their son be an achiever, but also demanded he do so while maintaining two character traits revered in their native Abruzzi: strength, or *forte*, and gentleness, or *gentile*.

When Tom was 14, Frank Abbruzese, a major sponsor of immigrant Italian families in the Rossis' adopted home of Philadelphia, requested that Julia and Raimando enroll Tom in the South Philadelphia High School for Boys.

"The people who rule this city won't respect Italians until we have our own lawyers, doctors, and teachers," Abbruzese, known to South Philadelphians as *Padron*, or 'the boss,' had preached to Tom's parents.

The Rossis agreed to Abbruzese's request, and set Tom on a path that would lead him to the District Attorney's Office.

"You're lucky to be going to school," Julia told her son. "Most poor Italians would have you working a job by now to help out with the family."

One of only a handful of Americans of Italian descent at the high school, Tom excelled before attending the University of Pennsylvania undergraduate and law schools. Though the Rossis were unable to afford the education, Tom found support through The Sons of Italy of America, who made it possible for him to have an education through full scholarships.

Tom's classmates taunted him and his friend Henry with ethnic slurs, making their first year of high school difficult. Not a day went by when someone didn't refer to one of them as a "dago" or a "wop." Their mothers bagged their lunches, which usually consisted of Italian pepper and egg sandwiches, unknowingly drawing ridicule onto their sons because their food was different than the usual ham and cheese sandwiches enjoyed by the other boys.

Tom never forgot the look in his mother's eyes when he came home from school one day and asked, "Why do the boys call me a 'guinea'?"

Tom had grown up in the same years, and the same neighborhood, as Giorgio DiSipio, when Philadelphia was a swirling mix of immigrant tribes trying to find a foothold. Tensions were sometimes high.

Tom and his friend Henry experienced the same racism that Giorgio dealt with. On one trip home from school, Tom and Henry were splattered with eggs and axle grease. Before the terrified boys could clean themselves off, four local boys were on the offensive.

"Get out of our fuckin' neighborhood, greasers!" a local boy waving a baseball bat sneered at them.

"Guinea! Wop! Go home!" a redheaded, freckled-faced kid shouted.

Henry shrunk back, all but hiding behind Tom, as he glared at his tormentors. The bully suddenly sprinted at Tom, waving his bat. Tom gritted his teeth and angrily wrestled the club from him. With all the power he could muster, he swung the bat at the boy's arm. The bone in his arm shattered, bringing everyone to a stop with the sickening sound of crackling bone. The boy cried out in pain and fell to the ground, clutching his now limp arm.

"You bastard!" Tom now shifted his attention to the stocky bully.

The boy froze in his tracks, then backpeddled. Tom chased his tormentor and gained on him easily, his squat frame not built for speed. There was a sickening thud as Tom whacked him in the back of the head, sending him down like a domino. Now filled with fury, Tom looked up to see the remaining bullies vanishing down the street.

"Fuckin' cowards," Tom shouted.

The incident had almost caused an ethnic riot in South Philadelphia. Local toughs standing on the north side of Washington Avenue gathered with clubs and chains, exchanging insults with Italian pedestrians as they passed by on the south side of Washington Avenue. The sudden arrival of horse-drawn police wagons had caused the crowd to scatter.

It was an atmosphere that toughened both Tom and Giorgio. Now, the two Italian boys were grown men headed toward a showdown.As Giorgio explored Eva, Tom was exploring Lillian's neighborhood. He was determined to find Lillian's secrets, and he was convinced she had a co-conspirator somewhere.

# Chapter Ten

As he took in the imposing colonial and Tudor mansions, Tom understood why Lillian Stoner wanted to continue living in Chestnut Hill. It was the city's gem. There were manicured lawns and tree-lined streets with hand-set Belgian paving blocks. By marrying Reggie and buying a home on the "Hill," Lillian assured herself access to the highest plateau of Old Philadelphian society—the same circle that had granted Bill Evans his power and means.

From Lillian's doorstep, Tom couldn't help but notice the beautiful, brown Tudor situated across the street. Looking closer, he saw the blinds in one of the second-floor windows shut. Tom walked across the street to meet Lillian's nosey neighbor.

Before he could ring the doorbell, the door cracked open on its own. A frail, white-haired woman in her 70s stared at him through a three-inch opening between the door and chain guard.

"Hi. I'm Tom Rossi from the district attorney's office," he said, flashing his credentials.

The old woman nodded.

"Took you long enough," she said. "I'm Bertha Brooks. Come in."

Bertha seated Tom across from her on a couch in her living room. "Rossi ... is that an I-talian name?" she asked. "I read you're investigating the death of my neighbor, Mr. Stoner. He's a victim of hanky-panky."

"Hanky-panky?" Tom asked, trying to hide his amusement. "Mr. Stoner hailed from fine stock," said Bertha. "I knew his parents. But this Mrs. Stoner—her father made money by selling beer to the morally weak. It's why decent citizens convinced Congress to ban booze nineteen years ago."

Tom nodded patiently.

"In a homicide case you look for motive, then opportunity," Bertha said in the tone of an expert. "Once a week for the last two months, I saw a man drive Mrs. Stoner home—at night. He'd park his car in the street. On occasion, Lillian Stoner's head would disappear from view. Minutes later, her head would pop up again. Then, like clockwork, she's redoing her lipstick. What do you think? Were they playing squirrel?"

Tom bit his lip to keep from laughing.

"It's entirely possible," he said. "Do you know this guy's name?"

"No. But he drove a black '38 Plymouth. I never wrote down the license plate number because of darkness."

"Can you describe him?" Tom asked, taking notes on the tiny pad and pen he always carried. "His age, height, weight, or facial and bodily characteristics?"

"He's about forty—medium height, with black, slicked-back hair. He looks like the movie actor Rudolph Valentino."

Tom thought, *That sounds like one of Lillian's boyfriends, not necessarily a murderer*. "What's this got to do with the death of Reggie Stoner?"

"On the night before Lillian found Reggie dead, this Valentino character drove to the house with Mrs. Stoner," Bertha said, as though stating the obvious. "About midnight, I saw the two of them get out of the car and go into the house together."

*Bingo!* Tom thought. "Do you think you could pick this guy out of a line-up, or identify him from a mug shot, Mrs. Brooks?"

"Of course. I've seen all the Valentino movies."

"Did you see this Valentino guy leave the house?" Tom asked, hoping for more evidence.

"No. I fell asleep after they first went in."

"Thanks so much," Tom said. "Someone from my office will be contacting you very soon."

Later that day, Tom and Mike sat across from Pat Connors in his office. They couldn't wait to give their boss the results of the investigation.

"Chief, the plot thickens," Mike began. "We've been to at least thirty insurance companies over the last few days. Reggie Stoner was insured alright."

Pat smiled. "Has Mister Motive raised his ugly head?"

Mike took a puff from his pipe. "Lillian found an insurance broker named Phil Reardon. He processed four policies on Reggie's life, totaling twenty-thousand dollars. Each policy was written by a different company, without Reggie knowing about it."

Pat whistled. "Wow. How'd you find this guy?"

"A detective never reveals his secrets, Pat," Tom joked. "We've had him sitting in Room Four for the last five hours. He's already chain-smoked two packs of cigarettes."

Pat looked pleased.

"Good—but a word of caution. As you know, Evans has at least two of our assistant D.A.s in his pocket. They're watching every move you two make and reporting back to him. Don't leave them rope to hang you with."

The veteran D.A. rose from his chair, a signal that the meeting had ended.

Once inside Tom's office, they found Detective Joe Horner sitting beside Phil Reardon, a handsome man in his 30s, dressed in an expensive suit. He looked anxious.

Mike started with his bad-cop routine. He pointed a finger in Reardon's face and shouted at him, "You were screwing Lillian Stoner!"

Reardon turned white with fear.

"What? I ... I don't know what you're talking about. Look, do I need a lawyer? Can I ... can I smoke?"

Tom nodded at Reardon. "Go ahead. Light up."

Reardon's hands shook as he lit a cigarette.

Tom now took a turn. "Tell us how you did four policies for Reggie Stoner without him even knowing it. His signature got forged and we have the paperwork to prove it. Reardon took a long, hard puff on his cigarette then looked up at the ceiling as if God might deliver him. "It's ridiculous. His wife handed me the endorsements with his signature. How am I ... how am I suppose to know the signatures were forged?"

Mike stared at Reardon in disbelief.

"One clue could be that you never met, or spoke to, the man you were insuring. Secondly, it's a large amount of money and insurance companies won't insure anyone without a physical exam. So you had to meet him, at least once—unless someone else took the physical for him ... someone like you, maybe?"

Reardon lit another cigarette, forgetting he had one still burning in the ashtray.

Mike continued the attack. "You and Lillian set Reggie up. Then you poisoned him. You're going down for Murder One, buddy!"

"Hey! If anybody knocked off Reggie, it's his slut wife," Reardon fired back. "Me? I'm a Boy Scout ."

"Why would he be slandering a society lady like Lillian Stoner?" Tom asked.

Mike glared at Reardon. "Because he's one of many sticking it to the bitch."

Both men stared at Reardon. He had glued his eyes to the floor, no longer responding to anything.

"I've lost my patience, Mr. Reardon," Tom said. "Mike, book him for Murder One and conspiracy to commit murder."

Mike stood and pulled out his cuffs, moving slowly, waiting for Reardon to panic.

"OK! OK! I did it as a favor for Lillian. She told me Reggie didn't believe in insurance and she needed security. But I didn't kill him!"

Tom picked up the phone and pressed a buzzer. "Lynn, come in and take a statement."

Lynn Sullivan, 30, a dirty-blonde Irish girl with deep-set dimples, entered and sat next to Tom. She prepared to take a statement by shorthand. Lynn, one of the D.A.'s official stenographers, also served as Tom's secretary.

"Tell us the full story," Mike demanded, "with all the details. I like details."

Reardon exhaled a huge white cloud of smoke and slumped his shoulders. "On Fridays I take weekly collections from a few of my clients who patronize this dumpy bar called Big Bill's."

"Where's Big Bill's?" Tom asked.

"Kensington and Allegheny Avenues," Reardon said. "While I'm there, a guy named Marion Moore's drinking at the bar. He introduces himself and buys me a drink. Then Moore asks me if I'm interested in selling twenty grand in life insurance. Naturally, I said yes. He asks for my card and tells me a Lillian Stoner will call me."

"When did this occur?" Mike asked.

"Two months ago."

"How well did you know Moore before he approached you?" Tom followed up.

"I didn't. He's always drinking at the bar when I make collections. He knew I sold life insurance. Hell, everybody knows I sell life insurance."

"Did Lillian Stoner call you?" asked Mike.

"The next day she called. She made an appointment to see me at my office. Well, she turns out to be a gorgeous, married blonde. She asks me to get twenty grand worth of insurance on her husband—a guy named Reggie. But she said she wanted me to write it with four different companies."

"Did she tell you why?" Tom asked.

"She said her husband didn't trust insurance companies. If one got all the business, it might go bankrupt—you know, the Depression and all."

"And it's much easier to get four illegal policies, totaling twenty grand, than one," Mike added. "But weren't you at least a little suspicious?"

"No. She gave me a Chestnut Hill address, so I figured her and her husband were loaded."

"Did you tell her that her husband had to undergo an insurance physical?" Tom asked.

"Sure, I had to."

"Well, we know Reggie didn't undergo a physical exam. So who posed as Lillian's husband?"

"I think this Marion Moore guy. Anyway, the next day she calls and asks me to meet her for a date at a Center City movie theater. We got settled in our seats and the next thing I know, she unbuttons my fly and gets me real excited."

Tom and his men were curious about the particulars but refused to give Reardon the satisfaction. Lynn continued to take notes, but her beet-red face belied her embarrassment.

"Well, did you or didn't you?" Mike asked.

"Hell. She's a sexy broad and I'm human."

"You still screwing Lillian?" Mike asked.

Reardon let out a big laugh. "After she got the policies, she says, 'I'm through slumming with you.' People think Lillian Stoner's a classy society lady, but she's a snotty bitch."

Tom thought Reardon might be telling the truth. "We're going to hold you in protective custody as a material witness for now. We'll continue the interview tomorrow."

Just then, Sam walked into the office, bent down, and whispered into Tom's ear. "Bill Evans is outside. He wants to speak to you…says it's urgent."

Evans, puffing a cigar, entered Tom's office uninvited. Everyone knew it would be wise to exit, so they did.

"Tom!" Evans bellowed. "I've been reading a lot about you in the papers lately."

Tom pointed to a wall sign. It read: "CIGAR SMOKING IS NOT PERMITTED IN THIS ROOM." Evans reluctantly snuffed his cigar.

"I'm sorry I haven't returned your phone calls," Tom said. "As you know we've been pretty busy."

"Tom, I won't mince words with you. I want you to withdraw the autopsy request on Reggie Stoner's death. The coroner won't object, and your political future will be instantly assured."

"I'm sorry, Bill," Tom replied, "but I'm afraid it's out of my hands."

"What do you mean?"

"Just what I said," Tom said, rising from his seat to leave.

Evans grabbed his shoulder and spun him around with a jerk. "Listen, you wop bastard! Don't you ever turn your back on me. Answer me … why is it out of your hands?"

Fueled by his anger, Tom exploded. "Lillian Stoner got one of the many guys she's fucking to secretly insure her husband, then another one of her boyfriends to knock him off."

"You bastard," Evans said. "The people you care about are gonna get hurt because you're too stubborn to back down. Your girlfriend is going to be fired because of your stubborn stupidity! I'll have her blackballed from ever getting a decent nursing job again. It'll hit the newspapers. Then, everyone will know. The candidate for D.A. is fucking his nigger girlfriend!"

"Burn in hell!" Tom yelled.

"Oh, don't worry, Rossi. The fire I have planned for you will be hotter than any Hell you can imagine. You have twenty-four hours for a change of heart."

Evans stormed out.

Tom quickly dialed Hope's number at the hospital. A female voice answered. "Nursing obstetrics."

"May I speak to Miss Daniels, please?"

"She's out to lunch. Would you like to leave a message?"

"Yes. Ask her to call Tom Rossi, she has the number." He hung up the phone and gazed out the window. People were roaming City Hall courtyard below.

Mike reentered. "What did Evans want?"

Tom continued to gaze out the window, not ready to look anyone in the eye. "Threats … nothing but threats."

Mike shook his head. "Well, maybe this is good news for a change. Marion Moore's on the phone. He says it's urgent he speak to you."

# Chapter Eleven

As Tom and his men searched for clues to the death of Reggie Stoner, Giorgio DiSipio was plowing ahead in his chaotic life. His appetite for women was fanatical. He tried to bed every woman in his sphere of existence, and once he had them under his thumb, he squeezed. Today, his web vibrated from the footsteps of a recent captive.

Joanna Napoli strutted down Passyunk Avenue holding a straw basket with lunch for Giorgio. Joanna operated a successful gift shop on the Avenue, a few doors down from Giorgio's shop, and she had been seeing Giorgio for about a month. She wore a bright, floral dress that pushed her breasts up and hugged her hips. It was a gift from Giorgio. Joanna used to dress in business attire: a suit-dress, blouse and a fedora. Her shop had been in her family since 1895, when her late parents emigrated from Rivella, a village situated in the mountains high above the Amalfi Coast. Joanna was working-class, and a stable influence in Giorgio's life. She wasn't rich like Lillian and she wasn't wild like Eva.

Joanna was introduced to Giorgio when Eva persuaded him to date her.

"You'll like her," she told the tailor. "You know her. She's attractive, 40-years-old with a baby face. She's a little chubby."

Giorgio laughed. "Ya mean the gray-haired broad who wears the rimless glasses?"

Eva gave him a devilish smile. "Just because she can't see doesn't mean she can't fuck. Anyway, she told me she's got it bad for you. Joanna would love to tie you up and sink her teeth into you."

Giorgio laughed. "Ya know, ya got me curious. What gives with her husband?"

Eva shook her head. "She's been married for 20 years and no kids. Her husband, Antonio, is 50 and crippled. She doesn't cook for him. He can't screw, and he spends most of his free time playing bocce with his friends at the park. He drinks wine all day, comes home tired and drunk and passes out."

"She sounds like my type."

Giorgio's tailor shop was only a few doors down from Joanna's gift shop, and the two had known each other in passing for almost twelve years. To Joanna, Giorgio was freedom. He was daring and handsome and virile, all of the things her husband wasn't.

As a way of introducing the two, Eva mentioned something to Joanna about asking Giorgio to make her some suits. Next thing Joanna knew, she was humming the tune of a Giuseppe Verdi aria on the Victrola, while disrobing to try on the tailor's new creations.

Giorgio peeked through the curtains to see what lay beneath the bulky suits Joanna had been wearing for a decade. Once he got a glimpse of her in her corset, he knew he wanted her, especially her huge, firm ass.

Ready to spring into action, he quickly placed the "CLOSED" sign on the inside of the shop's front door and snatched open the curtains.

"What do you think you're doing?! Are you crazy? I'm not dressed," she said, hoping her words wouldn't discourage him.

Giorgio was experienced in seducing women and he knew by the look of intrigue on her face that she wanted to be seduced.

He unhooked her bra and began to kiss her breasts, fondling the surprisingly firm flesh until her nipples were hard. She tore at his clothes as he struggled to unlace the rest of her corset.

"I hate these goddamn things," he chuckled. Finally out of patience, he grabbed a pair of scissors and trimmed the lacing away, giving him a full view of her pale white skin.

He touched the softness of her breasts and the rounded flesh of her belly. Giorgio and Joanna groaned as the bell on the front door jingled. Someone had entered the shop.

"Christ," he whispered. "I forgot to lock the front door. But it ain't gonna stop us."

As the customer walked further into the shop, he was greeted by the sounds of passion emanating from behind the rear curtain, Joanna's shrill soprano accompanied by Giorgio's loud grunts and groans. The young customer smiled. His new jacket could wait.

Everyone in the neighborhood knew Giorgio's habits. They called Giorgio the "Don Juan of Passyunk Avenue," thinking that his constant lust for women came from a love for the fairer sex. But Giorgio had a deeper motivation, one driven by the death of his mother. By dying, she had abandoned him. She left him alone. It was betrayal, and to Giorgio it meant he could never trust women.

Within a month of first sleeping with Giorgio, Joanna was captivated by him. To her, he was more than just a fling. He was a way out. *He's so handsome and charming. He makes me feel like a woman again. But there are so many other women, including Eva. And the attention he gives her, I don't know if I can deal with it.*

Today, Joanna decided to pay him a surprise visit and bring lunch. She entered his shop to find Giorgio standing over his boxed cutting board, adjusting material for a suit-coat. As he cut a pattern of cloth, he hummed along to the music of "La danza" on the radio, and his eyes stared aimlessly into space. He passionately grunted to the melody, "Ah! Oh! Oh!"

Then Eva's smiling face popped up from underneath the board. Joanna turned and stormed from the shop.

Giorgio didn't give Joanna a thought. "Christ, Eva," he sighed. "You made me cut this guy's new jacket in half!"

A week later, Joanna decided to forgive Giorgio, and again she went to surprise him with lunch in a basket. She entered the empty shop and heard opera music coming from behind the rear curtain. Suddenly, she saw a woman's leg protruding from the space between the curtains. Joanna hurried to the curtains and parted them. Giorgio, on his knees, was licking the feet of a naked, neighborhood wife. She was also one of Joanna's best customers.

Joanna offered no words, only the hot plate of penne pasta and marinara she'd brought for their lunch. She threw it all over Giorgio's trousers and the creamy legs of her former customer.

The next day, Giorgio showed up at Joanna's shop with a bouquet of red roses. He fell on his knees before she could speak.

"I beg ya to forgive me," he said. "I won't do it again."

Joanna looked down at him. *Please don't hurt me again*, she thought.

"How could I not forgive the 'Don Juan of Passyunk Avenue?'" she said.

*I can't wait to be married to Giorgio. I need him to take me away from Antonio. I can't live this life anymore.*

She shook a finger at him. "I forgive you. But I warn you, no more girlfriends!"

Giorgio came to his feet and gave Joanna a kiss. "I gotta meet a customer at the shop, but I'll see ya around six tonight."

Joanna watched Giorgio walk towards his own shop door. She saw him waving to someone inside. He entered, closed the door behind him and flipped his "OPEN" sign to "CLOSED."

*Why is he closing at two in the afternoon?* she wondered.

Joanna walked down the street to investigate. When she looked through Giorgio's front window, her knees buckled. Behind the partially closed curtains, she could see a woman she recognized as Rose Grady, naked and kissing the man who had just come to beg her for forgiveness.

Joanna walked back to her shop. She was hysterical by the time she reached the door. She dropped to her knees and made the sign of the cross. "I beg the Lord Almighty, help!"

To Joanna, Giorgio meant a chance at a permanent escape from the rut she was in. Her marriage was loveless. Antonio offered her no passion, no excitement and no support. She was alone and struggling for air. To Giorgio, Joanna was another woman with too many needs. He was able to convince her that he still wanted her but their relationship became strained. Joanna wanted more than he could give.

# Chapter Twelve

Giorgio tired of hearing Joanna complain about her husband and their lack of passion.

"Ya gotta see one of my insurance buddies, Joanna," he told her. "He'll get you a secret policy on Antonio's life, and you can end your nightmare."

She knew by his tone what he meant.

"Then what?" she asked.

"One night, when your husband's asleep, you shoot him with this .32," Giorgio said, showing her the revolver. "Then you call the cops and tell 'em a burglar did it while you were in the tub."

The color escaped Joanna's face. She didn't love Antonio, but she didn't want to kill him either. Though she had dreamed of his death many times, she wasn't a murderer.

"Giorgio, I thought if I divorced Antonio you were going to leave your wife."

Giorgio let out a deep sigh. "Joanna, Antonio will never divorce you. He doesn't make any money of his own, and you let him live on easy street. He uses your money to buy booze, and your money to spend time with his useless pals. This is the only way."

"Giorgio, promise me you'll be with just me."

"I promise, baby," Giorgio said.

"And what do we do with the insurance money?" she asked. "It would be enough to move away from here and start over with." Joanna couldn't hide the hope in her voice.

"I divorce my wife, marry you and we buy a house in the suburbs."

Joanna cried. He had given her the perfect answer.


Giorgio didn't know that Phil Reardon was in protective custody. When he couldn't reach Reardon, he went to someone else, and soon Antonio was worth more dead than alive.

Giorgio had a broker write two policies on Antonio's life: $3,000 for Joanna and $1,500 for him; the tailor had his friend issue a policy listing Giorgio as Antonio's nephew.

Two days later, Antonio came home from the park. He was drunk, as usual, and he went to bed and fell into a sound sleep. When he started to snore, Joanna entered the bedroom and pointed the .32 at his head. She was breathing hard and praying to herself. She placed her left hand over her eyes and pulled the trigger several times, but the gun didn't fire. Joanna panicked and tried again to discharge the .32.

*Bang!*

Joanna felt an excruciating, burning pain. She looked down and saw blood gushing from her fleshy thigh. "Oh, my God!" she screamed. "I shot myself!"

A neighbor heard her cry and summoned a police patrol wagon.

Joanna told the police she'd heard an intruder. They took her to St. Agnes Hospital for treatment.

The shooting didn't interfere with Antonio's sleep. He remained in bed, dead drunk and snoring, throughout the entire, futile exercise.

"Next time get the drunk with poison," Giorgio told Joanna. "Antonio drinks a glass of wine before going to bed, right? Lace the wine bottle with arsenic."

Joanna decided to wait for a night when Antonio had overindulged on wine and food. She didn't have to wait long. Three days after shooting herself—a mostly superficial wound that was healing quickly—Antonio went overboard. After he had eaten four dozen clams on the half shell with two bottles of wine at Maria's Italian restaurant, he staggered home. Once there, he drank a glass of *vino*, prepared by Joanna. He went to the bedroom and drifted off peacefully. But the peace didn't last.

Antonio clutched his belly and began twitching violently, his body racked with nauseating pain. He turned to his wife, who looked horrified.

"Oh, no!" she screamed.

Antonio vomited his clams, and the poisoned wine, on Joanna's body. He didn't die, and Joanna grew frustrated. She demanded that Giorgio help her kill her husband.

A week later, Antonio Napoli lay asleep in his bed. His loud snoring resonated off the bedroom walls. At midnight, Joanna attempted to shake him awake. He wouldn't stir. She gazed down at him, scowled, and then whispered: "He who acts like a sheep, gets eaten by a wolf."

Joanna knew her moment of freedom had arrived. She lived for Giorgio. *He'll change for me once we marry.* She walked downstairs, lifted the receiver of the phone and dialed.

"It's time," she said.

Five minutes later, Giorgio left the rear of his shop and walked down the back alley that ran parallel to the stores fronting Passyunk Avenue. He entered Joanna's shop from the rear.

"Is he asleep?" he asked.

"He's been completely out for two hours," she said. "Giorgio, I don't know if I can do this. Please, let's just forget about it. We'll run away."

"You know that won't work, Joanna. This is the only way we can be together."

Joanna followed Giorgio up the stairs to her apartment and they entered the bedroom. She handed Giorgio a glass of water, into which he dropped a teaspoon of white powder. He handed the glass back to her.

Giorgio raised Antonio into a sitting position. "Christ, the bastard's heavy," he griped, struggling to hold the man up. As Antonio slept, Giorgio pried his lips and mouth apart with his free hand and gave Joanna a nod.

Joanna poured the contents of the glass down his throat. Her husband gagged, opened his eyes momentarily, gasped, and then fell back to sleep.

Giorgio had never been so hands-on in the killing of one of his lover's husbands. But he was growing reckless. The money was too good, and he had orders.

The next morning, Dr. Testa, the family doctor, examined Antonio. He placed a stethoscope on the patient's heart. "He has a fever," Dr. Testa said. "With his chest pain, chills, and vomiting, he's being torn up. He's got a rapid heartbeat, too, and I'm concerned about the trouble he's having breathing."

"Will he be alright?" Joanna asked. "I mean, is he going to make it?"

The doctor shook his head. "I suspect lobar pneumonia. It's all over the city. Although Antonio doesn't have a cough, or bloody phlegm, not everyone exhibits the same symptoms."

"What can I do for him?" Joanna asked.

"Make sure he gets plenty of bed rest. I gave him an injection of morphine to help him sleep. Give him these sulfide packets three times a day with water. I'm also starting him on a series of anti-pneumococcal serum injections."

Joanna told the doctor she would do as he instructed. Within two days, Antonio died. Dr. Testa signed the death certificate and attributed the cause of death to lobar pneumonia.

Joanna cried the day of Antonio's death. Although she didn't care about him, she worried for her soul. What helped to get her through were her dreams of life with Giorgio. They could get married. But something about it all made Joanna uneasy.

*Can I really trust Giorgio? What do I do if he changes his mind?* Joanna couldn't sleep in the days following Antonio's death, despite reassurances from Giorgio. She thought about what she had done and whom she had done it for. Giorgio squeezed harder, telling Joanna that he was the only one who could still desire an aging widow like her. Joanna ceased worrying aloud. But her conscience grew heavy, and she started thinking about a way out.

# Chapter Thirteen

Eva Fitzgerald got on the phone to Nicky Fits. She had settled up with Fits following Dennis' death, but she had no intention of forgetting the way he treated her. Eva was a woman with a long memory and a penchant for payback.

"Hi, Fits, it's Eva," she said.

"What do you want?"

"I want $200 on Pywackit to win in the eighth," Eva said, referring to a race scheduled for that day in Florida. She didn't have enough to bet on the race, having blown through her insurance money. She needed Fits to front her the $200.

"You gotta be out of your mind, lady. That horse is twelve to one, and you didn't go so easy paying back the other race."

"Nicky, you know I'm good for it. I paid you back, didn't I?"

"Yeah, you did, when your husband blew up."

*Come on, Nicky,* Eva thought, *you can't turn down action like this. Come on ... come to mama.*

"Listen," Fits said, "I'll front ya the money this time, but you delay on me and I'll kill you dead."

*Yes! You're mine now, you son-of-a-bitch.* Eva was ecstatic. She took slights to heart and never forgot a betrayal or insult. Now, Nicky was in line for payback. Eva was wild-eyed.

What Nicky didn't know was that a pair of jockeys had fixed the race. Stevie Stearn, a jockey in the race and one of Eva's old boyfriends, had called her from the Sunshine State with a tip: "Bet on Pywackit to win in the eighth."

Nicky lent Eva the money and booked the horse.

"Remember what I told ya last time ya didn't pay on time," he said. "Don't make me come and beat the hell out of ya when you lose. Only a dope bets a horse at twelve-to-one."

"Maybe you're right," Eva said. "Maybe I better pass on this one. What do you think?"

"Look," Nicky said, "I ain't yer goddamn priest, yer doctor or yer lawyer. I ain't givin' advice here."

Eva paused for effect.

"Then I think I'll go for it," she said.

Pywackit won and Eva collected eighteen hundred dollars from an angry Nicky Fits. When he counted out her money, he bit his tongue and drew blood.

Fits always did his boozing at the Golden Dawn on Friday nights. He loved jazz and would sit at the same spot at the bar for hours, listening to the evening's entertainer. Around four a.m., as the band wound up their last number of the night, the phone at the bar rang for him.

"Hi! It's Eva. I wanna give you a chance to get your money back."

"I'm listenin'," Nicky slurred. He had been drinking Beefeaters for six hours and things were getting fuzzy. But Nicky never forgot losing a big bet. Never.

"I want Notre Dame tomorrow against Southern Cal, for fifteen hundred."

"Eva? Come see me ... later ... later this mornin'. "

"But I won't be in town later this morning," she argued. "Giorgio's taking me to Atlantic City."

Fits let out a sigh. He really wanted to go home and go to bed. "Well ... get over here now then. I'm at the Dawn."

"But they won't let me in the Dawn," Eva said. "I was banned for fighting with a broad last week. They won't even let me stand outside the place."

"What? Where the hell ... where are ya?"

"I'm at the corner of Carlisle and South Street, a block west of the Dawn. I'll be waiting for you." Eva hung up the phone.

"Goddamn, degenerate broad," Nicky muttered as he paid his tab. "I gotta get even with this bitch." He staggered out of the Dawn and turned right, stumbling toward Carlise Street. The intersection of Carlise and South Streets looked pitch-black. The gas street lamps were out of gas and people were in bed.

"Eva!" He called out. "Where ... where the hell are ya?"

Eva tapped him on the shoulder from behind. As he turned to face her, she plunged a six-inch blade into his chest just below the sternum, a perfect strike into his heart. The darkness prevented Nicky from seeing who had stabbed him. He slumped to his knees in pain, grasping at the knife. His hands were too weak to pull the blade all the way out. Blood erupted from Nicky Fits like lava, spewing out into the night air.

"I promised this, Nicky," Eva whispered. Her eyes were wide open as she stared past Nicky's face into the darkness. "Didn't I promise?"

"You hear about Nicky Fits?" Giorgio asked Eva a few days later, after the story hit the papers.

"No," she said. "What happened?"

"They found 'im dead on the sidewalk, near the Golden Dawn. Somebody stuck a

knife in his heart, then cut off his prick and balls."

"Terrible..." she said, turning her eyes away from his, "...just terrible." Eva smiled to herself.

Giorgio stared at his sometime-lover. *This chick is going to be the death of me,* he thought—*her or the other one.*

Giorgio stared at the floor in his shop and thought about the solar system of people he inhabited. Though he thought of himself as the Sun in the swirling mass of his life, he feared the meteor lurking beyond the light. The Lady in Black scared him. She was cold, and her companion, the Giant, could be a problem if Giorgio ever had to get to that cunt.

# Chapter Fourteen

Deputy Mayor Bill Evans read the *Globe* headline as Lillian sat across from him: "ROSSI ORDERS AUTOPSY IN STONER DEATH!"

He slammed the paper on his desk. "That greasy wop. Rossi can't keep his fucking hands out of things that aren't his business! He had to order a damn autopsy."

"What does it mean?" Lillian asked. "Are they going to arrest me? I can't go to jail … I didn't do anything wrong."

Evans shifted his hefty frame and rose from his office chair. He walked to his second-floor window and stared at the people and traffic on the north side of City Hall. Then he turned and smiled at his niece.

"Honey, you're the most important thing in this world to me. You're more important than power, prestige, or money. I'll do whatever it takes to protect you. Rossi will eventually make a mistake. Then, I'll make him wish he never set foot in City Hall."

Lillian's protection from Evans was beginning to look shaky. She worried she would be left out in the cold by the deputy mayor if things got dicey. Evans was a politician, and to Lillian that meant he was worthless if protecting her meant losing his place on the seat of power. Rossi was getting too close to her.

Lillian took solace in the planning she and Giorgio had done. It would have to be enough to hold off Rossi and his team of investigators. She was a careful woman, and in that she took comfort. She knew the same could not be said for some of Giorgio's other women.

Eva, lying nude after making love to Giorgio on his couch, smiled at her lover. "I collected two grand from Dennis' insurance. You were right. The cops thought the Lenzettis blew him away."

Eva didn't tell Giorgio that she'd blown the insurance money. She had her winnings from Nicky, and she had taken the cash he had on him when she killed him. But Nicky wasn't her only bookie, and she had debts to pay.

"I saw a train ticket to Buffalo on your kitchen table," Giorgio said. "What's it all about?"

Eva smiled. "Do you remember my old girlfriend Grace Russo?"

Giorgio looked surprised. "Ya mean the ugly broad? Christ. She wears her hair tied in a bun, her front teeth are missin' and her face is peppered with them black moles. Hell, as I remember, she's got the ugly-eye twitch."

Eva laughed. "Right. I got a letter from her. Her husband Michael just inherited seven-thousand dollars. She asked me to come visit her. So, I'll go visit her ... and her husband, of course."

Giorgio shook his head. "I don't know who's gonna be in more trouble after you visit—Gracie or her sick husband."

Eva played at being shocked. Giorgio knew what she had in mind. Eva was never one to let herself go unsupported, and Grace's husband was sitting on a lot of money.

*A girl has to do what a girl has to do*, Eva thought. *It's not stealing if he chooses me.*


Two days after Eva's rendezvous with Giorgio, on a snowy, Buffalo night, Eva, Grace and Michael sat drinking homemade wine as they listened to the music of *The Italian Hour* on the radio. It didn't take long for the wine to make Grace head for her second-floor bedroom. "I'm tired and I'm goin' to bed. Buono notte."

Within minutes, Grace's snoring could be heard throughout the house. After a half hour of talking with Michael about the days the three of them spent together in their youth, Eva got up from the couch and stretched, putting her body on display for Michael. *This greaser's going to oink like a pig just as soon as I get him excited*, she thought.

Michael sat on a chair in the living room and stared at her in awe. His mouth hung open, and perspiration covered his forehead and neck.

Eva gave him a smile. Then she began to disrobe, beginning with her shoes, then her dress and, finally, her slip.

Michael fixed his eyes on the rise and fall of her bosom; it seemed about to burst from her bra. He started to salivate and shifted in his chair to hide his erection.

"Baby," Eva whispered with a grin. "You're gonna get lucky tonight."

Michael was all smiles. He nodded and tried to rise from the chair. But Eva pushed him back down. "Steady, baby doll ... steady."

Eva unhooked her bra and gave him a wink. Michael wasted no time in burying his face between her breasts. He feverishly licked at her nipples. "*Bella putana*," he said. "*Bella putana.*"

Eva giggled. "Relax, baby doll. This doesn't have to be your last supper."

Michael couldn't speak English very well, but he understood Eva's actions.

She pulled off her panties and pushed his head into her crotch. After a few minutes, she laughed. "You like the taste of mamma's honey, don't you?"

Michael pulled Eva to the floor and struggled as he failed to get his pants off. He couldn't control his lust any longer; he exploded his seed in his trousers. "Oh, my God! Oh Lord ... God!" he shouted.

Eva was amused, but quickly placed her hands over his mouth in order to muffle him. It was too late. Grace came charging down the stairs to find Michael lying on top of her smiling, naked, best friend.

Michael packed his bags and left with Eva the next morning on a train to Philadelphia. He took his inheritance with him.


Michael married Eva in a quick ceremony when they got back to the city. She persuaded him to buy her another row house in South Philadelphia and he began working two jobs to provide her with the extra money she needed for her gambling habit. He wasn't home at night to keep Eva from her other habits, either.

Just a month after getting back from Buffalo, Eva came home at 2 a.m. after a Friday night with her "college boys," as she affectionately called them. She ascended her stairway and entered the bedroom to find her new husband sick. Dr. Pinto, Michael's doctor, claimed he had heart disease.

Michael lay in bed with his head propped on a pillow, barely conscious and struggling to breathe. With her back to the old man, she took an envelope from the nightstand drawer and scooped out a teaspoonfull of a white substance. She dropped it into a glass of wine and stirred.

"The doctor said wine would help you sleep." Eva put her arm around the old man and poured the wine down his throat. An hour later, she picked up the phone next to Michael's dead body. "It's done," she said. "Call your friend, the undertaker."

She made another call shortly thereafter. "Dr. Pinto, this is Eva Bell. I'm afraid my husband has taken a turn for the worse. I believe it's his heart again. Please come over right away. It's urgent."

Eva hung up the phone and smiled at Michael's corpse, the second husband she would bury in less than a year. "Good riddance to bad rubbish."

# Chapter Fifteen

Tom and Mike sat at the crowded Venice bar having lunch. "I'm going to the Yankees-A's game with the guys tonight," Mike said, playfully waving his tickets in Tom's face. "I've got an extra if you're interested."

"Damn. I can't go ... and I wanted to see Joe DiMaggio play. Marion Moore wants to meet me at Big Bill's tonight. Then we're supposed to go someplace private and talk."

"Why the cloak-and-dagger routine?" Mike asked.

"He said it's too dangerous to talk on the phone."

Mike shook his head. "I don't like it. Let me go with you."

"Thanks. But he wants me to meet him alone, and I don't want to spook him by showing up with someone."

"Just the same, pack your .38."

Later that night, Tom swung his legs out of his car and walked toward his meeting with Marion Moore.

A flashing red sign on the outside of the saloon read: "BIG BILL'S." The bright sign made the broken bottles in the street gleam.

Tom, intentionally unshaven and dressed in a ratty, gray shirt and matching pants, entered Big Bill's for his meeting with Moore. A long, warped pine bar ran along the wall, which was covered in peeling paint. The cheap floor tiles were cracked and chipped, and the barchairs looked like they hadn't been stained since the Civil War. The air reeked of ammonia and soap powder.

Earlier in the week, Moore told Tom he knew the cops were looking for him and that he feared for his life. He said he knew too much about the murder scandal. He suggested Tom wear work clothes to blend in with the patrons at Big Bill's. Once in the bar, Moore would secretly signal Tom to follow him to a second destination.

Big Bill, dressed in a dirty apron, chatted with three longshoremen as he tended bar. The longshoremen's thick beards proved they hadn't shaved for weeks and their odor said it'd been even longer since they'd seen a bathtub. Two "b-girls" were flirting with some patrons, a few stools down. Bill had hired the girls to hustle customers into buying drinks.

Marion Moore, a small, thin man with shifty eyes, sat at the bar's end. He held a bottle of beer and chain-smoked. Tom recognized him immediately from the description Moore had offered over the phone but he sat a few stools away and motionmed to Bill he wanted to order.

"A bottle of Schmitz," Tom said, signaling Moore he was ready to move.

Moore waited until Tom made eye contact then jerked his head toward the door. A few minutes later, he walked to the exit as Tom downed a glass of brew.

"See ya tomorrow night, Bill," Moore said with his back to all. After Moore left, Tom spent a few minutes finishing his beer. He dropped a quarter on the bar and murmured something about meeting a wife he didn't have and then strolled out.

Once outside, Tom saw Moore standing about five feet from the corner intersection, looking nervous. Seeing Tom, he jerked his head for him to come closer.

As Tom neared the corner, he noticed a black 1936 Buick pull up and stop alongside Moore. A brunette, dressed in black, sat behind the wheel, the veil of her hat pulled down. She smiled at Moore, who smiled back. It was a nervous smile. His eyes darted between the car and Tom. The brunette signaled for Moore to approach the car and, after a moment's hesitation, he did.

Moore had barely taken a step when a mustached man appeared from around the corner of the darkened building beside him. He grabbed Moore by the throat and slammed him against the brick wall. After a loud click, Tom saw a flash of metal.

Tom whipped out his .38 and ran toward the men. "Hold it right there, buster!"

He was too late. Moore's body slid to the pavement. Seeing Tom, the giant killer ran to the Buick. Tom pointed his .38 and fired as his target jumped through the opened passenger-side door. The Buick's tires screeched as the giant and his lady fled down the street. Tom fired three more shots, one of which shattered the car's rear window. Another made a hole just above the mud-covered, rear license plate before the car disappeared into the darkness.

Tom ran over to Moore's motionless body. The eyes were wide and the mouth was hanging open. Blood spurted from the cerotic artery. Death had claimed him.

The next day, Tom sat in his office and read the *Philadelphia Globe* headline: "EX-CON'S THROAT SLASHED ON KENSINGTON STREET CORNER." The Moore murder had left him shaken. He realized there were at least two more conspirators linked to Moore and Reardon and they were playing hardball. With the elimination of Moore, Tom now had only one witness to support his fledgling case against Lillian. Luckily, Reardon had been kept in protective custody.

Tom read the medical examiner's report. There were several items found on Moore's body, including: a Bulova watch, a gold ring, an apartment key, a leather wallet containing some cash, a membership card to the Golden Dawn, a Stevedore's local union #108 card, a business card for Robert Pearson, M.D., and a business card for Giorgio DiSipio.

Studying the items, Tom felt one thing didn't add up: *Why would a relatively poor guy like Moore have a custom tailor's card?* It could be nothing, but Tom had a hunch it might mean everything. Rather than ask a detective to look into DiSipio's background, he decided to visit the basement of City Hall and do a criminal record search himself.

Arrest records were kept in a dark, poorly ventilated and foul-smelling basement area known to City Hall workers as the "dungeon." Tom spent his free hours sifting through countless rap sheets in an effort to find one for Giorgio DiSipio. The temperature outside soared to a muggy 95 degrees on some days he was there, which was common for a typical Philadelphia Indian summer.

On a Friday afternoon, Tom sat in the sweltering heat of the dungeon and peered with hazy eyes at the yellowed rap sheets. Tom took off his seersucker jacket to reveal a white shirt soaked with sweat. He made constant trips to the ice-water cooler in an effort to gain relief from the persistent humidity, which was made worse by the ceiling fans being out of order.

Tom's fingers sifted through the nameplates of each file as he read the names. DiBona, DiDio, DiFrancesco, DiGrande. The sweat dripped from his brow. DiLuca, DiMento, DiDiego. "Christ," he muttered to himself. "Some half-wit failed to arrange the files alphabetically." He continued to plod. DiLulio. DiPietro. DiPorto. Bingo! Tom smiled and studied a rap sheet containing a photo of a young Giorgio, taken in 1921 at 23 years old.

| NAME | : DiSipio, Giorgio |
|---|---|
| DATE OF BIRTH | : September 1, 1898 |
| BIRTH PLACE | : Palermo, Sicily |
| ADDRESS | : 1700 East Passyunk Avenue, |
| HT | : 5'5" |
| WT | : 150 |
| HAIR | : Brown Philadelphia, Pa. 47 |

ARREST DATE CHARGE DISPOSITION

| 6-23-21 | Attempted Arson Not guilty 9-4-21 |
|---|---|
| 7-30-22 | Receiving Stolen Goods Not Guilty 8-5-22 |
| 5-9-23 | Illegal Lottery Not Guilty 5-11-23 |
| 12-21-23 | Drunk-Disorderly Not Guilty 1-2-24 |
| 1-3-25 | Illegal Lottery Not Guilty 1-4-25 |
| 5-6-26 | Pandering Not Guilty 5-8-26 |
| 10-2-30 | Pandering Not Guilty 10-3-30 |
| 3-7-31 | Counterfeiting Guilty (l yr. prob.) (Federal) |

After scanning the record, Tom thought of Giorgio as a small-time punk. But he couldn't be sure. He pulled the file out of the metal cabinet and threw his jacket over his arm. He knew his buddy "Gimpy" Stein might be able to give him the lowdown on Giorgio. Gimpy knew everybody who lived, worked, or played where Giorgio resided in South Philly and he owed Tom his allegiance.

# Chapter Sixteen

"Boo-Boo" Huff was Philadelphia's number-two distiller and distributor of illegal booze during Prohibition. His bodyguard had been Gimpy Stein. In 1928, Gimpy took shotgun blasts in both knees protecting his boss from an attempted hit by the Lenzetti gang. He even managed to shoot the attacker twice through the neck, killing him.

Tom, who had investigated the homicide, recommended that Gimpy not be indicted, as it was a legitimate case of self-defense. After the Prohibition Amendment was repealed in 1933, Boo-Boo lent Gimpy the money to buy a saloon, which he still owned and operated, despite needing two canes to get around. Gimpy was still grateful to Tom Rossi, and he tried to help him whenever he could—with some conditions. Gimpy still had his ears to the streets, but he wasn't a rat. His help was rarely in the form of direct information. After all, he didn't want someone finishing the job that started with his knees in 1928.

Tom didn't turn down the Dewar's the bartender served him on Gimpy's order.

"I need some information on a guy," Tom said.

Gimpy didn't say anything. Gimpy rarely said anything before Tom gave him specifics. He took a gulp from the glass of wine he held in his massive hand and waited for Tom to rephrase his question.

"I only want to know if he's connected with the mob in South Philly."

"Tom, even though I love you like a son, I'd rather take a bullet for you than be a fuckin' squealer."

Tom continued, as if the words had never hit the air. "I have the guy's rap sheet. I just want to know what his angle is."

"Spoken like a real fuckin' lawyer. What's this guy's name?"

"Giorgio DiSipio."

Gimpy exploded into laughter. "Giorgio? Connected? Are you kidding? Giorgio DiSipio ain't nothing but a little faggot dreamer. All his life he wanted to be a gangster but he didn't know how to go about it." He started to laugh again, but he forced his way through it.

"Let me tell you a story about this guy. Back in '21, the dummy burns his shop down to collect fire insurance. His business was going under. But when he goes to collect on the policy, he finds out the policy had lapsed. He had only made one month's payment, thinking he was insured for a year."

"Yeah, I guess that says a lot," Tom laughed.

"Says he's a dumb fuck."

"I take it you know him personally?"

"'Course I do. I got another story for you. In '26, the little bastard decides he's getting into the whorehouse business with another greaser."

Tom winced at the slur, but swallowed his pride. The info was far more important.

"The two of them import the finest broads they can get from Atlantic City. But what Giorgio forgets, or ignores, or probably didn't even know, is that anybody in the snatch business in South Philly has to pay tribute either to the Jew mob or the Lenzetti gang. After three months, he goes to the house one night and finds his wop partner and the madam dead in bed with their throats cut; they stuffed dollar bills in their mouths. Somebody tells him later the Lenzettis had warned his partner to start paying up. But the guy who gave the warning to his fresh-off-the-boat partner didn't know he didn't understand a lick of English."

"Does Giorgio ever come in here?" Tom asked.

"Yeah, he stops in every couple of weeks, flashes his bankroll and buys drinks for whoever's at the bar. He claims he hit the jackpot as a tailor. If you ask me, I think the little prick has become a fuckin' professional gigolo."

"Why?"

"In the last two years, he's been in here with at least six different broads, all of 'em married and not getting it at home, if you know what I mean."

Tom beamed inside at the first real break in the case. "Ever seen him with a blonde—about 29? Her name is Lillian Stoner. She's a 'merican?"

Gimpy thought for a moment. "I don't remember her name, but back in May he brings a blonde broad in. Said they had just been to the opera. The little creep ain't got no class. He bragged to me that he fucked her up the ass; meanwhile, she's standing less than a foot away."

Tom now had a handle on Giorgio DiSipio. *But does this mean this two-bit punk has suddenly graduated to murder*, he wondered. *And if so, why? It has to be love, sex, money or a combination of the three.*

Tom thought back to his conversation with Bertha, Lillian's neighbor. She mentioned a playboy who drove a '38 Plymouth and was present the night of Reggie Stoner's death. *I gotta find out what kind of car*, he thought.


The next day, Tom found Mike and Joe having lunch in the D.A.'s employee lounge. Tom skipped the "hellos" and jumped right in.

"Moore's wallet contained two business cards. One for a tailor with a shop at Passyunk and Pierce Avenues, named Giorgio DiSipio. I contacted the state office in Harrisburg and confirmed DiSipio owns a black 1938 Plymouth.

"What's the relevance of a black 1938 Plymouth?" Joe asked.

"A guy with that same kinda car drove Lillian Stoner home the night Reggie died. Then they were seen entering the house."

Mike wasn't impressed. "So what? Thousands of people in Philly own '38 Plymouths."

"But not all drivers of black 1938 Plymouths look like Rudy Valentino," Tom smiled.

"Come again?" Mike said.

"This guy DiSipio has a record. He's been booked for loan-sharking, pimping, and running cathouses. Here's his record and mug shot." Tom dropped Giorgio's record and photo on the table for all to see.

"So he looks like Valentino. So what?" Joe grunted.

"Sam Whittaker showed Giorgio's photo to a witness, one of Lillian's neighbors. She's sure it's the guy she saw go into Lillian's house on the night of Reggie's death."

Mike nodded. "OK, so now we have to look into this guy and his relationship with Evans' niece."

"I'd like you guys to gather more details, Mike," Tom said. "Have your men trail Giorgio and his girlfriends. I want to know their habits, hangouts and friends, down to how often they use the can. He's also a got wife who's paralyzed. DiSipio hired a colored woman to tend to her. He keeps them both holed up in their apartment above his shop. Check it all out."

Just then, Sam came in and rushed over to Tom. "Hope's on the phone in your office. She says it's urgent."

Tom ran to his office and took the phone. He knew that Evans was the reason for her call.

"Hi, Hope. What's up?"

"Tom, I've got bad news. An hour ago, the hospital's head nurse fired me."

"What reason did she give you?"

"She said I lied about my race on my original job application. She claims I concealed that I'm part colored. Tom, I know Evans did this, but can they do this legally?"

"Unfortunately, yes," Tom said. He let out a sigh and looked down at his desk. It was covered in evidence files and legal briefs. There was also his toothbrush and a clean shirt. *How do I protect Hope*, he thought. Tom was tired. Since he'd gotten the call from Pat Connors a month before, he hadn't gotten much sleep.

"This is Evans at his best," he said. "Yesterday, he told me you'd lose your job if I didn't protect Lillian. I tried to call, but you were at lunch. Listen, I've been thinking. You want me to play ball with Evans? If I do, I'm sure he'll give you your job back and help me become D.A."

"Absolutely not," Hope said. "Especially not with what happened at the bar. Just promise me. Make him pay for all of this. Our city doesn't need the likes of him."

Tom leaned back and stared at the ceiling. "Thanks, baby."

"Can we get together this evening, though?" she asked. "I need to see you."

Tom looked at his watch. "We have a staff meeting at six. How about 7 o'clock, sharp? We can meet at our usual spot in Rittenhouse Square, then go to dinner."

"Great. We love each other," Hope whispered.

"We do love each other," Tom said. He stared at the ceiling.


Tom and Hope sat on their favorite park bench in Rittenhouse Square. Tom's face was sallow, and he had bags underneath his dark eyes. His suit was wrinkled. Hope wore an ankle-length, flower-patterned dress, and her hair was pulled in a bun. Though she was upset, her expression was one of defiance.

"How will you manage to live while you look for another job?" Tom asked.

"I've already accepted a position as a nurse-midwife with a group of former nursing-school classmates. The job is only part-time, but it's better than nothing."

Tom shook his head. "Evans is such a bigoted bastard."

She looked Tom in the eye. "If we continue to see each other, many bigots like Evans will cross our path."

"I told you, your colored blood doesn't matter."

"I'm sure you're being very sincere today, but tomorrow worries me. I'm a normal woman, Tom. I wanted to be married, and I wanted a family and home. But life isn't always fair, and sometimes the bad guy wins. Are you ready to defy today's conventions and tolerate the people who won't tolerate us?"

Tom was pensive. "We could move to another city where people don't know us. Hell, I could get a job with a law firm and we could raise a family."

"Tom, I'm not about to lead a life of quiet desperation, fearing someone, someday, will discover my colored roots and hurt me. More importantly, I fear bringing children into this world where they'll be persecuted because they're a product of a mixed marriage. My grandfather went through hell because he was a mulatto." As soon as the words were spoken, Hope regretted being so honest.

"I'm 40-years-old and, for me, life's time-clock is running out," Tom replied. "I want the same things you want. I can't live without you, Hope." Tom hung his head. His frame draped over the park bench and he thought of the years he's spent as a prosecutor. *So much sacrifice. Hope is worth it, though.*

Hope smiled, kissed Tom tenderly on the cheek then hugged him. Finally, she had the courage to tell him. "Why don't we call time out for a month or so and think about our future?"

Tom placed his hand under her chin. He held the necklace he'd given her with the other hand. "I don't need a time-out, but I'll respect your wishes, OK?"

"OK," she said, uncertain of it all. They smiled and shared a final kiss, for the time being at least.

# Chapter Seventeen

Only 2,000 homes per year were built in Philadelphia during the Depression, hardly enough to accommodate a city of almost twomillion people. To control the housing shortage, many people became boarders in a single-family house. A boarder's rent usually included dinner, the use of a spare bedroom and access to a shared bathroom.

If you were lucky enough to be a male boarder in Sadie Lamb's house, you could also share her bed, for an additional fee. Sadie, a friend of Eva and Giorgio's, inherited a large, four-bedroom house on Girard Avenue near 29ᵗʰ Street. The 47-year-old had a face of someone a decade younger and a petite but curvy frame to match. She had one condition on letting you between her sheets: you had to pretend to rape her. She told her boarders that it eased her guilt about being a whore. Plus, the very thought of men forcing themselves inside of her made her excited.

Officially, Sadie only slept with her happy-go-lucky-husband, Robert, a straight-laced 50-year-old brewmaster who worked the graveyard shift at the Schmitz Brewery. Robert never suspected his wife's infidelity … but then Robert rarely saw his wife. She worked around the house during the day, changing sheets and cooking, as Robert slept. The couple saw each on other in passing, and the passion they once shared was gone. Sadie never meant to run a house of ill repute with her boarders. But money was money, and her husband hadn't seen a raise in years.

Howard Rice, 28, rented the bedroom next to the Lambs. He was handsome, with short-cropped hair and a prematurely receding hairline. Howard didn't have to pay extra rent to Sadie for her services. She became infatuated with the idea that she could still turn on a stud almost 20 years her junior. But Howard, an auto mechanic, felt more for Sadie than just lust. He sincerely loved her and became increasingly jealous of sharing Sadie with the three other men living in the house.

Sadie shared Howard's feelings, and felt trapped in her marriage with Robert. Robert was a good man, but she craved passion. When Eva first met Sadie at an outdoor market, Sadie couldn't take her eyes off the redhead. Eva was brash and confident, and she owned her sexuality. At that point in her life, Sadie had only been with Robert. Eva encouraged Sadie to sleep with other men. "After all," she'd said, "you deserve to be taken care of."

Once Sadie opened her legs to other men, she'd found herself. She felt free. She also fell in love with Howard.

"Let's run away to Chicago together," Howard suggested once in the afterglow. "Then you can divorce that chump and be with me."

"We have to wait, baby," she insisted. "The doctor told me Robert's heart could blow out any day. Then I'll cash in on the policy and both of us will be set."

Robert knew about one life insurance policy, but Sadie had acquired others through Eva and Giorgio, the same way she'd acquired some boarders.

Carmine "the Mouse" DeLeo, an unemployed undertaker, became a boarder in Sadie's home after his pal Giorgio told him about an open room. Although people continued to die in the '30s, undertakers often had trouble collecting their fees, making it difficult for them to hire assistants.

Giorgio gave Carmine his nickname because Carmine only stood 5'3" and weighed 130 pounds, with deep-set eyes, a large mustache, and a huge nose planted on his tiny face. He also had a personality befitting his nickname; he was a shy and introverted man who kept to himself. Carmine looked to Giorgio as a big brother, and he was in awe of Giorgio's power over women.

Other undertakers, such as Albert Sacca, would frequently give Carmine overflow work when they were busy. But the jobs rarely lasted more than a day. Even so, he avoided contact with the public when he could. Carmine told Giorgio, "It's not the dead I fear; it's the live ones."

Giorgio always laughed when Carmine confided in him. "Why is the Mouse afraid of live ones?"

"When I first started as an undertaker, I got a job to do an ole man. His Sicilian wife tells me, 'For the viewing, make my husband's face look like a movie star.' Well, I'm not Leonardo DaVinci, but I try to make the ole bastard look good. Unfortunately, rigor mortis had set in. Jesus! He looked like Dracula in that friggin' casket. Before the viewing opened to the public, the wife takes a look at his face, then pulls a knife and chases me into the street, screaming, 'You butcher! I'll cut your balls off!'"

Though Carmine had been at Sadie's house for several months, she refused to service him when he lacked work and couldn't pay. "I don't extend credit," she told him the first night he tried to wiggle onto the mattress without the proper fee.

In the house with Carmine and Howard was Paul "the Cat" Squilla. Paul was the newest boarder in Sadie's house. He got the name Cat as a kid because he had once jumped from the second-story window of a home he had been burglarizing to avoid the cops. He landed on his feet, without injury. Paul spit nails and had a mean disposition, so much so the Lenzetti mob hired him as a strong-arm man and debt collector. Paul and Giorgio were his best friends.

Paul also availed himself of his landlady's unique services, but she charged him extra. As she explained to Paul, "You always end up doing me twice."

Paul had a rough history with Sadie. He was a heavy drinker and often came home drunk. Once, on a freezing March morning at around 2 a.m., Paul staggered to Sadie's house after spending hours at a Lenzetti-operated bar. When he got home he wanted to wet his beak again. Knowing Robert worked until 8 a.m., Paul stumbled into Sadie's bedroom, knocking a lamp off her vanity and breaking several bottles of perfume in the process.

Sadie got excited at the prospect of surprise sex. She said to herself, "Let's see how good he is at playing catch-me-if-you-can." Clothed in only a flimsy nightgown, she ran downstairs, through the front door and into the bitter cold with Paul in hot pursuit. She allowed him to catch her within fifteen feet of her house. He carried her back home as she lowered the volume on her feigned sobs and mock resistance in case there were witnesses.

Once inside the vestibule, Paul ripped off her nightie, slammed her to the floor and stuck his bulging cock into her wet and waiting womanhood. It surprised Paul each and every time that Sadie liked the idea of being raped. Tonight, however, even as he filled her with liquid desire, his mind was unfocused and confused.

"Now you've really been raped, ya little fuckin' whore!" Paul said as he began to put Sadie's nightie back onto her sweating body. "And I ain't payin' ya, either! Ya enjoyed it too much."

Then, hearing noises from upstairs, Paul and Sadie realized Carmine and Howard, awakened by the commotion, were running down the stairway from their bedrooms. They had heard Paul's tirade.

"Motherfucker!" Howard screamed as he ran at Paul. Howard swung his fist at the other man's head, but missed. Paul grabbed him by the throat and banged his head against the corridor wall several times, creating a gaping wound before Howard slid to the floor, bleeding and unconscious.

Paul grinned at his fallen foe. "Might is always right … stupid."

Later that morning when Robert arrived home, he got an earful from his neighbor.

"Your little saint of a wife raced down the avenue in her nightie," his neighbor said, hiding a snicker. "Then she let Paul Squilla catch her and carry her back to the house. God knows what, or who, went down on whom once they got inside."

"What the hell is going on?" Robert asked Sadie as soon as he crossed the threshold.

But Sadie had a plausible explanation, which each of the boarders confirmed. "I … I had a horrible nightmare…" she explained, whimpering. "A hungry wolf tried to bite into my flesh. Good thing Paul had just got home. He ran after me, woke me up and … and carried me home 'cause I didn't have shoes on. When you see him, please … please thank him. I don't want him to think I'm ungrateful."

Robert felt badly because he hadn't had more faith in his wife. He apologized to Paul and rewarded him with two bottles of Chianti.

But a week later, Robert Lamb realized he had a venereal disease. Yellow pus leaked from his penis like when he was in the Navy. So he immediately walked down the avenue to Dr. Clark's office for treatment.

Robert entered the waiting room to find Sadie's boarders also waiting to be treated. Howard Rice, Paul Squilla and Carmine DeLeo froze when they saw him.

"Gee," Robert said, greeting the boarders. "What a strange coincidence. What's wrong with you guys?"

Carmine got so nervous he started to stutter. "Er … I got … I woke up with…"

Paul interrupted, not wishing to take a chance on Carmine spilling the beans.

"Late last night, while you were working, I took home some cooked crabs. Ya know, for the guys. Well, we all woke up this mornin' sick as dogs. Our stomachs are killin' us."

Carmine and Howard nodded in agreement. Then Paul put Robert on the defensive. "So, what's wrong with you?"

Robert blushed. "I got … er … personal problems."

The boarders understood. They were quite familiar with his "personal problems."

Giorgio, Paul and Carmine got a good laugh out of the whole episode. Giorgio liked the swagger Paul had and the three men took great pleasure in seeing Robert Lamb's ignorant bliss. But Sadie wasn't as amused. She wanted out of the marriage, and she wasn't looking for a divorce.


Sadie finally tired of waiting for her husband to die. She contacted Giorgio and within a week the plot would be executed.

Sadie had complained her roof leaked for several weeks. She convinced her husband and the boarders to fix it. A week later, Sadie would find herself in a dangerous game.

Robert Lamb had a habit of arriving home from work at 8:30 a.m. on weekday mornings. Usually, his first order of business was to have coffee with his wife in the kitchen. But on this particular morning, Sadie lay sick in bed upstairs. She had a fever and had been vomiting for two days. Unbeknownst to Sadie and her boyfriend Howard, Giorgio had his friend DeLuca, the insurance agent, write a policy on her life for two-thousand dollars, naming Giorgio as a cousin and the beneficiary.

Paul and Carmine had placed arsenic in Sadie's coffee, and then watched her become violently ill right in front of them. They were supposed to place the poison in her coffee in small quantities over a period of days so the symptoms wouldn't affect her all at once. But they got carried away. After examining Sadie, Dr. Clark concluded she had pneumonia.

The diagnosis got Howard suspicious. He decided to stay home from work to take care of her. He hadn't been made aware of Giorgio's murderous plot to eliminate Sadie, only the scheme to put Robert six-feet deep. In fact, he was supposed to push Robert off the roof.

As Robert entered the kitchen, he found Carmine, Paul and Howard having coffee at the table.

"Hi," Howard said. "The doctor said Sadie's looking a lot better this morning. He just left, maybe ten minutes before you got home."

Robert smiled when he heard the good news. "Thank God. This pneumonia shit is killing too many people."

When Robert finished his coffee, the men were ready to repair Sadie's roof. The flashing surrounding the chimney loosened, causing water to seep into the third-floor ceiling. All four men climbed the ladder to the roof and inspected the defective flashing. Robert bent down to inspect the area of the lower chimney, located three feet from the rear of the roof.

Paul nodded to Howard, who was standing directly behind Robert. Suddenly, panic gripped him. Howard turned white and started to sweat, then clutched his stomach as he vomited all over his shoes.

"Are you OK?" Robert asked, looking at Howard with some hesitation. He was growing tired of the boarders in his house and the strange happenings he'd seen in recent weeks.

Carmine and Paul shot Howard ugly stares, knowing he had lost his nerve.

"Er … I suddenly don't feel so good," Howard said, embarrassed. "I'm leaving." Robert ignored Howard's illness. *I just wanna to get the damn roof done so he could get some rest.* He started to rip up the worn out flashing.

Paul gritted his teeth, ran at Robert's back and gave him a powerful shove. The brewmaster rolled over and off the roof, screaming before his head shattered thirty feet below on the concrete sidewalk.

Giorgio and his friends were now killing anyone they could insure. To Giorgio, it was a solid arrangement that kept him in the money. The scrutiny from the authorities could be cause for concern, but he didn't really care. "Cops ain't nothin' but scum," Giorgio was fond of saying. His father's attempts at joining the local authorities in Sicily stayed with him. If it weren't for cops, he'd never have ended up leaving his home. If it weren't for cops, he'd still have his family. Those scumbags had lied to his father. They told him they could protect him. *Well, nobody can save anybody,* Giorgio thought.

During his years as a tailor, Giorgio had built himself quite the menagerie of local married women, and now many of the members of the group knew each other through him. As carefree as Giorgio was, he still feared the Woman in Black and her big friend. Her influence was threatening to supersede his, and that could prove costly.

# Chapter Eighteen

Bill Evans didn't know that District Attorney Pat Connors had secretly ordered Tom and Mike to investigate him. His dealings with hopeful businessmen looking to curry his favor had led to the arrest of two wealthy housing developers. They were arrested for bribery and in order to obtain lenient sentences, the suspects secretly admitted to giving thousands of dollars in payoffs and kickbacks to the deputy and various license inspectors, and they would testify against them in court.

Connors sat behind his desk, reviewing the thick file on Evans' personal and political history while Tom and Mike looked on. Connors shook his head. "Evans is one of the only survivors of the old Philadelphia political Vare gang. They were successful power brokers in a corrupt Republican machine that rivaled New York's Tammany Hall. During their twenty-three-year reign, Philadelphia had a national reputation for being the most politically corrupt city in the U.S."

"How can anyone forget Bill Vare?" Mike chuckled. "After winning a U.S. Senate seat back in '26, he fought for three years to be seated. Both Democrats and Republicans accused him of buying the primary election. Then in December, 1929, the Senate denied him his seat."

"According to this,"—Tom began reading from an old *Globe* article—"William Vare allegedly told reporters, 'Evans will be given a job in the mayor's office as an administrator. Soon, he'll become one of our most trusted lieutenants. Within two years, we'll make him chief of patronage for the party. Because of Evans' pedigree, we'll groom him to be our future mayor.'"

"I know a guy who went to school with Evans," Connors chimed in. "He said his circle of friends didn't hold the deputy in high regard. Growing up, nobody saw him as anything but fat and ugly. Women didn't even want to be seen with him. It's no wonder he became such a bastard once he got in office."

"Exactly," Tom said. "A couple of years ago, we had two of his female workers complain that he only promoted females if they gave him sex, but the mayor dropped the hammer on the case. Both girls quoted Evans as saying, 'Every beautiful woman has a weakness. The trick is to find it and exploit it.'"

"Well, he's done plenty of that," Mike said. "I could never prove it, but I think that son of a bitch did more than squeeze one gal. He might as well have pushed Esther Baron off the roof of City Hall."

Life had been good to Esther and Harry Baron. They were orthodox Jews adhering to all the rules and customs of their blood religion. Harry had a well-paying political job with Philadelphia's Licenses and Inspections Bureau, and had been one of Bill Evans' Republican ward leaders in an area of West Philadelphia inhabited by middle-class Jews.

Evans often bragged about Harry to his wife Gert. "He always gets out 90 percent of his ward's registered Republican voters, and they always vote with the machine." Evans would give Gert a big wink whenever he talked politics. "He also hands me an extra fifty bucks every few weeks for ... extra licensing fees."

The Barons managed to keep up with their bills and they owned a large, four-bedroom row house in West Philly's Cobbs Creek Park section. Their sons, ages thirteen and ten, were happy and getting good marks in school.

"Study hard and get all A's," Esther preached to the boys. "They only accept bright, ambitious boys to medical school."

At 33, Esther was a shy but strikingly attractive brunette. She had a firm, full figure and wore dresses that looked as if they'd been drawn across her shapely curves. Her breasts were unusually large for such a petite girl, so much so they made her self-conscious. She also had long, pretty eyelashes shielding her dark, glistening eyes. When Esther smiled, her face would flush, accentuating her dimples. She always carried herself with grace and decorum.

In September 1935, Esther awoke one morning to the loud clanging of her alarm clock. Harry had his back to her.

"Harry, wake up already." When he didn't stir, she shook him again. "Harry!" She rolled Harry over and screamed when she saw his face. His lifeless eyes were staring at the ceiling above them, his mouth wide open. "He's dead!" Harry's rheumatic heart had given out sometime during the night.

In the six months that followed, Harry's widow searched for a job to keep her and the boys afloat. But jobs were scarce, especially for an unskilled and uneducated Jewish woman.

"I'm terrified of financial ruin," she whimpered to her sister Ruth. "Harry didn't believe in life insurance and I had to use our savings to pay for his funeral and a new roof for the house. The mortgage is three months overdue and the bank's collectors send letters every week."

Esther agonized over her financial plight on a daily basis. She was developing stomach problems and her doctor told her she had an ulcer. *Without an income I'll lose the house and end up on a bread line*, she thought. *But I have an idea. I'll go to see Bill Evans for a job. He always used to flirt with me.*

Evans sat behind his desk, blowing cigar smoke towards the ceiling. Esther sobbed as she told the deputy her tale of financial woe. He let out a sigh and feigned interest. "You have my sympathy, my dear. Because Harry produced for the party, he had a good political job. But Harry's dead now and life goes on."

Esther went into shock, just as Evans had planned. He would usually fuss over her at parties, and embarrass her by gawking at her huge breasts, proclaiming to everyone: "Esther is the prettiest wife of all my ward leaders."

"I don't want a handout," she said. "What I need is a job." She pleaded with Evans to help her.

He shook his head. "I can't justify giving you a job. I already have people waiting in line who are more deserving and they have priority." Evans grinned at her. He detected desperation in her voice and that made him feel powerful. Now, he would ascertain how far she would go. "But maybe I could do something," he said.

Her eyes brightened at this glimmer of hope.

"Understand, I'm not promising anything," he said. "But what kind of work are you willing to do?"

"I'll do anything!" she said. She was anxious and it showed.

The Deputy knew he had another victim. "I'll put you on probation as a clerk in the Recorder of Deed's office. But in a month or so, you'll start to come and work for me on Friday afternoons."

Esther smiled. "Oh, what would I be doing for you on Friday afternoons?"

Evans grinned and winked. "You'll be doing what every good employee does for her boss: tending to my needs."

Esther reacted to his comment with a shy smile and disregarded his lascivious stare at her bosom. She would have to learn to disregard his rather suggestive sense of humor.

The job paid twenty dollars a week, but Esther was able to stay afloat by renegotiating her mortgage payments. For the first time since Harry's death, she felt financially secure. She could get back to properly raising her children without anxiety.


Three weeks later, on a Friday afternoon, Esther received a phone call at her desk at the Recorder's office. The deputy wanted to see her in his office immediately.

The widow entered the reception area where the deputy's secretary, Holly, greeted her. Holly placed her hands on her hips and smirked as she gave Esther's body the once-over. "Have a seat. The deputy will be with you shortly."

After more than an hour, the door to Evans' office finally opened and a tall man exited. Esther recognized him from the newspapers. It was Jim Morris, the Director of Public Safety. He looked at Esther, smiled and shook his head as if enjoying his own private joke. She stared at him as he left the office, wondering what he found so funny.

The phone buzzed and Holly answered. She turned to Esther a moment later. "The Deputy will see you now."

Holly closed the office door behind Esther. The room looked dark to her. The blinds had been drawn and she could smell the foul odor of stale cigar smoke. Evans stepped behind her and locked the office door from the inside, startling her.

"How are you, Mr. Evans?" she asked, nervously. "What … what's going on?"

He stepped out in front of her, examining the new prize he had snared. His tie hung from his collar at half-mast and he sweated as he took a giant swallow from a snifter of brandy.

Esther felt anxious.

"Are you ready to tend to my needs, Esther?"

Her hands began to shake. *Now I understand why this… this pervert helped me. If I reject him, I'll lose my job and my home.*

"You can leave if you like," he said, "but I don't think you will."

Somehow she had known this would happen, but she had chosen to deny it. Now she stood in the darkness before Evans and thought of her husband and children. *Is there even a choice for me to make?*

Evans emptied his snifter and reloaded. "I'm an impatient man, Esther. If you're staying, get undressed. I've waited a long time to see those big Jew tits of yours. If you're leaving, then get the hell out … now." Evans' gaze bore through Esther. He looked at her with a possessive glee, and she felt dirty from the look alone.

*May God forgive me,* Esther said to herself as she unbuttoned her blouse, removing every shred of her dignity along with it. The deputy began to pant and sweat profusely as he locked his eyes on Esther's nude body. He smiled and advanced toward her. Esther closed her eyes and thought of her children.

A month later, Esther found herself staring out over Philadelphia, having taken the elevator to the observation deck atop City Hall. She had been a wreck after her encounter with Evans, but she kept going. She didn't want to lose her children, and if she lost her home there was a good chance the city would take her babies. Esther experienced severe depression and guilt after her first four Fridays in Evans' office. He had forced her to engage in depraved sexual acts. She had suffered sleepless nights and the daily anguish of knowing what waited for her at the end of each week. She became ill and began to lose weight. She couldn't eat. Evans didn't notice any of this during their time together. He would surely notice her final act.

Esther looked down at the cars and people five-hundred feet below. *Although my mind's clouded, I'm confident Yahweh and my sons will understand what I'm about to do. I must find Harry and seek his forgiveness.* Esther unlocked the gate of the fence surrounding the base of the statue then silently leaped to her death.

# Chapter Nineteen

The Golden Dawn, situated at the northwest corner of Broad and Lombard Streets, was a Philly landmark. Both negroes and whites patronized it because it was the city's best jazz club and performers like Lionel Hampton, Louie Armstrong and Billie Holliday performed there regularly. On most days, there was a colored trio that played jazz. The club also saw its share of bookies, hookers, drug dealers, con men and gangsters.

Giorgio sat among the sprinkling of patrons, flanked by his two dates: Eva and Joanna. All three were drunk.

Eva was jubilant because, even though she was previously barred for fighting, Giorgio had her reinstated at the Dawn. She wore a low-cut, lime green polka dot dress and her signature elephant necklace. Her glassy eyes were fixed on Giorgio as she played with the hair on the back of his head.

Joanna wore a bright yellow cocktail dress. One of her shoulder straps hung down her arm, showing off her tanned skin, and her rimless glasses slid down her nose. She giggled as she squeezed Giorgio's cheek. Though Joanna didn't like sharing him with Eva, she held out hope that he would somehow see her as the better option. To Joanna, Eva was unstable and unpredictable and she saw herself as a chance for Giorgio to be with a real woman that would take care of him. Though she appeared relaxed by the alcohol in her system, Joanna was tense around Giorgio and Eva.

Joe Whittaker sat at the bar, a few feet away from Giorgio and his ladies, trying to eavesdrop on the threesome. As he watched, the peace between Giorgio's competing girlfriends began to crumble.

Eva slipped her hand under the table and into Giorgio's lap. She rolled her eyes and squeezed the bulge in Giorgio's crotch. He grinned. Not to be outdone, Joanna slid her tongue into Giorgio's ear and then smiled at Eva before licking his earlobe. The friendly nature of the game ended as quickly as it started.

Like a cat, Eva reached across the table and rubbed her hand across Joanna's face, smearing her fresh lipstick over her cheek. Joanna retaliated, slapping Eva across the face with an open hand. Giorgio smiled, moved out of the way and watched his two lovers attack each other.

Stunned by the slap, Eva pounced on Joanna, drawing blood from her neck with a fierce swipe of her fingernails. In moments, their table overturned and the two women were rolling around on the floor.

Joanna pulled at Eva's hair. Grabbing Joanna's forearm, Eva sank her teeth into it. Then, turning, Joanna jammed her fist into Eva's nose.

"You fat, four-eyed pig! Your mother should have named you Harriet the Happy Hippo!" Eva shouted as she kicked Joanna in the face, shattering her eyeglasses.

"Who you callin' a pig?!" Joanna said. "You slut! You're fuckin' so many guys they could fill up every seat in Madison Square Garden." Joanna picked up a glass of wine from a nearby table and threw it directly into Eva's bloody face.

Two bouncers appeared through the crowd and pulled the women apart, but Eva broke free of the bouncer holding onto her arm and grabbed Joanna by the nose. She squeezed hard, but Joanna kicked Eva in the shin and she let go.

"You're just mad because we're getting married!" Joanna yelled. The words hit Eva harder than the kick to her shin. Her physical encounters with other men were merely scratching an itch. Giorgio was her real match.

The two huge, colored bouncers dragged Joanna and Eva toward the exit and Giorgio followed, shrugging his shoulders at the gawking but fascinated patrons as he bid them adieu.

During the ride home, Joanna decided she would stop Giorgio's unfaithfulness with whores like Eva. Joanna entered her apartment and put together an ice pack for her nose. She walked into the bedroom and sat at the edge of the bed she once shared with Antonio. She hadn't slept well since his death. Though she still saw Giorgio at his shop, he never stayed at her place. Her bed was empty without a companion and Joanna was determined to see Giorgio commit to her and her alone.

,

# Chapter Twenty

Tom Rossi's investigation into Reggie Stoner's death was yielding results. His men continued to look into Lillian Stoner's background and though he had hit a dead end in trying to find Marion Moore's murderer, he felt confident he would soon have enough evidence to link Reggie Stoner's murder to both Lillian and Giorgio. Tom secured an order for an autopsy on Reggie and as he waited for the results, his men looked into Phil Reardon's claims about Giorgio's insurance scam.

As Tom started putting together the pieces surrounding Giorgio DiSipio, an equally urgent push for answers was being waged by Giorgio's women.

Seven days of sweltering Philadelphia humidity ended with thunder and lightning at 4 a.m. on a Sunday morning. The storm crashed over the city like an explosion and cut through the thick air, cooling the city by ten degrees. A black 1936 Buick pulled into Lillian's driveway and stopped in front of the side entrance. As Lillian held the side door open, the driver, the Lady in Black, ran from the car to the house with an opened umbrella.

This time, the Lady wore a full black facial mask that hid her identity and disgjuised her natural voice when she spoke.

A colonial motif decorated Lillian's home, but only a few antique paintings, clocks, silver, furniture and rugs remained in the sparsely furnished house. The majority of her treasures had been sold.

Lady shook off the rain and handed her umbrella to Lillian. She scarcely glanced at Lillian as she moved past her into the house. Lillian was nervous. She hadn't met with the Lady more than a handful of times, and even in those instances she had felt uncomfortable.

*How can I trust her?* Lillian thought. *She's too close to this whole thing. She isn't looking out for me.*

Lillian and the Lady descended the steps to the basement. Curtains covered the windows, making it dark but for candles flickering from sconces embedded into the stone walls. Six additional women, including Eva and Joanna, were waiting in the basement. The women sat at a large table and no one spoke.

As Lillian and the Lady in Black made their way to the table, a tension filled the air. All eyes were on the Lady. None of the women knew her true identity. But, each of the women in attendance knew what influence she held over Giorgio—something none of them had been able to muster—and her demeanor was ice cold.

Lillian and the Lady took their places at the table. The Lady was the first to speak.

"Each of you has made your own decisions in this matter," she said. "You each chose money over your husbands' lives. If you're nervous about the investigation into Reggie's death, you ought to be. Tom Rossi is determined to find the truth."

"We need to do something about him, I think," said Eva. "Why don't we take care of him like we did the rest? You could do the deed yourself."

"No one is going to kill the assistant district attorney," the Lady in Black said. "If you think things are getting hot now, you can't imagine what it would be like if he was killed."

"Yeah, well, what are we supposed to do?" Eva asked. "If he gets to Giorgio, we'll all be in for trouble."

"He's not going to get to Giorgio," Lillian said. "Giorgio wouldn't rat to save his own life. Besides, Bill Evans is going to keep Tom Rossi on a leash. He's got some things up his sleeve."

Giorgio's women looked at Lillian. Their looks said that each of them was worrying about their own chances at staying out of prison. Each of the women in attendance was linked to Giorgio and each of them was a widow through unnatural means. Eva was a double offender and, like the other women, she knew that Giorgio had been involved in more than a handful of killings.

The Lady continued. "Everybody better keep her mouth shut," she said. "You each know what you did; each of you is looking at your own execution or life in prison."

Eva looked at the Lady. "We better all hope your foolproof plan really works."

"I'll be just fine," the Lady replied. "You worry about your-selves."

With that, the meeting was over. The Lady in Black rose from her seat and left Lillian's home. It was still dark outside and each of the women left a few minutes apart to avoid being seen togeth-er. The thunder crackled in the sky as Lillian stood at the side en-trance of her home. She looked out over the stately homes in her neighborhood and prayed that Bill Evans could keep Tom Rossi at bay.

# Chapter Twenty-One

"Giorgio is screwing a host of married women." Joe was sitting in Tom Rossi's office on a Monday morning, reading from the pages and pages of notes he and the other detectives had gathered while following Giorgio. His report was part of a debriefing Tom had asked for from him and Sam.

"He uses the couch at his shop as his own little flophouse, while his crippled wife listens to the radio upstairs," Joe said.

"This guy is trying to act like Valentino alright," Sam said. He smiled at the thought of a lowly tailor living out a Hollywood-inspired dream. "Some neighbors claim that at different times on a given day, as many as three married women enter his shop for an hour apiece. And nobody thinks they're having dresses made. " Tom and his detectives laughed.

"You know the old saying," Tom said. "Old wives make the best soup."

"He's known in the neighborhood as the 'Don Juan of Passyunk Avenue,'" Joe said. "Joanna Napoli has lunch with him three times a week and Eva Bell and Lillian Stoner usually visit him at night once or twice a week. Turns out Eva and Joanna's husbands died within weeks of Reggie Stoner."

"Eva's second husband died of heart problems," Sam said. "Her first hubby got blown away by a car bomb last year—that was Dennis Fitzpatrick, the bookie. Homicide wrote it off as a hit by the Lenzetti mob, but she collected well on each husband's insurance. She's a heavy gambler and owes big money to loan sharks ... sharks most likely recommended to her by loverboy Giorgio. I also managed to find out one more thing about Eva," Sam said. "She gets her kicks out of screwing young boys."

"Jesus," Tom said as he let out a laugh. "Is there anything this broad isn't into? What did you dig up on this Joanna Napoli?"

"Her husband stopped working due to a crippling injury," Sam said consulting his notes. "Afterward, she supported him by running a gift shop down the street from Giorgio's place. The doctor listed her husband's cause of death as lobar pneumonia. Apparently, the only vice Joanna's got is her hots for Giorgio."

"Interesting," Tom said. "Both lobar pneumonia and heart failure can produce the same symptoms as poison. An unsuspecting doctor could be fooled and misdiagnose the cause of death in both cases."

"The doctors who approved Lillian, Eva, and Joanna's insurance applications all positively identified Marion Moore as the guy they examined," Joe said.

"Alright," Tom said. "I'm petitioning the court to exhume the bodies of Eva and Joanna's husbands. You did a great job, guys. Thanks."

Joe looked at Tom and smiled. "There's one more thing which may interest you. We have reason to believe Lillian is having an affair with your favorite politician ... Bill Evans."

"What? I thought Lillian and Evans were uncle and niece."

"They are," Sam said. "I trailed her for three weeks. Lillian visited her uncle in his office at City Hall on three consecutive Wednesdays. She arrived by cab at about 8 p.m. and stayed about an hour. During the most recent visit, I stood in the hallway outside of Evans' office door—locked, by the way—and I didn't hear any conversation, just plenty of giggling and the sound of Evans moaning. Afterward, Lillian left and entered a waiting cab, which took her home or to Giorgio's shop."

Tom shook his head. "Evans is a sick bastard. The real reason he's protecting Lillian is because he's afraid of losing a piece of ass. Did you check the records of Yellow Cab?"

"Yep. For two years, a cab has been picking her up once a week at her house at about 7:30 p.m. Each time it drives her to City Hall. The cab then picks her up at 9 p.m. and usually drives her home. For the past few months, like clockwork, she's been driven to Giorgio's shop."

"Doesn't she own a car?"

"Yeah, a Ford roadster. But, she never used it to visit Evans. They probably didn't want anyone spotting her car and getting suspicious."

Tom turned to Sam. "Do Pat and Mike know about this?"

Sam nodded. "Yeah. Pat said not to use this info unless you double check with him first."

"Okay, fellas. Keep me posted."

As the men left, Mike entered with the day's *Globe* in his hand. He wore a grim look. "Seen the paper?"

Tom could always tell when Mike brought bad news. "Hit me."

Mike handed him the paper. "This shit is getting vicious."

The headline read: "D.A. Candidate's Girlfriend Fired from PGH for Lying About Colored Lineage."

Tom read from the accompanying story: "Hope Daniels, who has frequently been seen in the social company of Deputy District Attorney Tom Rossi—a possible replacement for outgoing D.A. Pat Connors—was dismissed from her post as a supervisory nurse at PGH for lying about her racial background."

"Damn it!" Tom said. "This is Evans' work! That son of a bitch just couldn't let go. He made good on his threat to get her blackballed, and for what? A lousy piece of ass."

"It's even worse for you," Mike said. "A lot of people won't vote for you in the primary if you're dating a girl with colored blood."

Tom stood and walked to his office window, shaking his head in disbelief. "Hope predicted this would happen." He looked down at the floor and thought about what the news meant to his chances at being elected D.A. *This isn't good.* He turned back toward the room and pounded his fist on his desk, scattering papers across the floor. "I care more about Hope than being elected D.A. Screw it!

We're arresting that whore Lillian and her playboy boyfriend for Murder One. Lillian Stoner's not getting away with this because of who her uncle is."

"Are you crazy?" Mike asked. "The autopsy results aren't even in yet. What if Reggie Stoner hasn't been poisoned after all? You've got nothing if the autopsy doesn't confirm homicide, especially since your only witness turned up dead! Evans will get you disbarred as a lawyer for malicious prosecution!"

Tom didn't flinch. "If the Stoner autopsy doesn't prove death by poison, I'll pose nude in Wanamaker's window."


A squad car containing two uniformed officers pulled up in front of the Stoner house with lights flashing. Mike pulled up behind it with Tom in his passenger seat and Joe and Sam in the back. Tom and the detectives strolled to the front door as the two uniformed officers moved to cover the house's other exits.

Mike pounded on the front door, but there was no answer. He tried again, harder this time.

A moment later, Lillian appeared holding a glass of wine. She was drunk and naked under her robe. Her hair was in disarray, and she had to lean against the doorframe to remain upright. "What's … goin' on?" she slurred.

Mike flashed a warrant and eased her out of the way as the other men entered the house. Caruso's voice blasted from the phonograph as he sang an aria from *Pagliacci*.

Giorgio sat on the living room couch trying to pull up his pants. An unlit cigar dangled from his mouth. Tom looked at Lillian and Giorgio with contempt. "Giorgio DiSipio and Lillian Stoner, I'm arresting you for the murder of Reginald Stoner."

Lillian looked confused and dazed. She pointed at Giorgio, still trying to pull up his pants. "He … the … the gangster did it."

"Shut up!" Giorgio yelled. He was stunned, and his face flushed red as his eyes bore into Tom. Giorgio started for Lillian, but Joe grabbed him by the arm before he could get close enough to slap her.

Mike clamped cuffs on Lillian's wrists as Joe tended to Giorgio.

Lillian turned to Tom as he walked her out of the house. "I'm reporting ... reporting you to Deputy ... Deputy Mayor ... Evans. False ... false arrest!"

On the ride to the police station, Tom thought of what Mike had said earlier. *What if I'm wrong? But then why did Lillian point the finger at Giorgio?* Tom figured he would worry about it later. For now, he wanted answers from Lillian and her lover.

# Chapter Twenty-Two

The headline of the October 20, 1938, *Philadelphia Globe* declared: "Society Wife and Lover Arrested in Love Triangle, Insurance Murder!" The scene at the district attorney's office was pandemonium. Phones rang off the hook behind Joe, Sam, Lynn, and the other detectives as they took statements from newly acquired witnesses.

Tom ordered the arrests of each of the widows his detectives had been able to trace back to Giorgio. The arrests were made in one sweep as police cars swarmed the homes of a half dozen women.

Uniformed cops led a line of seven handcuffed suspects: Lillian, Eva, Joanna, Giorgio, and three more wives suspected of complicity in murder with the Don Juan of Passyunk Avenue. The officers removed each of the suspects' cuffs and seated them next to each other against a wall. Lillian was indignant. Her hair looked so oiled one might have thought it wet. Eva, wearing orange polka dots, flirted with one of the patrolmen keeping watch over her. Joanna, wearing a fedora and suit, sobbed into the handkerchief between her hands. The three newly discovered members of Giorgio's wives' club stared at the floor. Giorgio smirked at the gathering of his conquests. *What a bunch of no good dames*, he thought.

Lynn took a steno statement from Alice Cionci, an elderly woman in her late sixties. She insisted one of Giorgio's ex-girlfriends had murdered her ex-husband and then fled the city.

"Some people call her the 'Kiss-of-Death Widow,'" Alice said. "The bitch buried her first three husbands."

Lynn stared at Cionci in disbelief.

Joe stuck his head into Tom's office. "This bit of news shouldn't surprise you.

Reardon recovered from his amnesia after Giorgio's arrest. He now remembers meeting him several times with Moore, even before he met Lillian. He also claims Giorgio introduced him to as many as four other wives and gave him a detailed description of the sexual habits of each wife."

Tom smiled. Things were coming together. "Good. Make sure Lynn takes his statement."

Mike walked into Tom's office with Lillian in tow. She raised an eyebrow and placed a hand on her hip, giving Tom a defiant scowl.

Tom shook his head as he addressed her. "Our handwriting expert informs me your husband's signature, which appeared on four life insurance policies, was forged. The signatures are your handwriting. We call it forgery and, more importantly, a motive for murdering your husband, Mrs. Stoner."

"Well, Mr. Rossi, according to my attorney, forgery is an unauthorized signature. Reggie knew about the policies. He told me to get the insurance and sign his name, which means his signatures were authorized."

"Did your late husband also authorize you to commit adultery with Mr. Reardon, Mr. DiSipio and … a certain City Hall politician?"

Lillian froze. She hadn't known the extent of Tom's investigation.

He continued. "And did your husband authorize Marion Moore to take his place for the insurance physicals?"

Lillian turned red. She didn't know Moore had spoken to the police before his murder. "My lawyer told me if you made any defamatory allegations, I should inform you I intend to sue for libel and slander after I'm declared innocent."

"Truth is the only defense I'll need to counter," Tom said.

Lillian folded her arms and stared at Tom. He seemed determined to put her behind bars and she refused to give him the satisfaction. "My husband died of pneumonia. Why have I been arrested for murder?"

"Your confession at your house, for starters," Tom grinned. "Maybe it's because we have an eyewitness. Giorgio entered your house the night before you found your husband dead. That means you lied to me when you told me no one had been in your house the night before."

"Prove it!"

Tom smiled and gave Mike a nod. The detective then left the room and returned with Bertha Brooks, Lillian's neighbor.

Lillian stared at Bertha as she was brought into the room. "I refuse to answer any more questions. I want to see my lawyer immediately!"

Tom looked to Mike. "Mike, escort Mrs. Stoner back to her cell and on your way ask Lynn to take Mrs. Brooks' statement." He looked at Lillian and then at Bertha. "I understand Mrs. Brooks will give us—how can I put this delicately—a blow-by-blow account of Lillian's habit of playing a game called 'squirrel'… a game she liked to play with a certain gentleman while parked in his car outside her house at night."

Lillian glared at Tom as Mike escorted her away.

Five minutes later, Joe brought Giorgio in and they both took a seat across from Tom. Giorgio crossed his legs and smirked. "I don't know nothin' about no murders, The only thing I'm guilty of is bangin' married broads."

"Let me ask you a question," Tom said. "What were you doing with a bottle of arsenic in the trunk of your car?"

"What bottle of arsenic?"

"The bottle in the hardware store bag, which also contained the hardware store receipt you forgot to remove. The owner, Ray Dickson, identified you as the purchaser from your mug shot."

"Oh, yeah, I use arsenic to kill rats. They come into my shop from the restaurant next door sometimes."

"OK," Tom said, making a note on his pad. "In the last three years you deposited a total of eighteen thousand dollars into four different banks. What's the source of the money?"

"I got a successful tailorin' business."

"Your income tax returns indicate you've lost money with your business for the past three years. You know, playing games with the IRS got Al Capone his own cell."

"Al Capone had a lousy lawyer."

"No," Tom said, "Al Capone had a lousy doctor who failed to diagnose gonorrhea."

"What the hell does it gotta do with me?"

"After examining the arrested wives, the commonwealth doctor sent us his report. It seems the last two wives you were screwing had gonorrhea. Has your dick been leaking yellow stuff lately?"

Giorgio's jaw dropped. "I wanna see a doctor."

"I've got a couple of questions first. What were you doing at Lillian Stoner's house the night her husband died?"

"I was doin' the same thing to Lillian you were doin' to your nigger girlfriend," Giorgio said. "I hear she ain't gonna be around too long."

Without hesitation, Tom hit Giorgio across his jaw with a right cross, knocking him out of his chair and onto the floor.

Mike rushed into the office when he heard the thud. "What the hell happened?" he demanded, looking down at Giorgio just as he spit out a wad of blood.

"Giorgio took a swing at Tom and he defended himself," Joe said.

Mike looked at Tom, who gave him a wink. "Get him out of here," Tom said.

Joe recuffed Giorgio and led him out.

Mike picked up the fallen chair and took a seat in it just as Connors entered the office. He pointed at the hectic scene outside. "Somebody giving away turkeys out there?"     Tom     smiled.

"DiSipio's arrest brought in a deluge of tips about other wives who may have conspired with him to waste their husbands."

Pat scratched the back of his head. "How many wives are we talking about?"

"At least six, maybe a dozen."

"Spread word to the press then. You're the only person authorized to talk to reporters. From now on you report directly to me. I don't want any surprises with this thing."

Suddenly, Tom and the others heard women screaming and men shouting. Tom, Pat, and Mike exchanged glances and rushed outside.

Grace Russo and Eva were in the middle of a ferocious skirmish. Grace, still wearing black to mourn her ex-husband, was scratching at Eva's face and Eva was kicking at Grace as both women screamed obscenities.

"You cunt! You killed my husband. You killed Michael!" Grace spat on Eva.

"Nobody killed that greaser. He died on his own."

Sam and several uniformed cops separated the women as they continued to glare at each other.

"What the hell is going on?" Tom asked.

Sam shook his head. "Grace Russo, the gal in black, claims Eva Bell stole her ex-husband from her. Michael Russo married Eva after he divorced Grace."

"So what?"

"She also swears Eva poisoned Michael to collect his life insurance."

Grace sneered at Eva, her bad eye twitching. Eva smiled at Grace then stuck her tongue out at her.

"I seen the evil whore do it!" Grace snapped.

"Seen her do what?" Tom asked. "Poison your ex-husband?"

"No. When I was married to Michael, I caught Eva screwin' him on my livin' room floor."

Amidst the chaos, the phone rang. Lynn answered it, then handed Tom the receiver.

"Rossi here."

"Tom, this is Evans. The coroner's physician ruled Stoner died of pneumonia, not homicidal poisoning. Reggie's body didn't contain arsenic. You falsely arrested Lillian for murder, and there is no murder. You're in deep shit, wop!"

Tom placed his forefinger over his lips in an effort to silence Mike then held the receiver so he could listen as well. "Come again?"

"I knew if I bided my time you'd screw up eventually. We filed a compliant against you with the Lawyers' Disciplinary Board for unethical conduct. It looks like you're getting disbarred, asshole!"

"Listen to me, you son of a bitch," Tom said, but Evans slammed the phone down before he could finish.

"He's really greased your chute this time," Mike said.

Tom had to sit down. He was shocked. "I can't believe it! Do you think Evans got to the coroner?"

"Wouldn't surprise me. But you'd better come up with a reason to justify Lillian's arrest."

# Chapter Twenty-Three

Mike escorted Joanna outside Tom's office and seated her in a chair. She stared at Giorgio, seated next to her, and closed her eyes, dreaming of an escape from the nightmarish humiliation she had experienced during the past hours.

Detectives had barged into her shop and greeted her with an arrest warrant as she served customers. The cops handcuffed her and marched her outside and into the rear of a police wagon. Neighbors stared at Joanna as she was taken away in tears. Many of them had expected Giorgio would one day run afoul of the law, but Joanna was considered a decent woman.

Distraught, Joanna sat and pretended she was Muzetta, the former mistress of Marcello—in her mind played by Giorgio—in Puccini's opera *La Boheme*. Joanna loved operas and the characters whose lives were played out in their scenes. To her, the romance and passion in the lives of these characters was so much purer than anything she'd experienced. Joanna closed her eyes tight, losing herself in her role.

Joanna saw herself in a Paris café on Christmas Eve. She arrives with her paramour and sees Marcello. In an attempt to see if she still has amorous powers over her former lover, she sings Muzetta's Waltz: *Quandro m'en vo'*.

When I strode out alone along the street,
the people stopped and gazed

at me to seek out my beauty from head to toe

and then I tasted the sly desire that gleams from admiring eyes.

They can see all my beauty, which lies concealed in my heart,

perceived from my outward charms

and you know who remembers and fret,

you flee from me like this?

I know very well you will not speak of your anguish

and yet I sense you are ready to die!

Moments after Joanna fell into her fantasy, Mike snatched her from it and led her into Tom's office. She looked unkempt and anxious.

Mike smiled. "Tom, say hello to Joanna Napoli. I remember reading the surveillance report on this beauty queen. She got involved in a cat fight with Eva Bell."

Mike read from his notes. "After reading about Giorgio's arrest, her insurance man gave us a tip. She and Giorgio had her husband Antonio insured. When we arrested her, she demanded a lawyer. But when we showed her photos of a dozen of Giorgio's current girlfriends, she threw up her arms and wanted to confess."

Lynn entered and sat at the desk with paper and pen ready.

"Okay, Joanna," Tom said. "Talk to us."

Joanna let out a howl and burst into tears before stopping herself. "I loved Giorgio so much! He said if I poisoned my husband, I would be his only girlfriend and we could get married. He lied to me!" Joanna's body heaved up and down as she gasped for air. She spoke nonstop for an hour. All of the lies she'd been told and all of her regrets about Antonio's death poured out.

When Joanna was done talking and Tom had finished asking questions, he signaled for Joe to escort her back to her cell. Joe placed the cuffs on her and led her away.

"We don't have Giorgio's full harem," Mike said, taking a puff from his pipe. "Rose Grady fled town. She's the gal who had four husbands."

"Is her latest husband dead, too?"

"Husbands," Lynn said. "Giorgio may have helped her lose three of them. She's called the 'Kiss-of-Death Widow,' and she always dresses in black as if she's in mourning, with a black veil over her face."

Tom snapped his fingers. "She fits the description of the woman who drove the getaway car in the Moore murder. Put out an APB for Rose Grady right away. Don't forget to warn everyone she's probably in the company of a large man, and give the description I gave you."

"Do you think Giorgio ordered the hit on Moore?" Lynn asked.

"Probably. We're dealing with a group of conspirators and chances are they'll keep killing to keep from going to jail."

As Lynn left the office, Tom dialed Hope's number. It was 8 p.m. and he was exhausted.

"Hello?"

"Hi, babe."

"Tom? Are you OK? I've been worried about you since the newspaper article about us."

"I'm fine. What about you?"

"I won't lose sleep over people knowing my secret, but I will lose sleep if this hurts your chances in the election."

"Keeping you is more important to me than politics."

"I see you made your first arrests."

"Yeah, but it seems like this bullshit is never going to end, and I have a second reason for calling you."

"What is it?"

"Giorgio threatened your life this afternoon. I lost it and decked him."

"Great. If you stick with me, you'll end up in jail."

"I'm serious, Hope. You may need police protection."

"From what I've read in the papers, Giorgio isn't very smart, especially when he threatens your girlfriend in front of eyewitnesses. Tom, I think the jerk was trying to get under your skin. Anyway, you're invited for dinner tomorrow night—seven sharp."

"I love you," Tom said.

"I love you more," she said. She hung up as tears came to her eyes. *Tom, I love you more than you'll ever, ever know.*

# Chapter Twenty-Four

While Giorgio and his ladies stewed in jail, Tom and Mike decided to search his shop and apartment. Tom was convinced there would be some evidence at Giorgio's shop, even though his detectives said they hadn't found anything incriminating during a previous search.

The search turned out to be a distasteful ordeal for Tom. Giorgio's wife, confined to her bed and wheelchair, looked like an old lady waiting for death's arrival. Most of her teeth were missing and her facial bones were sickeningly prominent because of malnutrition. Her hair was straggly and unkempt. *This lady's just waiting to die*, Tom thought.

"Don't tell me about Giorgio's troubles," she told Mike. "I got too many of my own."

Tom and Mike spent a day in Giorgio's shop. They began their search by checking his sewing machine drawers, boxes, closets, and the cutting board compartments. They worked from an inventory list prepared by Joe.

Tom reviewed business records and phone call lists retrieved from the desk drawers.

"What have we here?" he said as he pulled a bong from the top drawer.

Mike examined the long stem of the bong. "Opium."

"Don't tell me Giorgio's an opium addict," Tom said. "If he goes into withdrawal, I'll have my answer, I guess, but I doubt if it's him. There are remnants of lipstick on the edge of the bong and your men told me Lillian's been known to do opium."

Mike double-checked the search list prepared by Joe. "Here it is. Item twenty-two: Indian peace pipe."

"Your detectives probably never worked narcotics," Tom said as he inspected the rear door of the shop. "Where does this door lead to?"

Tom opened the door and found himself entering the rear yard as Mike followed behind him. The yard, enclosed by a wooden six-foot fence, measured fifteen 15 feet by fifteen 15 feet. To the left of them stood a fig tree with fresh fruit on its branches.

"What kind of tree is this?" Mike asked.

"Nothing unusual. Giorgio's Italian and a lot of us keep a fig tree in our back yards."

To the right of the tree were two tomato stalks with tomatoes on their branches. Mike pointed to the plants and smiled. "I know. Italians also grow their own tomatoes, too, right?"

Tom smiled. But as he looked at the tomato plants he noticed something that caught his attention: a plant resembling parsley that stood four feet high with leaves that looked like white parsley on purple, spotted stems.

"I'll bet it's parsley," Mike said.

"I'm not so sure," Tom said. He pulled off a few leaves and twirled them in his fingers. He sniffed the leaves, and then tasted them.

"Well?" Mike asked. "Is it parsley?"

Tom spit the leaves out and shrugged his shoulders. "Not sure yet. I'm gonna take some of this and have it tested. I don't want to let anything get by us. Who knows what Giorgio's into?"

The next day, Tom was sitting in his office reading a file when Lynn Sullivan entered carrying an envelope. "Some guy from the Horticultural Society delivered this for you. When did you become interested in plants and flowers?"

He took the envelope from her and removed the letter inside. After reading its contents Tom was excited. "I'll be damned!"

Tom rose from his desk and rushed past Lynn. "I'm going to the medical library."

Lynn shook her head as Tom disappeared down the corridor. He rushed to the Philadelphia College of Physicians' library and asked for books on pathology and toxicology. The librarian there brought him book after book as he pored over the pages looking for answers. He read from *Toxicology* and *Elements of Pathology* and asked for more texts as he thought of more questions. A librarian wearing horned-rimmed glasses arrived and piled another stack of books on his desk. Tom stayed at the library until it closed.

# Chapter Twenty-Five

While Giorgio and his ladies stewed in jail, Tom and Mike decided to search his shop and apartment. Tom was convinced there would be some evidence at Giorgio's shop, even though his detectives said they hadn't found anything incriminating during a previous search.

The search turned out to be a distasteful ordeal for Tom. Giorgio's wife, confined to her bed and wheelchair, looked like an old lady waiting for death's arrival. Most of her teeth were missing and her facial bones were sickeningly prominent because of malnutrition. Her hair was straggly and unkempt. *This lady's just waiting to die*, Tom thought.

"Don't tell me about Giorgio's troubles," she told Mike. "I got too many of my own."

Tom and Mike spent a day in Giorgio's shop. They began their search by checking his sewing machine drawers, boxes, closets, and the cutting board compartments. They worked from an inventory list prepared by Joe.

Tom reviewed business records and phone call lists retrieved from the desk drawers.

"What have we here?" he said as he pulled a bong from the top drawer.

Mike examined the long stem of the bong. "Opium."

"Don't tell me Giorgio's an opium addict," Tom said. "If he goes into withdrawal, I'll have my answer, I guess, but I doubt if it's him. There are remnants of lipstick on the edge of the bong and your men told me Lillian's been known to do opium."

Mike double-checked the search list prepared by Joe. "Here it is. Item twenty-two: Indian peace pipe."

"Your detectives probably never worked narcotics," Tom said as he inspected the rear door of the shop. "Where does this door lead to?"

Tom opened the door and found himself entering the rear yard as Mike followed behind him. The yard, enclosed by a wooden six-foot fence, measured fifteen 15 feet by fifteen 15 feet. To the left of them stood a fig tree with fresh fruit on its branches.

"What kind of tree is this?" Mike asked.

"Nothing unusual. Giorgio's Italian and a lot of us keep a fig tree in our back yards."

To the right of the tree were two tomato stalks with tomatoes on their branches. Mike pointed to the plants and smiled. "I know. Italians also grow their own tomatoes, too, right?"

Tom smiled. But as he looked at the tomato plants he noticed something that caught his attention: a plant resembling parsley that stood four feet high with leaves that looked like white parsley on purple, spotted stems.

"I'll bet it's parsley," Mike said.

"I'm not so sure," Tom said. He pulled off a few leaves and twirled them in his fingers. He sniffed the leaves, and then tasted them.

"Well?" Mike asked. "Is it parsley?"

Tom spit the leaves out and shrugged his shoulders. "Not sure yet. I'm gonna take some of this and have it tested. I don't want to let anything get by us. Who knows what Giorgio's into?"

The next day, Tom was sitting in his office reading a file when Lynn Sullivan entered carrying an envelope. "Some guy from the Horticultural Society delivered this for you. When did you become interested in plants and flowers?"

He took the envelope from her and removed the letter inside. After reading its contents Tom was excited. "I'll be damned!"

Tom rose from his desk and rushed past Lynn. "I'm going to the medical library."

Lynn shook her head as Tom disappeared down the corridor. He rushed to the Philadelphia College of Physicians' library and asked for books on pathology and toxicology. The librarian there brought him book after book as he pored over the pages looking for answers. He read from *Toxicology* and *Elements of Pathology* and asked for more texts as he thought of more questions. A librarian wearing horned-rimmed glasses arrived and piled another stack of books on his desk. Tom stayed at the library until it closed.

# Chapter Twenty-Six

Tom sat beside Mike as he drove down East River Drive past the houses lining Boathouse Row. They were headed back to the office after grabbing lunch together.

"Are you ready for tomorrow's Disciplinary Board hearing?" Mike asked.

"I sure as hell hope so."

"Good luck."

"Thanks. But I'll probably need divine intervention."

"Are you worried about Evans exerting his influence on any of the board members?"

"Pat warned me about a guy named Lord who's definitely in Evans' pocket. All I can do is maintain my decorum and present my case."

After Mike left the office, Tom opened his wallet and stared at a faded photo of himself with his older sister and parents—a prized possession. He'd carried it on board the ship that had taken him and his family to America. A tear came to his eye. *I'm the only surviving family member left and I'm not going down in disgrace.*

The next morning, Tom made his way to the Pennsylvania Supreme Court's disciplinary board. He was assigned a seat at a small, rectangular table a short distance from Roger Flowers, the disciplinary board prosecutor, and a stenographer. Both were seated at an adjacent table. Three men, whose name placards gave no hint of what positions they held, sat facing the principals. They were the lawyers chosen to sit in judgment of Tom: Keith Lord, Richard White and Vincent McDermott. Tom had no way of knowing how many of the lawyers were in Evans' pocket. He looked at the men and wondered if he would still have his job at the end of the day.

Mike, Lynn and Hope sat in the first row behind Tom. Evans and a bodyguard were sitting behind them. Tom flashed Hope a smile as the hearing was about to begin, and she responded with a quick wink before Keith Lord made the first move in the proceedings.

"Thomas Rossi's been accused of egregious professional conduct. Deputy Mayor Evans has filed a complaint. Roger Flowers is representing the State Supreme Court. Mr. Flowers, would you please state for the record the charges filed against Mr. Rossi?"

Flowers rose and addressed the panel. "The charge is the wanton and malicious false arrest of Lillian Stoner. Mr. Rossi has charged her with the homicide of her spouse, Reginald Stoner, by poison."

"Let's proceed," Lord said.

Tom was sworn in by the stenographer and he took his seat, hoping that he would be able to hold his own.

Lord spoke. "Let the record reflect Mr. Rossi wishes to represent himself. Am I accurate, Mr. Rossi?"

"Yes, sir."

"Rossi's dumber than I thought," Evans whispered to his bodyguard in a tone loud enough for all to hear. "Doesn't he know a lawyer who represents himself has a fool for a client?"

Hope and Lynn both turned and glared at Evans. He, in turn, offered only a sheepish grin.

"You may begin with your questions, Mr. Flowers," Lord said.

"Mr. Rossi, did you order the arrest of Lillian Stoner?"

"Yes, I did."

"Did you order her arrest before you received the coroner's autopsy report?"

"Yes." Tom shifted in his seat.

"Lillian Stoner's arrest warrant alleged she murdered her husband by poison, correct?"                    "Yes, and I believe it's accurate."

"But the medical examiner's autopsy report concluded Reggie Stoner died of pneumonia and not poison, correct?" Flowers stared at Tom. His voice was calm and methodical and Tom could tell he wasn't going to ask questions he didn't have the answers to.

"Correct."

"Mr. Rossi, you've had years of experience prosecuting homicide cases, correct?"

"Yes."

"Then, tell us, how does a man with years of experience make such an egregious, impetuous error?"

"I don't believe I committed an error," Tom replied. "We ... we had a witness named Moore. Lillian conspired—"

"Yes," Flowers interrupted. "The dead ex-con."

"Our suspicions were confirmed by an insurance broker named—"

"We're only interested in scientific evidence justifying arrest before autopsy," Lord interrupted.

Evans gave Lord a slight nod, which few managed to notice, and Lord gave a slow blink in response.

"Now, why don't we discuss the motives for your actions?" Flowers said. "Deputy Mayor Bill Evans refused to endorse you as the party's candidate for district attorney. In an effort to retaliate, you maliciously had his niece, Lillian Stoner, arrested and imprisoned, and you did this without an autopsy to support your theory."

Tom seethed inside, but maintained his cool. "Mr. Flowers, that allegation is totally false."

"You were playing Russian roulette with Mrs. Stoner's freeedom, Mr. Rossi!"

"That's total nonsense! I demand an opportunity to explain my motives," Tom exploded, rising to his feet to look Lord dead in the eye.

"You're completely out of order!" Flowers said. "I object."

Lord bent his head to confer with his colleagues. "The objection is overruled," he said. "We will allow Mr. Rossi to testify, but we, as well as Mr. Flowers, will reserve the right to ask questions as he proceeds. Also, please confine your remarks to relevant, scientific evidence, Mr. Rossi."

Tom took a moment to breathe. *I'm the defense now instead of the prosecution. But I can do this. I have to.* "As a prosecutor, I've always had an interest in homicidal poisoning—"

"Please avoid lecturing us and get to your defense." Lord was pushing the issue.

"I'm aware of poisons," Tom continued, "their effects on the body, and a victim's symptoms. We established motive and—"

Flowers interrupted. "Cut the nonsense, Mr. Rossi. What's the scientific basis for your arrest of Mrs. Stoner? You had nothing beyond circumstantial evidence and a confession that was given under the influence of alcohol."

Tom knew he'd made a mistake in arresting Lillian when he had. He'd made his decision when he was angry with Evans and now he was paying for his stupidity.

*I'm not losing my license to these puppets*, he thought. *I'm not losing everything I worked for.*

Tom ignored Flowers and kept going. He lied to the board.

"Because of Stoner's symptoms, I concluded we were dealing with a poisonous alkaloid, such as *conium maculatum*, also known as hemlock. I did not expect the coroner's physician's autopsy to show traces of hemlock." Tom was bluffing. He hadn't thought of hemlock as the murder weapon until he got word back from the Horticultural Society. "But, even without autopsy evidence of poison, we had irrefutable evidence proving Lillian Stoner and Giorgio DiSipio's guilt in poisoning Reggie Stoner."

Lord smirked. "I spent twenty years prosecuting homicide by poison cases in this city. I'm not aware of any case ruled a homicide before the poison was identified."

"Hemlock is an alkaloid which dissolves and disappears from the body," Tom said. "It's the reason why it's not found after lab tests or autopsy."

"But most of these toxic substances contain obnoxious odors," Flowers said, "Can you identify the odor of an alkaloid?"

"Most toxins do have unique odors," Tom replied. "Conium has the odor of a mouse's urine. For this reason, most humans and animals will avoid the ingestion of any substance containing conium. However, if one were to disguise conium in orange juice, liquor, or poached eggs, more likely than not the intended victim would not detect the pungent odor. Stoner's mother said her son complained, in the weeks before his death, that his bourbon tasted funny. We think conium ended up in his alcohol."

Flowers smirked. "I'm confident I can prove your alkaloid theory is flawed, Mr. Rossi. Can you cite us just one homicide poisoning case which supports your theory?"

"The 1855 London case of Palmer-Cook is similar. Palmer was tried, convicted, and executed."

"1855? Over 74 years ago," Flowers said. "Surely there's been scientific advancement in modern-day autopsies involving issues pertaining to toxicology."

Tom knew his use of the case was a risk, but he had to keep the board focused on the possible use of poison so that he could bring the discussion around to Giorgio's garden. "Of course there's been advancement in pathology, but the chemical composition of an alkaloid and its effect on the body has not changed."

"You were about to tell us about this Palmer-Cook case," Lord said.

Tom nodded. "Yes. Palmer killed Cook with another alkaloid called strychnine. Doctors couldn't find poison in the body in the Cook case either. But prosecutors got a conviction. The victim's symptoms and the evidence proved Palmer's guilt."

Richard White turned to Lord. "Keith, you remember … we studied the Palmer case in law school. It's legitimate precedent."

Lord turned to look at Evans and found the deputy mayor staring directly at him.

"But Stoner drank excessively," Lord argued. "How'd you rule out cirrhosis of the liver as the cause of death?"

"The autopsy report said the ulcers in Stoner's liver were large and rough," Tom said. "Ulcers caused by cirrhosis are smaller and smoother. I'm no pathologist, but Stoner's autopsy liver plasma tests were normal."

"Right you are, Mr. Rossi," said Flowers, "You're no pathologist! Maybe that's why you can't explain away the pneumonia diagnosis made by an expert pathologist who is a little more qualified than you at making a diagnosis of cause of death."

"The side effects of poison and pneumonia are the same," Tom said. "Hard breathing, nausea, vomiting, stomach pain, and diarrhea—"

"Mr. Rossi, this is 1939," Lord said. "The number-one killer in America is pneumonia, and the symptoms you just listed are completely in keeping with pneumonia."

"Yes, but Stoner had jaundice and nerve damage in his legs, symptoms of poison, not pneumonia. The coroner's physician didn't address these facts. It has to be a case involving hemlock poison. No heavy-metal poisons, such as arsenic or bismuth, were detected in the body."

"Nothing but conjecture from an amateur," Flowers said. "I read the homicide report in this case. You found arsenic in Giorgio DiSipio's car, not poison hemlock."

Tom's moment had arrived. "True, but we later found a plant growing in Giorgio's backyard."

Tom presented the letter from the Horticultural Society, which confirmed the plant was hemlock, also known as *conium maculatum*.

Lord tried in vain to dispute Tom's letter, saying it wasn't evidence the plant had actually been used. Flowers reminded the panel that Giorgio's possession of the plant did not prove Reggie Stoner died of hemlock poisoning. But White and McDermott had seen enough.

"Gentlemen, I'm willing to listen to Mr. Rossi," said McDermott. "Please refrain from interrupting."

Tom explained how hemlock could be turned from a plant into a viable poison and presented additional information from the texts he'd read at the library.

"Gentlemen," he said, spent, "I rest my case." Tom turned and looked for Hope, but she had gone.

Lord shrunk back in his chair and, after a long discussion with his fellow hearing examiners, finally spoke. "The panel will adjourn and deliberate. We'll reconvene and issue a decision and opinion one week from today."

# Chapter Twenty-Seven

Deputy Mayor Bill Evans' campaign against Tom was beginning to cause real damage. Tom's personal life was now fodder for the local media, and his career was in jeopardy following Evans' attempt to have him disbarred.

But Tom wasn't the only victim in Evans' fusillade. In trying to protect Lillian Stoner from prosecution, Evans had shattered much of Hope Daniels' world. He had caused her to lose her job under humiliating circumstances and the public revelations about her race caused people she had known for years to suddenly ignore or avoid her. But most importantly, she knew Evans had given Tom reason to hesitate in asking her to marry him. Though Tom professed his love for her, she knew he was hurt to find out Hope had kept secrets from him, especially a secret that seemed likely to hurt his chances at becoming D.A.

The weight of her situation had hit Hope in the chest as she sat through Tom's hearing, and she rushed home before its conclusion. Several hours later and Hope was still sitting in her living room, trying to figure out what to do.

*Damn! If only I'd been honest with Tom about my background sooner, I know he would have understood and we wouldn't be in this situation. But would he have ever really have loved me if he knew? He's so ambitious and now I'm holding him back.*

Hope knew that Tom was more hurt about losing his chance at being D.A. than he let on. She felt a divide growing between her and the only man she'd ever really respected and loved.

As Hope smoked a cigarette and listened to jazz from her living room radio, the

phone rang. "Hello? This is Hope."

"Good evening, Miss Daniels." It was Evans. Hope shifted in her seat when she heard his voice and her grip on the phone was turning her knuckles white.

"Miss Daniels, I believe it would be in everyone's best interest for you to hear a proposal I have. It may help save everyone a great deal of trouble."

Hope didn't respond right away to Evans. She sat on the couch and stared straight ahead; her breathing was slow and deliberate as she used the silence to gather her thoughts.

*How does this guy have the audacity to call me? And how did he manage to get my private telephone number?*

Hope could feel Evans waiting for her response. "How may I help you, Mr. Evans?"

"Good, Miss Daniels, very good." As Evans' voice came through the phone, Hope could feel her skin crawl. Everything about the situation felt wrong.

Evans continued, "I'm glad you're willing to listen, Miss Daniels. I know my remarks in the past may have upset you, but I assure you I meant no harm. Politics can be a dirty business and sometimes things get out of hand. It seems Tom allows his Italian temper to be his worst enemy, and perhaps I've responded in kind. Ma'am, I'd like to meet with you personally to give you my proposal. If you're not satisfied, we can always compromise."

"Why must we meet in person?" Hope asked. "Give me whatever proposal you may have over the phone and we'll discuss it right now."

"I know you have cause to doubt anything I say," said Evans, "but I assure you we'll meet alone. Neither my bodyguards nor anyone else will be present. I'm just as anxious as you to resolve my differences with Tom. I've found in my experience such things are better resolved by one-on-one mediation."

"Suppose I tell Tom I plan to meet with you? Do you have any objection?"

"Look, Miss Daniels, as far as I'm concerned, if you must tell Tom, so be it. But you know and I know he'll never approve of us meeting."

*He's right*, thought Hope. *But I'm not going to meet on his terms unless I'm sure I'll be safe.* "Suppose we meet in one room for our discussion while Tom or anyone else I choose stays in another room?"

Evans laughed. "I'll meet you under any conditions. But, again, I believe it would be best if Tom were not aware we're meeting. If we got together in my office, whomever you choose could sit outside in my reception room … or anywhere you want; it could be a restaurant, a church or the public library."

"OK, Mr. Evans, I'll meet you in your office tomorrow at 8 p.m. I may bring someone with me, or I may come alone."

"Done. See you tomorrow night."

Hope hung up the phone and stared at the ceiling as she thought about what to do. *Should I call Tom? There's no way he'd agree to me going, but I've got to make up for what's happened.*

The next day, Hope prepared to meet Evans. She hadn't spoken to Tom since his hearing and she had no plans to until she could do something to help fix the situation. As she stood in front of the mirror in her bedroom, she took one last look at herself. Her long, black, velvety hair shined, as did her long eyelashes. Her emerald dress—her favorite— matched the color of her eyes. The dress hugged the curves of her body and revealed just enough cleavage to announce femininity. Lastly, she wore Tom's favorite Oriental perfume.

Thirty minutes later and Hope was standing outside of Evans' office, her hands shaking as she gently tapped on the door of Room 224 at City Hall.

The door opened immediately and the deputy greeted her with a warm smile. "Hello, hello." Evans looked behind Hope, expecting to see her friends.

"I decided to come alone," she said as she smiled. "I didn't want you to feel uneasy if we're to have a serious discussion."

Evans smiled, and a look of relief crossed his face. He was glad to have her alone. He couldn't help gawking at her full breasts and healthy figure. "Come in. Come in," he said, and his eyes locked on the movement of her hips as she entered his office foyer.

Hope walked passed Evans and into his office. To her, the room spoke of power and arrogance with its old, red leather furniture and photos of glad-handing politicians. The smell of cigar smoke made its way into her nostrils as she took a seat in a leather chair across from Evans' large, oak desk. The size of the office matched Evans' girth, and Hope felt small in the open space of it. The chair swallowed her slight frame, and she felt her feet dangling above the floor.

Trying to ease some of the tension, Hope quipped, "I believe you need a decorator to bring this office into the 20th century."

Evans let out one of his famous belly laughs. "You know, I believe we'll be able to do business. What can I get you to drink?"

She pointed to the bottle of Scotch on the desk. "It would appear we enjoy our booze, Mr. Evans. Hopefully we have other important interests in common." Hope smiled a weak smile and played with her hair.

Evans laughed again. "Well, as far as I'm concerned, a woman who drinks can't be all bad." He opened a draw and retrieved two glasses then reached for the brandy and Scotch bottles.

Hope smiled again, but her eyes held no amusement. "I'm a nut about cleanliness. Do you mind washing the glasses first?"

"Of course. Please excuse me, the washroom is in the office lobby."

As Evans waddled out of the room, Hoped opened the brandy bottle, poured a powdery substance into it, capped it and shook it. She moved to the couch and waited.

The deputy returned, poured her a Scotch and then gave himself a generous portion of brandy. Hope looked at her glass. "Mr. Deputy, could you please double my drink? It's not often I get to enjoy a fine Scotch."

Evans' eyes gleamed as he poured more alcohol into her glass, which she abruptly clinked against his. "Here's to solving all our problems."

"Absolutely," he said as he emptied his glass in one swallow and poured another.

Hope sipped from her glass. *I have to stall him for a while. Then things should get interesting.*

Evans sat so close to her on the couch that their legs rubbed together. Hope didn't move, but placed her hand on his knee and rubbed his inner thigh. The deputy's tongue protruded slightly and he became sexually excited.

"Look," he said, "if Tom agrees to the autopsy findings, everybody will be happy. I'll hold a press conference announcing that the party is endorsing his nomination for D.A., and he's guaranteed to win, even considering recent developments. But everything depends on you convincing Tom to play ball. From what I hear, he'll do anything for you."

Evans got up and poured himself another brandy while Hope nursed her Scotch.

When he sat back down, their legs touched again. This time, he placed his hand on her thigh and rubbed it. "What do you think?"

Hope nodded. "Sounds like a good opportunity to me. But what about my old job at PGH?"

"You can have your old job back the minute Tom does what he has to do," Evans said.

"No deal. I don't want my old job back … I want to be the new chief executive nurse at the hospital. As a matter of fact, I want the nurse who dismissed me fired for incompetence. Her name is Florence Obermayer."

Evans shuttered. "I can't fire her. She's the wife of one of my ward leaders."

Hope rose from the couch. "Then I can't recommend your deal to Tom!"

Evans looked up at her from the couch, clearly annoyed. "Alright. No problem."

Hope took her seat next to him on the couch. "One more thing: I want a ten-year contract."

Evans looked down for a moment, then unbuttoned his shirt and loosened his tie.

*Maybe he's getting sleepy,* Hope thought.

Evans made his way back to his desk and refilled his glass of brandy without noticing that Hope had taken very little of the original Scotch he'd poured her.

The deputy raised his glass. "OK. Do we have a deal?"

She stood and clinked his glass. "We certainly do."

Hope gave him a kiss on the lips as she began unbuttoning his shirt. He looked at her with a silly grin, then yawned; he was sinking fast. Evans sat on the couch in an attempt to fight off the dizziness he was feeling. He couldn't keep himself upright and he slumped back on the couch. He tried to speak, but his words were slurred and incoherent. Hope moved quickly to the couch and took off the deputy's shoes, socks, and pants. As he rested his head on the back of the couch, she removed his underwear and pulled him onto the rug in front of the couch. As the nude deputy passed into unconsciousness, Hope gathered all of his clothes and placed them in a mail sack. She quickly emptied the remainder of the brandy bottle onto the rug beside him and placed the empty bottle at his feet. Then she put the bottle of Scotch away in his desk drawer and put the glass she had been using in the mail sack.

Before leaving, Hope blew a kiss at the snoring deputy then threw a match into a wastebasket in the office foyer. Flames rose above the rim of the wastebasket as Hope moved into the hall and tripped the fire alarm. After checking the hallway for city employees, she walked down the concrete steps to the first floor and exited City Hall.

Within five minutes, Hope saw two fire engines with sirens wailing, accompanied by three police cars. They were headed toward City Hall.

*My time as a nurse is really paying off,* she thought.

While in nursing school, Hope had learned about a knockout drug known as a Mickey Finn or a 'Mickey.' The drug was chloral hydrate, and it was used to treat insomnia. The drug got its nickname from its use in a drug-laced drink used to incapacitate robbery victims before they were rolled in Mickey Finn's Chicago bar. The robbery technique was most commonly referred to as "slipping one a mickey."

Chloral hydrate treats deep insomnia by depressing the user's blood pressure and respiration; it can also cause confusion and nausea. Hope had taken no chances with the deputy—she had given him a double dose. Bill Evans wouldn't remember how he ended up naked on his office floor in a cloud of black smoke.

The next day, Hope read the *Globe* headline: "A Nude & Confused Deputy

Mayor Evans Felled by Smoke Inhalation in his City Hall Office." She couldn't help but smile. *So much for the despicable deputy's future in this town!*

# Chapter Twenty-Eight

Tom's petition to exhume the bodies of Eva's second husband, Michael, and Joanna's husband, Antonio, was granted by the court several weeks after his disciplinary hearing. It was spring 1938, and Tom's investigation had been building for months.

Michael and Antonio had died within one week of each other and Tom wanted to find out if all of Giorgio's women were involved in the murder-for-money scam.

Several weeks after his hearing—and one day after Evans was found naked in his office—Tom, Mike, Sam and Joe looked on as two cemetery workers hoisted Michael Russo's remains from his grave with chain pulleys. Mistakes made during exhumation could often jeopardize a valid autopsy, so Tom wanted to be there for the collection of his evidence. Earlier in the day, Tom had supervised Antonio's exhumation as well. Because he suspected death would be attributed to homicidal poisoning, he secured samples of the soil above, below, and surrounding the coffins.

"Check for water inside the coffins, too," he told Mike. "Sometimes water will leak into a coffin from underground springs. This cemetery also uses arsenic as a pesticide and remnants occasionally find their way into coffins."

"Why take samples of the soil, though?" Mike asked.

"If a body contains poison after autopsy, we can prove it wasn't acquired from the soil, as long as the chemical tests of area elements prove negative."

Tom cautioned the cemetery workers to handle the coffin with care. "Guys, I've seen dozens of bodies after exhumation, and I've seen excellent preservation after 10 years of death if everything was done right in preparation for burial. I've also seen significant decomposition after a few weeks of burial, so the body may be in a delicate state."

Tom stared at the wooden box as it was pulled from the ground.

"I'm worried about decomposition," he said. "I have a hunch they used the lowest grade of embalming fluid."

As Michael's coffin rose above the lip of the grave, rain came down to soak the detectives.

"Damn!" Mike said. "Look at the water and mud pouring out from the bottom. Eva's poor bastard of a husband worked two full-time jobs to support her and this is what she buries him in?"

Sam pried the lid open with a crowbar. Everyone gasped. Fungal growth had distorted Michael's face beyond recognition after only a few months of burial. Tom ordered the detectives to wrap the coffin in a tarp so that it could be taken to the medical examiner's office.


Howard Summers, the coroner's physician, sat at his desk reviewing his report on Reggie Stoner as Tom and Mike sat across from him.

"I owe you an apology," Summers said. "After going through the autopsy again, I now agree with you on the cause of Reggie Stoner's death. To think this guy DiSipio grew hemlock in his backyard."

"What about the tests on Joanna and Eva's husbands?" Tom asked.

"The good news is we found arsenic in the liver, kidneys, bones and hair of both husbands, just as you suspected."

"And the bad news?" Mike asked.

"The husbands were embalmed with arsenic trioxide."

"Arsenic trioxide?" Mike repeated.

"Arsenic was frequently used as an embalming fluid before January 1 of this year. They changed the law and made it illegal. I guess the undertaker didn't know of the new requirement."

"Didn't know, my ass," Tom said. "The same undertaker, Sacca, buried both husbands. This isn't a coincidence. They used arsenic to poison these guys, then covered their tracks by having them embalmed with arsenic."

Call a few of our friendly reporters," Tom instructed Mike outside of the coroner's office. "Let's let word out: Sacca is wanted for murder. But tell them off the record I'm willing to cut him a deal if he cooperates."

"You can't guarantee a deal in a homicide case without the approval of the trial judge," Mike said.

"Don't worry … if this guy identifies Giant and the Lady in Black, I'll convince any judge to be lenient."


Tom entered Connor's office to find him seated behind his desk, smoking a cigar. "You wanted to see me, Chief?"

One of my spies on the Disciplinary Board called me this morning. They're sending a letter to you today with their decision. Charges against you were dismissed by a vote of two to one. Congratulations."

"Thanks, Chief," Tom said, truly relieved.

"I suppose you won't be surprised to learn Lord's the one who voted against you."

"No. I've got it on good authority Lord needs Evans' backing to become a common pleas judge."

"If you have ambitions about being D.A., you can't keep going to war with Evans, Tom. Other politicians might get worried you'll come after them next, and they'll put you through this kind of thing again and again. My advice is to ignore Evans. He'll self destruct on his own."

"Thanks, Chief. I'll remember that."


Later, Tom drank his Dewar's at a table in the Venice Lounge, with Mike sitting next to him. Despite the drink, Tom couldn't stop thinking about the case. "Any luck on leads for the Giant and his veiled lady?"

"Nope. They've vanished."

Mike saw a waiter and held up his index finger, then turned to Tom. "Did you hear about last night?"

"I heard Eva attempted suicide."

A waiter appeared with a bottle of beer and Mike chugged it down in one shot, slammed the bottle to the table and wiped his mouth with a napkin. "Yeah. A matron called me last night from her cellblock. Eva tried to choke herself to death with a hanky, but after five minutes she

realized it couldn't be done. I don't get this chick. She acts all tough when we arrest her and we know she killed at least two guys. Now she's trying to off herself. I mean, this lady went all out. She married Michael Russo, and then bought nine life insurance policies on his life within six months. When we confronted her, she clammed up ... like she was afraid of someone."

"Scared of someone?" Tom asked. "Didn't you tell me Eva spent time at Grace Russo's house in Buffalo before she married Michael?"

"Yep. She apparently went up there shortly after her first husband was blown up. As a matter of fact, I remember Grace Russo saying Eva drank quite a bit when she went up to Buffalo. Are you thinking she knows something?"

"I'm not sure. But Eva doesn't seem like the type to be afraid of anyone. Giorgio's involved with a lot of women, and most of those women have killed their husbands, right?"

"As a matter of fact, yes. We picked up another one yesterday, a Helen Sherman."

"Christ!" shouted Tom. "What if Eva spilled the beans to Grace? What if Grace knows something that could put Eva away for good?"

"I don't know," Mike said. "Eva may have realized that Giorgio never really cared about her. I mean, having all those women paraded through the station couldn't have been easy for her."

"Mike, Eva's a whore. She sleeps with anyone moving, and she had to have known about Giorgio's other women."

"I know, but she's still a woman. And I overheard some of the other girls chuckling about her marriage to Dennis being more of a ploy to get back at Giorgio than a real romance."

"At this point it could be anything. Maybe being in prison was too much for her; maybe she really is scared of something. I don't know. There's something here we're not seeing, and I want to find out what it is."

Mike shook his head. "I guess the next thing you'll be telling me is all of our murdering wives are members of the same witch order."

"Could be," Tom replied. "It just seems like Giorgio's too stupid to mastermind a conspiracy. I don't know if I'm just too deep into this case to really see everything clearly, but all of these pieces keep floating around in my head."

Tom picked up his glass and swirled its remains around. "You've got Giorgio romancing these women, and using a rare poison to kill some of their husbands; there's an insurance man saying he helped set up the policies; and his accomplice is now dead. Now we find out that an undertaker was likely involved, and that he used arsenic to cover up arsenic poisoning. We've gotta get Eva to talk. Where's her handkerchief?"

"In her evidence file in City Hall."

"Bring Grace Russo to my office in two hours. I have a plan."

Tom and Grace entered City Hall at 11 p.m. The place was deserted except for the criminal cellblocks on the seventh floor and the duo was anxious as they exited the elevator. Tom didn't want anyone to discover his visit and Grace was upset about having to see Eva again. They left the bank of elevators and walked to a caged door that stood beneath a sign reading: "WOMEN'S CELL BLOCK."

Tom pressed a buzzer and a tall, muscle-bound matron with short blonde hair appeared. She nodded to Tom and unlocked the door. Tom and Grace followed the matron down a narrow aisle of prison cells to the last one, where, through the jail bars, Grace saw Eva lying on a cot.

Standing outside of Eva's cell, Grace could see that Eva had lost weight during her time in prison. She wasn't the full-figured woman she once was and the prison issued-uniform she wore hung around her shoulders. As Eva lay on the bare cot in her cell, Grace could see the red marks around her neck. Though the handkerchief hadn't been strong enough to kill her, it had left its mark.

But sympathy wasn't on Grace's agenda. "Muori, putana!" she said. "Die, you whore … you know what you did to Michael and I know what you did to Dennis. They didn't die on their own."

Eva pulled herself off the cot and moved to the bars of the cell. "You're never gonna prove anything, you hear me? Everybody knows Dennis was killed by the Lenzetti mob. Just because you couldn't keep your husband's hands off me doesn't mean you know anything about Dennis."

"You don't hold your liquor so well, Eva," Grace said calmly. "Maybe you should think about what you blabbed to me and Michael before you start denying things."

"Eva, you're looking at life in prison," Tom said. "I think you should reconsider your stance. You're defending a man who clearly didn't care very much about you. To Giorgio, you were just another piece of ass."

"Giorgio loves me!" Eva said. But she couldn't keep her façade up. Her time in prison was wearing on her, and she was beginning to realize that she could spend the rest of her life there. Her hands began to shake as Grace screamed insults at her. She moved back to her cot and curled into a ball with her back to Tom and Grace.

"Eva, I want you to think about what you're going to do in the next 24 hours. It may save you from the electric chair."

Tom turned to Grace, who was still cursing Eva. "You made your point. Now let's get the hell outta here." He grabbed her hand and they sprinted through the opened cage door. The matron slammed it behind them as she shook her head in bewilderment. The next morning, Tom was dressing for work when the phone rang. He looked at his ticking alarm clock, the sound loud and insistent. It was 7 a.m. "Rossi here."

"It's Mike. I don't know what came over Eva, but she woke up singing like the fat lady. Get down here. I'm sure you'll want her statement as soon as possible.

# Chapter Twenty-Nine

Mike entered Tom's office with Eva. She was dressed in a white and black polka dot dress with black shoes and a white handbag. Because she was cooperating, Tom had arranged for her to wear her street clothes and keep make-up in her City Hall cell. He felt it was important to keep Eva's morale up because, in the days following her suicide attempt, she had shown signs of deep depression. Mike and Eva sat in the two chairs in front of Tom's desk, across from Tom and Lynn.

"She wants to keep singing," Mike said.

Tom nodded to Lynn, who had pen and paper ready to transcribe. He smiled at Eva, hoping to assure her he was someone she could trust. "Eva, this morning you said Giorgio supplied the poison to murder your husband Michael and that he got him insured. Was Giorgio the only person involved with you in this? We know Giorgio had other women he was working with, and I think there's more to this than you, or anyone else, has been letting on. Were you a member of a larger, secret conspiracy of women?"

Eva's jaw dropped. To this point in the day, she'd been in good spirits; dressing up always made her feel better. "Why ask me such a question?"

"Eva, we both know Giorgio isn't smart enough to run something like this on his own and we know you killed Michael with arsenic," Tom said. "What do you have to lose now? This is about saving your own skin. I don't want to see you go down alone for something other people made you do."

Eva felt a chilling rush of anxiety. She feared the consequences of violating her relationship with Giorgio, but she also feared what the Lady in Black might do to her if she found out she was spilling the beans on their group of wives. Eva stared at Tom for what seemed like forever and then spoke. Her voice was quiet and subdued. "Look. I'll help you convict Giorgio and some of his conspirators. But I won't answer any questions about the other wives I know. If you can't accept that, I won't say another word."

Tom didn't want to push his luck. Eva's testimony would seal Giorgio's doom and he felt as though he could convict some of the other wives without Eva's help. "Okay, fair enough. What can you tell us about this Giant and his Lady in Black?"

"I don't know anything about a Giant and a Lady in Black, except what I read in the papers."

"What part did this Sacca character play with Giorgio?"

"Sacca was Giorgio's close buddy. He also thought he was some kind of ladies' man. The undertaker got his kicks out of taking care of lonely wives, if ya know what I mean."

"This Sacca ever take care of you?" asked Mike.

Eva couldn't hide an embarrassed smile. "Once in a while I cooked up spaghetti for him."

"Al dente, I'll bet," Mike said.

Lynn blushed and Tom and Mike exchanged a glance. "Did Sacca help Giorgio in the murders?" Tom asked.

"Sacca embalmed husbands with arsenic. He knew it was illegal when he did it to Michael. But I thought it would make it impossible to prove my husband died of arsenic poisoning. How did you know I killed Michael?"

"I didn't know for sure until now," Tom said.

Eva's smile disappeared.

"Where's this Sacca now?" Tom asked.

"I don't know. He skipped town when Giorgio was arrested."

"What else can you tell us?"

"Giorgio has another close friend from South Philly, a real weirdo named Boris Feldman. He thought he was a witch doctor. Giorgio used to refer to him as the 'Rabbi.'"

"Is he a real rabbi?" Mike asked, concerned about anyone making the Jewish community look bad.

Eva laughed. "The way this guy acts? Hell, no. He's a lowlife who makes a living conning little old ladies and lovesick wives. Check this out: There's a rumor on the street he and Giorgio seduced two Polish broads, had their husbands insured, and then conspired with the wives to murder them. Both hubbies were bakers."

Mike asked, "Do you know the names of the wives?"

Eva thought for a moment. "As I recall, Giorgio referred to them as Big Mary and Judy, the Polish beauty queens. I never caught their last names."

"I thought you said you weren't going to help us convict wives?" Tom asked.

"I said I wouldn't help you convict wives that I know," Eva said, correcting him. "And I don't know the bakers' wives."

The phone in Tom's office rang and Lynn picked it up. "Mr. Rossi's office…" After a few seconds she handed the phone to Tom, but covered the receiver. She whispered in his ear, "I guess your headline flushed him out. Sacca's on the phone."

"Get Eva out of here," Tom whispered to Mike. After Mike and Eva had left, Tom took the phone from Lynn. "Yes?"

"All I did was embalm dead people," Sacca said, the words tumbling out. "You hear me? Dead people. I didn't kill anyone."

"What are you willing to do to prove your innocence?" Tom asked.

There was nothing but silence on the other end of the line. "I need the identity of the whole gang," Tom said, "like the Giant and his mystery woman."

"I'll identify them. But first I want a letter which guarantees me a deal signed by the D.A. himself."

"Call me in 24 hours," Tom said. "You'll have your letter."

"Twenty-four hours," Sacca repeated then hung up the phone.

"Lynn, when does Pat Connors get back from vacation?"

"Tomorrow," Lynn said as she put the receiver back on the phone.

Mike re-entered the office. "Eva Russo's lying," he grunted. "She knows the identity of the Lady in Black and the Giant."

"I agree," Tom said.

Just then, Joe walked into the office with a big, muscular woman in her 50s who could have passed for a female jailor. He sat her across from Tom and introduced her. "This is Helen Sherman. As you know, her husband died in 1936. Upon exhumation, the body was so badly decomposed the coroner's physician didn't have a clue as to whether he was poisoned. We're releasing her today."

Tom looked at her and smiled. "It's true, Helen, we were going to release you today. But instead we're re-arresting you for consipiracy. We know all about your little group of women."

Tom was lying. No one had given them anything of substance on a deeper conspiracy, but he hoped Helen wouldn't figure that out.

"Of course, if you cooperate, things could change." Tom held a file in front of her face. "We know all about it, Helen. Eva sang like a bird. How long have you been involved with these women?"

Helen's face turned white. She quickly placed a hand to her mouth and stared at the floor in silence.

"I do my research, Mrs. Sherman," Tom continued. "The women Giorgio was involved with, they weren't acting alone. Right?"

Mike continued the assault. "How long have you been involved with these women?"

She continued to stare at the floor as Mike scowled in an effort to intimidate her. "We know Eva is also a member of your secret club, Mrs. Sherman. And she told us you were a member. And to make it worse, she's thinking of testifying against you to stay out of the chair."

Helen finally lifted her eyes to Mike's. "I don't believe you. The only person I'll hang for you is that creep Giorgio and his buddy the Rabbi. But I won't testify against Eva or any other wife."

On Mike's cue, Joe took Helen by the arm and led her out of the office.

"Honor among wives?" Mike said, scratching his chin. "That's a new one."

"Maybe, but something is keeping their mouths shut, and it's not Giorgio."

# Chapter Thirty

Old Moyamensing Prison was located at Moyamensing Avenue and 11th Street in South Philadelphia. Locals called it "Moco." The prison dated back to the Civil War when Confederate prisoners were held there. But now, on warm days, the whole place smelled of manure from the police horse stables next door.

John McBurn, Giorgio's lawyer, sat with Tom at a large table, awaiting the prisoner's arrival. The steel door to the interrogation room clanged open and Giorgio shuffled in, escorted by a single guard. Chains were locked around his ankles and wrists. The guard put him in the chair directly in front of the room's only window so the sun would shine in his face.

McBurn offered him a cigarette, which Giorgio accepted. He took a long drag and then put on his routine smirk. "Should I be worried?" he asked. "My lawyer shows up with the prosecutor?"

McBurn had a reputation as one of the finest criminal lawyers in the city and the Board of Judges appointed him to represent Giorgio. Giorgio said he had no money for a defense lawyer when he was arrested since the D.A.'s office had temporarily frozen his bank accounts. McBurn didn't like Giorgio, but he was a consummate professional and was unaffected by personal feelings.

"Mr. Rossi has something to say to you. I thought you should hear it from him personally," McBurn said.

"Oh, yeah? Well, I got somethin' to say to the counselor first." Giorgio looked Tom in the eye. "There's people on the street who wanna get even with you for knockin' some of my teeth out. You better take my advice and hide your nigger girlfriend. We wouldn't want her to get herself hurt, would we?"

Tom bristled but remained mute. He had expected this, but McBurn appeared livid.

"Mr. DiSipio! One more veiled crack of disrespect or another threat and I resign as your lawyer, effective immediately. As a matter of fact, what you've stupidly accomplished is to make me an eyewitness to your threats of physical harm. I'll declare this meeting over if you can't understand."

Giorgio's smirk faded. "Look, John, I..."

"My name is Mr. McBurn to you."

In acquiescence, Giorgio shrugged his shoulders and showed his lawyer the palms of his hands. Then McBurn gave Tom a nod to proceed.

Tom looked straight at Giorgio. "Two of your girlfriends are pleading guilty and will testify against you. In addition, we have two insurance brokers and your hemlock plant. We've got more, which we'll show your attorney later if need be."

Giorgio grinned. "I'm impressed."

"I'll make this simple," Tom continued, ignoring Giorgio's arrogance. "You must identify the Giant and the Lady in Black, and then testify against them and Lillian. You'll get life instead of the chair."

Giorgio took a deep breath, then exhaled. "I wanna tell you a story, counselor," he began. "Me, my aunt and uncle, we fled Sicily when I was 6. I woke up one mornin' and found my Pop dead. They hung 'im from a tree outside our house. The Mafia put five slugs in his brain and stuffed a cork in his mouth. He had disgraced our family by rattin' out the local loan shark."

Giorgio took a puff from his cigarette, then exhaled a cloud in the attorneys' faces, waiting for them to respond.

"An interesting story," Tom replied, knowing what Giorgio was going to say next, but playing along just for the hell of it. "But what's your point?"

"I'm Sicilian, counselor. I'd rather burn in hell or in your chair than be known as a fuckin' squealer."

"Mr. DiSipio, I want you to consider Mr. Rossi's offer," McBurn said. "We can go to trial if you want, but if he's telling the truth about witnesses, I think you should consider it."

"Counselor, you can go to hell," Giorgio spat. "I'm not saying anything. I don't care what Mr. Rossi has; and besides, maybe I know somethin' he doesn't."

Tom rose from his chair and called for the guard. "Very well, Mr. DiSipio. I'll see you in court."


Tom waited for Hope on her living room couch. Louise, Hope's elderly, colored maid entered. She had worked for Hope a couple of days a week for the past five years. The thin, sixtyish woman liked Tom. "Mister Tom, Miss Hope be out soon. She be making herself pretty for ya."

"Thanks, Louise," Tom said. "Enjoy the rest of your evening."

Hope entered just as Louise left. She had just showered and looked in the mirror as she brushed her long, black hair. Tom looked at Hope and realized how much he had been missing her. *Her green robe matches her beautiful emerald eyes*, he thought.

"Would you like some Scotch?" Hope asked as she poured herself a Napoleon brandy and picked up a bottle of Dewar's.

Tom nodded. "You're still wearing the perfume that drives me nuts, huh?"

She winked then placed a Billie Holiday record on the phonograph. Hope poured him a drink and handed it to him. "To old times," she said as she sat beside Tom on the couch.

Tom and Hope clinked glasses and sipped their drinks.

"I spoke to Giorgio in his cell today. He threatened to harm you again. Let me get you some police protection."

Hope shook her head. "Absolutely not. If I agreed, I'd be no better off than Giorgio, trapped in a cage."

She paused for a moment, as if she were collecting her thoughts about something. "I've been reading about you almost every day in the papers, Tom. How are the cases of the wicked wives going?"

"We caught a break. An undertaker named Sacca phoned me and said he'd identify this mysterious Giant and his Lady in Black."

"I'm glad it's going well."

Tom smiled at a framed photo of Hope and himself on an end table.

Hope watched his eyes lock onto the image. "I've made a decision," she said. "In your heart you do love me, and I also know you're willing to suffer the consequences which would inevitably spring from our marriage. But I won't be the reason you can't achieve your goals in life."

Tom winced. "You've decided it's over between us, haven't you?"

Tears rolled down her cheeks as Hope started to sob. "My God … this is the most difficult decision I've ever had to make."

Tom held her face in his hands and wiped away her tears with his fingers. "When we first met, I had lived most of my adult life dealing with the dead. But during our relationship, you once told me we're born to love the living. It's the reason we exist and the only end. Please reconsider this."

Hope grabbed Tom's hand and pulled him up off the couch as she stood. She flicked out the living room lamp and dropped her robe. Tom saw her nude silhouette in front of the moonlit window.

"I'm going to remind you why love is life's one and only pleasure," Hope said. She took his face in her hands and tenderly kissed each cheek.

Tom's hands dropped to her inner thighs. He felt wetness. She feverishly slid her tongue into his ear, then frantically tore the buttons off his shirt and pulled down his pants. Hope wanted to feel her man inside her one more time.

# Chapter Thirty-One

Few lights burned in the semi-detached homes of the northeast neighborhood of Bridesburg. A milkman made deliveries from a horse and wagon, but otherwise the dark street appeared deserted except for a few parked cars. Sacca peered out of a partially opened, walnut-stained wood door. He was a tall man with a long nose; Giorgio's gangster friends had given him the nickname "Hose-nose."

Sacca looked left and right down the street as he peered out into the early morning darkness. He was staying at an apartment rented by his girlfriend while hiding from Giorgio's associates. He knew that word would get out he was looking to cooperate and he didn't want anything to happen to him before he could reach police protection. He moved out of the doorway and walked quickly to a parked car, unlocked it and got behind the wheel, locking the door behind him. He let out a sigh of relief as he turned the ignition. Then he saw someone in the rearview mirror.

Tom looked hungover as he entered his office. After being up all night with Hope, he was a mess: hair uncombed, in need of a shave and dark bags hanging under his eyes. Lynn snickered as she saw him enter the office, but it was nervous laughter. She could tell Tom had been with Hope and she was jealous.

"Get me some coffee, will you?" Tom said as he headed for his desk.

As Lynn left to get coffee, the office phone started ringing. Tom's headache was pounding, so he answered the phone himself.

"Rossi here."

"Tom, this is Mike. We found Sacca dead in his car this morning at 7. He had been hiding out at an apartment that a girlfriend rented a few months back."

"Son of a bitch! Was there anything about the killing that may give us some clues?"

"Yeah. Whoever did it wanted to send a message; he slit Sacca's throat."

"Sicilian," Tom said. "We have any witnesses?"

"A milkman saw a '36 Buick with both our suspects inside."

"What about Sacca's car?"

"We're dusting it for prints," Mike said.

"Have your men question the girlfriend and search the apartment."

"Will do," Mike responded, ending the call.

Five minutes later, Lynn walked into Tom's office with a cup of coffee. "Joe Whittaker's on the phone. He's got bad news.

Tom picked up the phone. "Yeah, Joe."

"Helen Sherman hung herself last night."

"Great. Where are you now?"

"I'm at her house; it's 1560 South Juniper Street in South Philly."

"I'll be there in thirty minutes."

"Better hurry. The coroner's men want to take the body out as soon as possible."

The scene in Helen Sherman's living room was a gruesome one. Her body was suspended above the floor by a rope that had been tied to a rafter and a chair lay turned over at her feet. Her eyes were bulging and her tongue protruded from her mouth, and as Tom arrived he could see her body swaying silently in the tidy space of her living room. The sound of the rope pulling on the rafter was loud in the silent room, and it bounced off the family photos and tidy furniture as a photographer took pictures.

Joe was talking to a young doctor from the coroner's office when Tom arrived. He turned and walked toward Tom, trying not to look at Helen's body. "Her daughter found the body. She came over to take her shopping. The woman didn't leave a note or anything."

Tom stepped onto a chair and examined the hanging corpse. The rope had left abrasions on the neck.

"This is an obvious case of suicide," the doctor said.

"I don't think so, Doc." Tom pointed to the abrasion under the area where the rope rested. "The final resting place of the rope created this ring. If you look closely, you'll see a second abrasion below the rope mark."

The doctor stared at the neck and found it. "I'll be damned."

"I'll be goddamned!" said Joe.

"The first abrasion caused strangulation," Tom continued, "then the murderer hung the corpse to simulate suicide. The rope rose up her neck as her body slumped, causing the second ring-like abrasion."

"Who could have done this?" Joe asked.

"In order to lift a big woman like Helen, the killer had to be very strong, like our mysterious giant."

"Ya know, Helen was the first wife to be released of all the arrested wives," Joe said. "Do you think word got out on the street she was ratting for us?"

"It's possible," said Tom. "Someone didn't want Helen talking, and they silenced her. More likely than not, it was the same people behind this murder conspiracy. Let's get additional search warrants for all the arrested wives. I suspect we'll find some sort of connection between at least a few of them."


The main reception room of the D.A.'s office resembled a sea of people. The crowd included detectives, uniformed police, Pat, Tom, Mike, Lynn, Joe, and Sam. Everyone held sketches of the Giant and the Lady in Black. Tom raised his hand to quiet the room.

"Our giant's about 50; he stands six-foot-four, wears a mustache and has thick, gray hair. I've seen this guy in person; he looks like the movie actor Cesar Romero. He dresses in a suit and hat and travels with a brunette. She drives a black '36 Buick and dresses in black with a hat and veil. We think her name's Rose Grady, 35, alias, the 'Kiss-of-Death Widow.' Check hotels, dives, and cathouses. We're going to put the heat on every mobster, bookie, thief and hooker. Their way of life comes to a halt until we find this bastard ... and his whore."

Mike approached Tom as everyone started to leave. "Your theory about a larger consipiracy looks like it's accurate. We found matching, handwritten notes in Joanna and Lillian's homes; they look like coded instructions to a meeting place somewhere."

"Anything in the homes of the other arrested wives?"

"No luck there. But the note in Joanna's home mentioned something about a bond among the women involved. It looks almost like a threat to any woman who turns on the others."

Mike handed Tom the paper. "A meeting for the widows," Tom read. "My God! This crew is working together and someone is killing anyone who knew too much. In view of what happened to Helen Sherman, do you think Eva, Lillian or Joanna fear they may be next on the hit list?"

"I don't know," Mike said. "But it doesn't matter. Lillian and Joanna both have lawyers who won't let us get near them and Eva won't say a word about the other wives."

"It figures," Tom said. "Every time we get a little closer to solving the big puzzle, the lights go out."

"Yeah … and one more thing," Mike added. "Guess which one of our wicked wives is having serious withdrawal in her cell?"

"Lillian?"

"Constant complaints of excruciating stomach pain and severe sweats and chills, according to the matrons."

"Are the prison doctors treating her?"

"They've sent her to the drug addiction unit at PGH for outpatient treatment—" Mike stopped mid-sentence and snapped his fingers as though a light had gone on in his head. "I've got an idea which could supply most of the missing pieces."

Tom waited for Mike's miracle idea. "Which is?"

"Instead of letting PGH doctors wean her down every time she goes into opium withdrawal, let's subject her to 24 hours of closed-door questioning when we know her lawyer isn't visiting. We could dangle the opium and pipe we took from Giorgio's shop in her face as an inducement for a full confession. The broad will succumb in no time."

Tom shook his head at the idea. "If anyone found out, I would get disbarred, we would lose our pensions, and then both of us would be sentenced to a long prison stretch at Eastern State." But Tom wasn't ruling out Mike's idea altogether. He wanted answers and the thought of having Lillian talk was a huge temptation. "Let me give your idea a little more thought. We may be able to work something out."

# Chapter Thirty-Two

*Moyamensing Prison Conference Room*

Two days after Eva Russo implicated Boris "Rabbi" Feldman as a conspirator in the deaths of Henry Bolsky and John Ashten—the two Polish bakers—police issued an arrest warrant for him.

Detectives learned that upon hearing of Giorgio's arrest, Feldman had fled to Brooklyn where he and his family were operating a Jewish deli. The New York City Police Department granted Joe and Mike permission to to apprehend Feldman in Brooklyn, even though they also wanted him for questioning on a private criminal warrant. They claimed he had raped a 70-year-old grandmother while posing as a doctor.

But when Joe and Mike went to Brooklyn to apprehend Feldman, he'd already fled town.

A few weeks after their trip to Brooklyn, Mike got a tip from a source in Feldman's old South Philadelphia neighborhood that the guy they were looking for was working as a waiter at Grossinger's in the Catskill Mountains under the alias "Jacob Zimring." With clearance from the New York State Police, Mike and Joe went to the Catskills and arrested him.

The day after Mike and Joe arrested "Rabbi" Feldman, Tom, Joe and Mike sat waiting in a meeting room at Moyamensing. Tom was hoping to get Feldman to flip on his friend Giorgio and he also wanted to test Eva's stories about the two men.

Suddenly, the barred prison door to the conference room clanged open. Feldman shuffled into the room, followed by a prison guard. As the guard seated Feldman across from Tom and the detectives, Tom thought, *This guy is even uglier than his arrest photo.*

Feldman was a dark, stocky man of 5-feet-5-inches, with jet-black hair, a large, pointy nose and a head too large for his body. His right eye was made of glass and he appeared to look straight ahead, even when his left eye moved. His appearance was made even more unsettling because he kept his left eye almost completely closed. Feldman was dressed in a shabby, blue serge suit, a soiled gray shirt and a stained, blue tie; the soles of his shoes were worn away. His hands were shackled and he had walked with a noticeable limp while entering the conference room. He wore bandages on his head because Mike had clobbered him with a slap-jack during his arrest.

Despite his appearance, Boris Feldman seemed confident, and his demeanor didn't reflect his current predicament. After being seated, he looked at Tom and his detectives as though they were students waiting for a lecture.

Mike wasted no time in letting Feldman know that he looked disheveled. "What a *schlepper*," he said, using Yiddish to describe the Rabbi's appearance.

"Good morning, Rabbi," Tom said. "We've never met before. These are my associates, Detective Mike Fineman and Detective Sam Whittaker. Of course, you've met them."

Mike and Sam nodded at Feldman, who was squinting in the bright room.

"Gentlemen, this is Boris Feldman," said Tom, "a/k/a 'the Witch Doctor,' a/k/a 'The Man with the Evil Eye,' a/k/a 'Rabbi.'"

Feldman smiled at the floor as Tom read his aliases. He seemed proud of his notoriety. Then, speaking with a heavy Russian-Hebrew accent, he proclaimed, "Gentlemen, I have degrees from Grodno University—"

Mike interrupted him. "Spare us. It was a Ph.D. in flim-flam economics, right?"

"What do you mean? I'm Dr. Boris Feldman, an educated aristocrat."

"You mean an aristocratic asshole!" Mike said.

Sam asked, "What makes you think aristocrats don't burn in the electric chair?"

"You're a schmuck," said Mike.

Tom read from Feldman's arrest record and investigative report. Feldman was wanted on multiple warrants or criminal complaints and Tom hoped to leverage a possible death sentence to make Feldman flip.

"You moved to South Philly in 1927 and opened a grocery store at 7th and Emily Streets. You soon figured out that it was more profitable to con superstitious and ignorant immigrants. By 1930 you were working as a 'doctor,' and treating mostly women with domestic problems." Tom smiled at his detectives. "Rabbi specialized in helping lovesick females cope with errant husbands."

Feldman gave Tom a self-deprecating shrug.

Sam said, "Rabbi, in 1934 you were charged with fraud. You sold people a liquid to chase evil spirits from their homes—"

"It was faith healing," Feldman said. "If you had faith in my liquid, evil spirits would disappear from your house."

Mike looked disgusted. "Chemical analysis proved your liquid was nothing but vinegar and turpentine. You're a crank!"

Feldman showed no signs of remorse at Tom's criminal roll call.

Tom continued. "In 1935, you made a call on a gullible old Italian lady, saying you would clean her cellar coal heater. After you left, the woman heard a croaking sound in her basement. Thinking that her dead husband's spirit was hiding there, she asked you to rid the house of the ghost. You went down the cellar carrying two lit candles, waved the candles in the air and shouted Oriental incantations. When you came upstairs, the croaking sound was gone. The little old lady was so grateful, she paid you $100, but the next day she discovered a dead frog in her basement and—"

Feldman interrupted. "You can't prove I put a frog in the basement." He crossed his legs and leaned back in his chair as he waved his hand in the air. "If a widow thinks the croaking of a frog is evil spirits ... that's her problem."

Mike was visibly angry. Feldman represented the kind of con artist that had taken advantage of his family when they'd first come to the United States.

"Let me take this *schlemiel* downstairs for five minutes," Mike said. "He'll talk sense afterward."

Sam stared at Feldman. "In 1936, you told a woman you'd bring her husband's voice back from the grave. She brought you to his gravesite and a muffled voice identifying itself as the woman's husband was heard. The voice told the woman it was all right to marry again and she paid you $200 for the session, only to later discover the voice was none other than Giorgio DiSipio."

"I can't help it if the widow heard voices in the cemetery."

"Mr. Feldman, we know why you fled Philly," Tom said. "Your deeds are following you and, among other things, we have statements from women you've treated. These women were unhappy because their husbands rejected them sexually. You told them that once you freed their bodies of evil spirits, their husbands would again love them. They claim you hypnotized them, made them disrobe in your basement and raped them while they prayed."

"Rabbi, you're looking at 90 years hard time," warned Mike.

"There was no rape," said Feldman, "The sex-starved women consented! They knew what they were doing. They just wanted an excuse to cheat on their husbands."

"You really enjoy playing the clown, don't you?" Mike said.

Tom had heard enough. "Well, let's see if the Rabbi thinks this is funny. We're having a press conference at noon today. Based on the affidavit of Eva Bell, we're identifying you as Giorgio DiSipio's co-ringleader in the South Philly poison ring. We're charging you with first degree murder in two homicides: Henry Bolsky and John Ashten."

Tom had intentionally misled Rabbi. Eva had told Tom she had suspected him of being involved in the murders, but she insisted she had no real proof. Tom decided to gamble anyway; he needed someone close to the inner circle of conspirators to talk.

"We're also charging you with conspiracy in the death of three other husbands."

Mike stood up from the table and walked toward the door, away from Feldman. He looked at Boris as he sang, "Burn, baby, burn," before calling for the guard.

The guard entered the room and walked toward Boris, who by now was realizing that his options were limited.

"Take this funny man away," Tom ordered.

Tom and Sam rose from their seats and collected their notes as the guard stood watch over Feldman, who stayed seated and appeared to be calling Tom's bluff.

But Feldman knew that Giorgio faced execution and that Eva and another wife might link him to other homicides. As the bulky prison guard pulled him out of his chair and moved him toward the exit, Feldman panicked. He was a comical sight, limping forward with his head twisted backward in an attempt to address Tom.

"No, no, wait ... I'll help you solve ten murders," he shouted.

Tom motioned for the guard to stop. "Are you serious, or are you going into your comic routine again?"

"Gentlemen, I'm deadly serious. I'll tell you what I know." Feldman searched the detectives for a response as he strained against the prison guard's grip.

Tom motioned for the guard to leave the room and led the reprieved man back to his chair.

Feldman gathered himself and wiped the sweat from his forehead with his soiled tie. Suddenly his voice resembled an arrogant Cossack general. "I'll help you solve murders," he shouted. "Me," he said, pounding his chest, "Boris Feldman. I'll help you convict people. Me," he said, again pounding his chest, "Boris Feldman."

"Are you proposing a deal?" asked Tom.

In a shirt now soaked with perspiration, the Rabbi studied Tom. "May I have a cigarette?" he asked.

Sam gave him a Lucky Strike.

Feldman looked down at his shoes and took a drag from the cigarette before speaking again. "I want a guarantee of life imprisonment," he said. "I don't want to burn in the chair."

"If you give us one fact we can't corroborate, the deal is off," said Mike.

Feldman nodded.

Suddenly, Mike couldn't control himself. "I want you to know something, 'Rabbi' Feldman. My parents are Polish-Russian Jews just like you and they came from Eastern Europe, just like you. As I sit here, I'm ashamed we share the same ethnic background, you fuckin' *yentzer*!" Mike used the Yiddish word that meant 'swindler.' It took the con man by surprise.

Mike stood and walked around the table. He looked down at the now trembling Boris. "You lie to us just one time and, dammit, I'm going to personally twist your fuckin' balls off! Have you got that, *putz*?" Mike didn't wait for an answer. He grabbed one end of Boris' tie and pulled the other end upward so that the tie wrapped tight around his Adam's apple. Boris' eyes widened as he stared at Mike and began turning blue. Only then did Mike release his hold on the tie.

Mike leaned in close to Boris and looked directly into his eyes before grabbing his tie and yanking it upward. "Then, I'll stretch your neck like this." Mike lifted Rabbi's tie so far above his head, he nearly lifted him off the chair. Boris gagged and his eyes bulged. Mike wasn't through. He reached down with his left hand and gave Boris' scrotum a hard squeeze, then pulled harder on his tie. "You understand where I'm coming from, Rabbi?"

Boris turned blue, but managed to nod that he understood.

"I can't hear you, *putz*!" Mike said. Boris could barely nod as Mike tugged on his tie. "If I squeeze his balls one more time, he'll qualify as a soprano in a boys' choir," Mike said to Tom as he released his hold on Boris' tie.

Tom nodded and shouted for Lynn, who was waiting for Tom's signal outside the interrogation room. "Lynn! You can come in and take his statement now!"

The door to the room clanged open and Lynn entered. She recoiled at the sight of Boris, who was still gasping for air after being released from Mike's grip. She nodded at Boris and then looked away, as though his appearance might dirty her. Lynn sat beside Tom and pulled steno paper and a pen from her briefcase.

"Okay, Boris," said Tom, "it's time to start talking."

When Boris hesitated, Mike snuck his hand under the table and into the Rabbi's crotch. He squeezed and Boris coughed loudly and grimaced.

Lynn jumped and immediately looked up at the Rabbi and frowned. Without taking her eyes off him, she turned to Tom and asked, "Is he sick or something?"

"Don't worry about him," Mike said. "He's just nervous."

Sam lit another cigarette for Boris and handed it to him. While taking a drag from his cigarette, the Rabbi whispered, "I have a photographic memory and the ability to recall names, dates and places. I can tell you everything I was involved in and who was involved with me."

"Were you the ringleader of the South Philly gang?" Tom asked.

"No! The ringleader was Giorgio. He *schtupped* wives, then made them poison their husbands."

"What was your part?" Mike asked.

"Well, I sometimes supplied poison and on occasion helped him ... send their husbands to California."

"What the hell does that mean?" Mike asked.

Boris winked. "To send them to a better life ... in heaven."

Tom asked, "I guess you provided leads, too?"

"Once in a while, I gave Giorgio a lead or two," Boris said.

Tom bent forward so he'd be closer to the Rabbi. "Tell us about the inner workings of the ring."

The Rabbi grinned and clasped his hands together. Though shaken by Mike's lecture, he was relishing the opportunity to give a sermon.

"The insurance murder system prospered because we were able to take out small policies without the insured being examined," he said. "Opportunities were plentiful and we didn't have to work too hard to find our 'clients.' Every family quarrel or love spat was grist for our mill. We let a frustrated housewife suspect her husband's affections were wandering and one of the bosses would give her a 'love potion' to recapture him." Boris laughed and murmured something to himself. "The basic ingredient was conium, bismuth or arsenic. Meanwhile, we made sure the husband was insured. If a boarder in a lower-class home became infatuated with the wife of the household, the poison ring was there, providing a lucrative way out for both parties. A lot of our leads were supplied by neighborhood fortune-tellers, or even by the wives themselves, like Eva Bell, Joanna Napoli and Helen Sherman. When we discovered a vulnerable wife, one of our gang would tell her that the stars said her husband would die soon, or that she would never really be free until her husband was dead. Then, we would instruct them to take out insurance on their husbands and we would refer them to one of the insurance men we kept on the books."

"Why did you use arsenic and conium?" Tom asked.

"Arsenic was cheap and easy to find," Boris answered. "It always fooled the physician because the symptoms were almost identical to pneumonia. Conium was very expensive and we only used it for jobs with bigger insurance policies." Boris giggled. "The stupid doctors never suspected foul play and you can't find conium in vital organs after the autopsy."

"Whose idea was it to use conium?" Mike demanded.

"I don't know! Giorgio was never clever enough to figure it out, and I have a feeling there was someone pulling his strings because he once slipped and said he had to meet a woman to pick up some supplies."

"Was there a pattern the gang would follow?" Tom asked.

"The wife was told to wait until her husband had a bona fide illness, such as a common cold, indigestion, or upset stomach. If the prey had ongoing physical illnesses, such as diabetes or a bad heart, she was told to wait until he complained. The wife would call the local physician and get treatment for her husband. After the doctor left, she would place a teaspoon of poison, per day, in his food, coffee, or juice. When the prey was on the verge of death, she would again call the physician and explain he suddenly took a turn for the worse. The confused physician, who arrived shortly before or after death, would list the cause of death as heart disease or pneumonia. The symptoms of those diseases closely paralleled conium and arsenic."

"When did you meet Giorgio?" Sam asked.

Boris chuckled and looked down at the table, his mind reliving his first encounter with Giorgio. The cigarette in his hand was burning down to his fingers, but he was oblivious. "In January 1932, I went to a futuro convention at Broad and Moore Streets in South Philly."

"What the hell does 'futuro' mean?" Mike wanted to know.

"It's a term Italians use meaning 'the future,'" said the Rabbi. "But it turned out to be the code name for poison. There must have been a crowd of 100 people there. They fancied themselves faith healers, fortune-tellers, witch doctors, or hex-doctors."

"Was Giorgio there?"

Boris nodded. "Giorgio went with his girlfriend at the time, Rose Grady. Every fortune-teller, old-world Italian and faith healer who lived in North or South Philly was there: Maria Fuentés, Sadie Buck, Josie Tete and Eva Bell, just to name a few. They had some real doctors, too. Dr. Larry Rosenberg compared notes with some South Philly physicians."

"How did John Ashten die?" asked Mike.

"His wife, Mary, came to me and said she had a double indemnity policy on her husband. She agreed to split the insurance money with us if we would make it look like an accident."

"Did you make it look like an accident?" Tom asked.

"Giorgio did … a hit and run by car."

"How did Judy Bolsky's husband die?"

"Giorgio gave Judy ground bismuth to put in his supper every night for a month. Her husband immediately developed a severe sore throat. Eventually he couldn't talk or eat and after being treated at PGH for several weeks, he died. The doctor diagnosed throat cancer as the cause of death."

"What the hell is bismuth?" asked Mike.

Tom answered for the Rabbi. "It's another heavy metal poison, like arsenic."

"Who the hell is this mysterious woman," Mike asked, "the one who dresses in black and drives a Buick with her boyfriend, the real big guy?"

Rabbi shook his head. "I never saw Giorgio with any real big guys, but as far as the Lady in Black, she may be his old girlfriend, Rose Grady. She usually dresses in black and some people called her 'The Widow.' I haven't seen her in a couple of years. You know, she once did a nude dance for her third husband and gave the son-of-a-bitch a heart attack."

Lynn stopped taking steno and stared at Boris.

Tom shook his head and looked at his watch. It was 6 p.m. and the Rabbi had been blabbing for almost eight hours. "Okay, let's call it a day."

After the Rabbi left the room, Tom turned to Sam. "Listen, I think we have something good here, but I need to know for sure. Boris is a braggart and I want to know whether or not he's putting on a show for us. Take him out and get him plastered. I'll let the warden know what's going on. I want to know if he tells one story while he's sober and another when drunk."


In the days that followed, Boris gave the detectives a pile of significant leads and expanded the number of suspects to eighteen people. Accompanied by detectives, he drank at a local tavern every night for weeks and rattled off names, dates and places with the amazing speed and accuracy of a thoroughbred horse race announcer, giving a wealth of information. Following up on Boris' leads took time, but many of them turned out to be valid.

In one case, Boris claimed that 31-year-old Iris Novak of West Philadelphia poisoned her mother-in-law. "She poisoned her 67-year-old *shiver*, Lena Novak, on February 9, 1936," Boris explained. "'*Shiver*' is Yiddish for mother-in-law."

Novak confessed in open court the day after her arrest. She had purchased arsenic from Boris and substituted it in her mother-in-law's medication capsules. Lena Novak had been a diabetic and died within hours.

In receiving Iris Novak's guilty plea, Judge Harry Crosby quipped, "It would appear Mrs. Novak had a personality conflict with her mother-in-law, so she DiSipio'd her." During the months of investigation involving Giorgio, his story had become headline material, and even his methods of killing were entering the common lexicon.

Boris' information led to additional arrests at the same time his entire, sordid history played itself out for the detectives. But not all of his stories led to convictions.

Boris claimed he had advised numerous, disenchanted wives experiencing domestic problems, including Elsa Berkowitz, a 56-year-old chicken-store proprietor in South Philly. Her husband Isaac, 57, died in July 1935 after he had refused to consent to Elsa's request for a divorce after 40 years of marriage.

When arrested, Elsa Berkowitz denied she had any part in her husband's death and insisted she did not carry one cent of insurance on him. She admitted she had purchased "bathing powders" from Boris, which were rubbed on the legs of her arthritic husband. However, upon exhumation, Isaac's body had decomposed, making an autopsy impossible.

Boris also accused Dr. Lawrence Goldberg, as well as Mike Gold and Giorgio DiSipio, of killing two of the physician's patients.

"Giorgio seduced a woman named Florence Frost," Boris claimed during one of his drunken testimonials. "He persuaded her to poison her wealthy mother, Edith Warrington, who suffered from acute kidney disease. Her mother had been Goldberg's patient for years, so Giorgio had Dr. Goldberg write a prescription for the mother's kidney medication, which Florence had filled at a pharmacy. She took the medicine to Mike Gold, who emptied capsules and substituted arsenic. That night, Florence administered a capsule to her mother, who died within an hour. Dr. Goldberg pronounced Warrington dead and said she died of 'acute nephritis.' Florence inherited an estate worth $30,000, but turned the $10,000 life insurance money over to Giorgio and the others."

Sam and the other detectives were amazed at how much the Rabbi was willing to tell them. They began to suspect that Boris was enjoying the attention of being a star witness.

# Chapter Thirty-Three

Mike spotted Tom and Lynn having lunch at a table at the rear of the Venice and approached them with a broad smile. "Our informant's tip checked out. We believe Rose Grady's holed up in a riverfront apartment near the Delaware River Bridge."

Tom was ecstatic. *Finally*, he thought, *we're going to get to the person in charge of the whole damn ring*. He stood from the table and started heading for the exit with Mike and Lynn in tow. "What are you waiting for?" he asked. "Let's go arrest the bitch."

Joe piloted the unmarked police car at full speed with Sam sitting shotgun and Mike and Tom sitting in the rear. He pulled the car up in front of a shoddy row house on the waterfront at Delaware Avenue, not far from the Port Authority Bridge.

Joe and Sam jumped from the car and ran to the rear of the house while Mike and Tom ran up the front steps. Mike kicked the flimsy front door open and rushed inside with Tom right behind him. After checking the hallway and the side rooms, Mike and Tom made their way to a bedroom at the back of the house. With his gun drawn, Mike kicked open the bedroom door and found Rose naked in bed with twin girls, 16. They were screaming and trying to get dressed. Mike leapt across the bed and forced Rose against the wall just before she could make her way to a window.

"What the hell's this?" Tom said. The room was lit only by daylight, and other than the bed, it had no real furniture. A single chair sat in the corner by the door and it was piled high with old comic strips and pornographic pictures. The two girls in bed with Rose were thin, almost waif-like, and their clothes were mere rags. Tom pulled them from the bed and ordered Sam to have uniformed police officers take them into protective custody until their parents—if they had parents—could be found.

"The Kiss-of-Death Widow's tired of men," Mike quipped.

Tom opened the only closet in the room. A black dress, slip and veil hung on a hanger; on the floor below were black shoes and black stockings.

"We've been looking for you for a long time, Rose," Tom said.

Rose said nothing. She stared at the wall and ignored Tom and the others in the room as though she was alone and nothing had happened.


Pat and Tom stood outside a soundproofed room and watched through a one-way mirror as Mike stood over a seated Rose Grady. Mike waved his arms frantically as he shouted at her.

"We know you killed your husbands, Rose. It's just a matter of time before we prove it. Just tell us what we want to know about the poison ring and maybe we'll make life easier for you."

Mike was leaning down so that his face was close to Rose's. He was staring into her eyes, waiting for her response. She just shook her head.

Pat turned to Tom and said, "I'm told Rose won't cooperate."

"She claims all her husbands died of natural causes ... and dares us to prove they were murdered," Tom said.

"Of course, she denies knowing the Giant or driving the Buick."

Pat and Tom continued to watch Rose through the window. She didn't say a word but continued shaking her head at a frustrated Mike. Rose wasn't easily intimidated or scared. The pressured interrogation with Mike was no different from the lectures on sin and religion delivered by her mother when Rose was a child growing up in South Philly.

In 1910, when Rose was seven, her father was killed in a saloon brawl. The hardship of being a single mother made Maureen Grady a strong and assertive woman. She struggled to support her family and worked as a domestic six days a week. She found solace in her Catholicism and instead of telling Rose normal bedtime stories at night, fed her the Catholic Church's dogma and history. Maureen told her daughter of the religious bigotry which Irish Catholic immigrants had to endure when they came to America and Rose remembered one night in particular when her mother explained the hatred between Protestants and Catholics in Philadelphia.

"We got persecuted, right up to the turn of the century," Maureen told her daughter. "We were Catholic and that might as well have been a sin. Protestants kept spreadin' rumors that the Pope was sending his army of Catholics to conquer America."

"Did Protestants respect priests?" asked Rose.

"Never, may God forgive 'em. They likened priests to whore masters, carryin' on with nuns."

"Why?" Rose asked, afraid to hear the answer.

"Some ex-nun from Canada, named Maria Monk, wrote this book about convent life. She lied, claiming nuns were forced to live in sin with priests; she said if they didn't, they were murdered. Monk said the nuns' illegitimate babies were slain and buried in the convent's dirt basement."

Rose stared at her mother in disbelief.

"When the book hit Philly in the summer of 1844, riots broke out and the Protestant Irish used Monk's book as an excuse to beat up on poor Catholic Irish. Your great uncle, Shawn Brady, got shot dead, right in the street."

"Did Catholics strike back?" asked Rose.

"Darn right. They raided this Orange meeting in Kensington and killed two of the murdering culprits. The next day riots broke out—a disgrace. Orangemen burned the homes of thirty Catholic families and then they went and burned down Catholic churches: St. Augustine and St. Philip De Neri. Jesus! Afterwards, the churches were nothing but charred timbers."

Rose's mother insisted her daughter become a nun so, at 16, she spent two years in a convent run by the sisters of St. Joseph. But Rose had to leave the convent because she became pregnant after having an affair with a janitor. Rose had chaffed under her mother's strict rules and she was beginning to give in to her lust for men.

Rose had a miscarriage after six months of pregnancy but she didn't slow her pursuit of the kind of lifestyle her mother had fought against. After leaving the convent, she sought financial support from the men of Philadelphia. She was a tantalizing seductress, especially in the eyes of tired, old men who had forgotten the excitement of sexual pleasure. They found the attractive, longhaired brunette irresistible. A flamboyant dresser, Rose loved to wear huge, light-colored fedoras with dark headbands and she always wore dark, silk blouses that were cut low at the neck. Rose wore tight-fitting skirts to accentuate her figure and she enjoyed walking with a wiggle through her South Philly neighborhood, especially when she knew men were gawking at her behind.

In 1928, when Rose was 25, she fell in love with and married a 20-year-old laborer named Bill O'Brien, with whom she had two daughters. Rose's romantic notion of marriage suffered a blow when O'Brien turned out to be a bum. After two years of marriage, she began to seek affection and support for herself and her daughters. She found what she was looking for in Giorgio DiSipio.

Now, years later, as Rose sat before Mike in a brightly lit interrogation room, she chose to keep her mouth shut about the man they called Don Juan. To find out more about Rose and her checkered past, Tom and Mike turned to the Rabbi, who gave them her detailed history during an hour-long visit at Moyamensing Prison.

"Within two years after marrying O'Brien, Rose met and commenced an affair with Giorgio DiSipio," Feldman told the detectives. "She found O'Brien dead in bed in September 1931. The examining doctor concluded the young man suffered a premature death due to a myocardial infarction."

The Rabbi smirked. "A little while later, Rose married Paul McDermott, a plumber who later died of 'pneumonia.' Then she married Umberto Conte. He was a lot older than her and owned a successful butcher shop in South Philadelphia. Incredibly, the physician also listed Conte's death as a myocardial infarction. Rose's neighbors figured the odds were high her fourth husband, Martin O'Meara, would meet a similar fate as her first three hubbies."

The detectives exchanged a glance and shook their heads in disbelief. Feldman continued, undisturbed. "Back when Giorgio was arrested, Rose took off. Poor O'Meara, he came home from his night job to find his rented house empty. She had sold all his furniture before she fled and left her daughters with their grandmother. Rose had collected insurance on three of her four husbands, but abandoned the idea of collecting on O'Meara, the fourth."

"Do you know for sure that Rose killed her husbands?" Mike asked.

"I only know for sure about Umberto because I was there," Boris said.

"You were there?"

"That's right. I saw the whole thing."

He proceeded to tell Tom and Mike how Umberto Conte had met his demise on his birthday.

The festivities started promptly at 8 p.m. on a Saturday night at Umberto's apartment, located above his butcher shop. As a recording of Caruso's melodious voice from *Veste La Jube* filled the air, Giorgio, Eva, Rose, Rabbi and Umberto picked at a large array of Italian food. Laid out across the kitchen table were Sicilian olives, roasted peppers, provolone cheese, imported Parma ham, artichokes soaked in olive oil and fresh Italian bread.

They washed down the delicacies with homemade wine and, by 11:30, Umberto had drunk a quart of the Italian wine known as "diego red." He was dazed and flushed as he sat on the couch next to Giorgio. Blood pounded against his temples and his reflexes slowed. Finally the old man's eyelids closed and he began to snore.

Giorgio changed the record on the Victrola to the seduction scene from *Samson and Delilah*. The loud music woke Conte from his deep slumber and he looked up to see the bedroom door flung open.

Rose made her grand entrance dressed like a belly dancer. A red silk scarf flowed from her hair, which reached to the middle of her back, and she wore a skimpy red bra. A transparent, light-linen skirt hemmed with red sequins was see-through enough that

Umberto could see she wore red panties underneath. With her hands held high, Rose clapped as she wiggled her hips to the fast-paced beat of the music. She moved across the room until she was right in front of her husband. "Umberto, baby, dance with me," she said. Rose smiled down at her husband then turned her back to him so he could see her firm thighs and buttocks. Every time she moved, the ankle bells she wore jingled.

The old man rubbed his eyes and arched his brows as he stared up at Rose. Giorgio and Eva stood behind her and roared with laughter. "Take her, Umberto! Take the *putana* now!" coaxed theRabbi.

Rose took delight in frustrating Umberto. She gyrated her hips and breasts two feet from his face and teased him by sticking her tongue out at him. Every time he tried to grab her, she spun away. His blood pressure rose, but he didn't give a damn and his lewd grin told Rose she had begun to reawaken his libido.

Rose plucked the silk scarf from her hair and wrapped it around Umberto's neck in one motion. As she danced, she pulled Umberto's face in close to her gyrating bosom. His 65-year-old eyes widened and a silly grin crossed his face amid more catcalls from Giorgio and Rabbi.

The beat of the music grew faster and louder and Rose shook her hips in rhythm as she tossed away her skirt. She teased Umberto by releasing enough scarf slack to expose her panties. Rose grinned down at Umberto and pushed her rotating belly inches from his face. "Does baby want some honey?" she asked as she whirled around so her buttocks bounced.

Umberto lunged to clutch the bobbing cheeks of her derrière, but his hands slipped away. Rose had coated her bottom with cold cream and Umberto laughed as she pulled out of his reach.

Giorgio, Rabbi and Eva were now rolling on the living room floor. They couldn't suppress their laughter at the sight of the stymied old man.

The tempo of the music increased and Umberto felt his heartbeat speed up. His breathing became labored, but his gaze never left Rose's body.

Suddenly, Rose whipped off her panties and tossed them in the air. She placed her hands on her rotating hips and hummed in tune with the music as she harassed the old man by pushing her naked crotch into his face in split-second segments. Then she abruptly withdrew her torso from his impatient lips.

"Baby, if you can grab it, you can keep it," she said.

Umberto couldn't hear the music anymore and perspiration poured from his forehead, eyes, nose and mustache. His tongue hung from his mouth as he watched Rose move back and forth into and out of his reach.

Rose squealed and raised her arms behind her back and un-snapped her flimsy bra, exposing her breasts. She clasped her hands above her head and smiled down at Umberto while waving her bosom with the beat of the music. She flicked her bra at Umberto's face.

"Down, baby, down," she teased.

"Grab the bitch!" Rabbi shouted.

"Now! Do it now!" said Eva.

Umberto could no longer restrain himself. He sprang from the couch, wrapped his arms around Rose's waist and locked his hands. He buried his face into her inviting bosom.

Rose stopped dancing and slipped her hands under his belt. She grinned as her hands slid inside his shorts until she found his erection. She squeezed hard, and Umberto gasped and clutched his chest. Suddenly, he felt an intense pain in his chest and he tried pulling away from Rose. But Umberto couldn't prevent his body from crashing face down onto the living room floor.

"Rosie! Phone his family doctor!" shouted Giorgio. "Tell him the old bastard had a goddamned heart attack." He looked at Eva and Rabbi. "Let's get the fuck outta here!"

After examining Umberto the next morning, the doctor told Rose, "He's had another infarction, his third in two years." He shook his head. "Your husband needs complete bed rest. Under no circumstances is he to have visitors. I doubt if the old man will survive this time."

Rose personally nursed Umberto and, citing the doctor's orders, refused visitors. She gave her husband sips of orange juice on the doctor's orders, but he died in his sleep. Later, the doctor signed the death certificate listing the cause of death as a heart attack.

# Chapter Thirty-Four

Tom and Mike had plenty of questions for Rose Grady, but they got more attitude than answers from her. She offered curses and threats when asked about Conte's death and her source for the arsenic. When asked if she was the notorious Lady in Black, her response was laughter, as it was when she was asked to identify the Giant.

The court appointed defense lawyer Peter Martin to defend Rose and he refused to allow anyone to speak to his client. A tall, black attorney known for his intellect and quick wit, the press touted Martin as Philly's answer to Clarence Darrow and, despite the rampant racism in some circles of Philadelphia's high society, Martin was respected by his colleagues because of his hard work and brilliant trial skills.

Mike was infuriated at the lack of access to Rose. "There's no doubt in my mind," he grumbled to Tom. "The degenerate bitch is the Lady in Black and I'll be damned if we can fuckin' prove it."

"I know," Tom replied. "It's frustrating."

Though Boris Feldman was proving to be a fountain of knowledge when it came to the poisoning ring and its participants, proving his claims was going to be difficult for Tom and his detectives.

"It might help if we had a witness who didn't admit to helping kill people," Tom said. "Feldman isn't exactly going to be a squeaky clean witness."

"That won't matter, though, if we can get some corroborating witnesses," Mike said. "I know we're probably not going to turn Giorgio, but Eva and Joanna seem ready to testify."

"It's not going to be hard for a competent defense attorney to say that these women killed their husbands on their own. Even with the hemlock on Giorgio's property, we'll have a hard time proving that he made them kill their husbands. His attorney can just say that these women killed their husbands so they could be with Giorgio and that he knew nothing of their plans." Tom knew that he had a large puzzle on his hands and that some of the pieces were easier to decipher than others. What he needed was a way to connect Giorgio and the wives to what he was sure was a larger conspiracy.

Tom lay in bed at his apartment, trying to catch up on some much-needed sleep after a night of boozing at Gimpy's. He'd been drinking heavily, but couldn't wash away the hurt he felt over the loss of Hope. Her decision to end their relationship was weighing heavily on him and he worried about her future. Tom was also worried about Hope's ability to regain her old life now that her name had been in the paper and everyone knew her as the assistant D.A.'s colored girlfriend. Now, Tom slept a restless sleep, trying to forget Hope.

At 2 a.m., the loud ringing of the phone interrupted his first dream: He had flunked an exam back in his law school days.

"Who the hell could it be at this hour?" he mumbled out loud. "Screw it. I'm not answering." After eight rings, Tom lifted the receiver off the hook and slammed it down only to hear persistent clanging a few moments later.

"What the hell is it?" he blurted into the mouthpiece, his knuckles turning white as he held the phone.

"Tom, this is Mike. Sorry to wake you up, pal, but it's important."

"Call me during regular business hours," Tom said as he hung up the phone again.

But Mike wouldn't be denied. He dialed again and let it ring until Tom lifted the receiver long enough to listen.

"Wake up, you dumb diego! Our prize witness is finally spillin' the beans. I'm in the D.A.'s library so get up and get the hell down here now!" Then he hung up the phone.

Tom almost dropped the phone, about to fall asleep for the third time. Then his eyes suddenly opened wide. *Who's the witness?*

Tom found the door to the library of the D.A.'s office thirty minutes later. Although it was locked, he could see light shining under the door and he decided to knock instead of barging in.

Mike creaked the door open a moment later. "Is anyone with you?"

"Are we playing 'Mother May I?' at 3 o'clock in the god-damned morning?" Tom asked.

Mike opened the door enough for Tom to enter, then locked it behind him.

Tom froze in his tracks when he saw the "witness" on the other side of the room. Rose Grady lay on her back on the couch and she appeared to be asleep. A short guy in his 50s, with a heavy crop of gray hair and a bushy mustache, checked her blood pressure with a stethoscope.

"She ain't sick," Mike volunteered. "The guy taking her blood pressure is Colonel Charlie Hayes, a doctor with Army Intelligence. He just gave her a mild sedative to put her to sleep."

Hayes looked up and nodded, then went back to his work.

Tom scowled at Mike. "Why the hell is a doctor from U.S. Army Intelligence taking our suspect's blood pressure?"

Hayes ignored Tom's question and continued to monitor his patient.

Mike smiled, and then spoke in a whisper. "The Army is experimenting with a barbiturate known as sodium pentothal. It's a truth serum, used to persuade spies to reveal confidential info."

Tom's eyes widened as he looked at Hayes. "Does this stuff really work?"

"Initial results are excellent," Hayes said—his first words since Tom's arrival. "Pentothal injected intravenously reduces a subject's inhibitions, forcing one to let his or her guard down as though hypnotized."

Tom gave him a skeptical look. "What's the bottom line?"

"The subject will answer questions truthfully," Hayes said. "But there's a catch: Sodium pentothal causes rapid depression of the central nervous system and it's contra-indicated in cases of heart disease, hypertension, and liver disease."

"Contra-indicated in what sense?" asked Tom.

"If I give a subject too much serum or fail to closely monitor her blood pressure, she might go into arrest and die."

Tom shook his head in amazement. "You mean once Rose is given this sodium pentothal, she'll really answer questions truthfully?"

"Most times."

A half-dozen thoughts raced through Tom's mind all at once. *Why not? Medical reports on Rose Grady indicated a healthy woman. She has a strong heart and no problems with lungs, bladder or kidneys. Besides, we'll finally learn the identity of the Lady in Black and her companion, and solve this damn case.*

"What's the percentage of a subject's death in these cases?" Tom asked Hayes.

Hayes didn't blink. "Maybe between one or two percent."

Tom suddenly realized the risks involved. He turned to Mike. "Jesus Christ! This idea is insane, illegal. If she dies and someone exposes us, we'll go to prison for second-degree murder and this guy Hayes gets off clean. Besides, if we do get her to talk, we won't be able to use what she tells us in court. It's goddamned illegally obtained evidence."

Mike tightened his jaw. "Are you tellin' me fuckin' due process protects this bitch from murder?"

Hayes rose from his perch beside Rose and quickly shoved papers under Tom's nose. "This is the City Surgeon's report on Rose Grady. "She's an excellent subject for the use of the barbiturate. Hell, she's probably stronger and healthier than all of us put together."

*I can't believe I'm doing this*, thought Tom. *But I have to know.*

"Screw it," he said. "This is important and maybe the end does somehow justify the means."

Tom gave Hayes a reluctant nod and the doctor nudged Rose's arm with his hand. She still had her eyes closed but she managed to push his hand away. Hayes picked up a syringe containing the sodium pentothal and injected it into a vein just below her elbow.

Rose let out a barely audible mumble and took a deep breath. Hayes then wrapped a blood pressure cuff on her arm, pumped it, then read her blood pressure.

"It's normal: 120 over 80." Hayes leaned in close to Rose and gave her a series of commands: "Rose, relax and count backwards, starting with the number ten."

"Ten, nine, three ... five, seven." Rose appeared to be in a stupor and Hayes kept the cuff on her arm and nodded to Tom.

Tom didn't move and he said nothing. He wasn't sure what to make of the situation.

"If you don't know what to ask her, then I'll do the questioning," Mike said.

His friend's words brought Tom back to the task at hand. He walked toward the couch where Rose was laying and sat on a chair set up by Colonel Hayes. "Rose," Tom whispered. "What's your maiden name?"

"Grady," she said, her eyes remaining closed.

"How old are you?"

"Forty-five." Rose's words were slurred.

"Tell me about your mother."

"A fine ... fine Irish lady. She raised four girls in spite of ... in spite of the drunk ... rogue she married."

"How many times have you been married?"

"Four."

"What's the name of the last man you married?"

"Martin ... Martin O'Mera."

"Did he get sick before you left him?"

"Yeah, I put ... I put bismuth in his beer."

*This is a damn miracle,* Tom thought to himself. *She's really cooperating.*

Mike and Tom exchanged looks of amazement and the Colonel seemed to be smirking to himself. Tom continued, "Why did you leave O'Mera?"

"Giorgio ... he got arrested ... thought they'd get me next."

Hayes pumped the cuff and checked her pressure again. He nodded to Tom.

"What caused Umberto Conte to die?"

"Heart attack ... danced for him, we ... we thought he'd die ... he didn't ... gave him arsenic ... he died within an hour."

Tom found his excitement difficult to control. "Rose, can you hear me?"

"Yeah."

"Who supplied you with the arsenic?" Tom's ears were perked.

"Razor's girl. He dumped me for her," mumbled Rose.

Tom scowled. "Who's Razor?"

"My ... my old boyfriend."

"What's Razor's real name?"

"Bruno."

Tom couldn't conceal his excitement. "What's Bruno's last name?"

"Salerno ... but it's his mother's maiden name."

"What's Bruno's born last name?"

Tears rolled down her cheeks. "Don't know."

It finally dawned on Tom. Moore and Sacca had their throats slashed with what appeared to be a razor ... by the Giant.

"Describe this Razor boyfriend … Bruno."

"Romero. He looks ... he looks like Caesar Romero."

Tom thought to himself, *Caesar Romero looks just like the Giant.* "Where does Razor live?"

"Live? Razor lives...he moved to ... New York."

Hayes interrupted Tom and Rose. He sat beside Rose and pumped the cuff around her arm to check her pressure.

Tom decided to go for broke. "Rose, did you drive the Buick for Razor when he killed Moore and Sacca?" His heart pounded faster. He'd finally learn if Rose Grady and the Lady in Black were one in the same.

"I love Razor."

It wasn't what Tom wanted to hear. "What? Were you the driver or can you identify him?"

"She's a bitch," she said, still calm.

"A bitch? Who is?"

"A bitch. She stole my lover." Rose's voice became barely audible.

"Where does she live?" asked Tom.

"She lives ... she ... lives in Philly and New York ... with Razor."

"Is Razor the Giant who's been executing witnesses?" Tom leaned forward, eagerly awaiting her response.

"He ... He dumped me."

"What's Razor's last name?" Tom was pressing for answers. He needed to know who was behind the poisoning ring.

Suddenly, Hayes looked at the blood pressure meter. "No more questions!"

"But, Doc," Tom protested, "I have a load of unsolved murders on my hands!"

Hayes gave him a look that said he should continue only at his own risk.

Tom turned back to Rose. "I'm asking again. Did you drive the getaway car when Moore got murdered?"

"My God!" said Hayes. "It's 240 over 90! Do you want her to die? Her pressure's going through the roof!"

Tom relented and Hayes began the process of bringing Rose back from her stupor. Before she came to, she was placed back in her cell.

The next day, Rose called for her attorney and told him, "I think the bastards drugged me." When she told him she thought she had been secretly interrogated, Martin became furious. But Rose couldn't remember the questions asked or how she answered. As a precaution, Martin filed an injunction against all future interrogations.

At the hearing, Pat Connors argued against the injunction in front of Judge Harry Crosby, saying, "The alleged drugging is a product of Rose Grady's imagination. It was only a normal interrogation, your honor. But, I assure you, Rose's lawyer will be present if the detectives have to question her in the future."

The interrogation had posed more questions than answers for Tom. He had corroborated that Rose's fourth husband, O'Mera, took violently ill after drinking beer and ended up at Methodist Hospital for two weeks. Fortunately, O'Mera had recovered from his mysterious chest and stomach symptoms, but the doctors had failed to make any diagnosis.

Rose had identified the Lady in Black as a "bitch," but that didn't get Tom any closer to finding the killer.

Tom issued an APB for "Razor" in New York and Philadelphia. An artist's sketch of Caesar Romero even accompanied the APB, but to no avail.

Hayes further complicated the enigma for Tom when he told him the day after the interrogation, "Studies have shown some people are immune to pentothal."

*Had Rose lied to me just before I had to abort the interrogation? Is she the Giant's Lady in Black after all? Yes!* Tom thought. *Rose and the Giant had to be lovers. And, besides, witnesses have corroborated that the Lady in Black is a tall, good-looking brunette. That fits Rose Grady's description.*

# Chapter Thirty-Five

Sadie Lamb and her boarders were among the people Eva implicated for murder, even though Sadie herself had been a victim of foul play in Giorgio's quest for more money. Sadie had managed to infuriate Eva by seducing Giorgio and, of course, Giorgio couldn't keep his conquest a secret; he bragged to anyone who would listen. Eva considered herself to be Giorgio's woman. She knew he had other lovers—and she had hers, too—but deep down Eva hadn't ever been able to get over Giorgio's refusal to marry her. Now that she was almost surely going to jail, she saw an opportunity to exact revenge on Giorgio and some his lovers.

Eva didn't give Giorgio the satisfaction of knowing she seethed inside, but she did put Sadie on her infinite revenge list.

On this particular morning, Eva was dressed in pink polka dots as she sat with Tom, Mike and Lynn in the D.A.'s conference room. Eva knew people associated her with polka dots, and it suited her fine. She loved the fact that Tom made sure her female jailers supplied her with freshly ironed dresses. He also permitted her to be driven for short car rides along the River Drives in the evening, something he felt necessary to prevent any further suicide attempts.

The door to the conference room swung open and Paul, handcuffed to Carmine, strolled in with Sam behind them. Carmine looked anxious as he eyed everyone in the room. Paul, on the other hand, looked like he couldn't have cared less. After Sam uncuffed them, he sat Carmine next to Eva and Paul to Carmine's left while Tom, Mike and Lynn studied the new arrivals from across the table.

"I'm sure Eva needs no introduction," Mike said just before she gave both men a half-hearted wave of the hand.

Paul glared at Eva. "Rat!"

Eva retaliated with an icy stare. She feared the bone crusher, but she'd never let him know.

Carmine had dated Eva back when he was a big spender, but when the undertaker came upon tough economic times, Eva gave him the quick heave-ho.

"Paul 'the Cat' Squilla, 55..." Tom began to read from his notes. "The State of New York allowed us to take you into our custody two days ago. I see you're currently their guest at Ryker's Island, doing two years for mayhem. It seems you cut out a piece of tongue from a guy who owed you money. First convicted of assault in New York City in '14; served a year. Convicted of assault and battery in '19…" Tom looked at Paul and shook his head. "…then graduated to murder in the second degree in Delaware County—"

Mike interrupted. "Murder?"

"Yep. Served 12 and paroled in '31. It seems Mr. Squilla here wanted to shoot his brother but shot a stranger instead who bore a resemblance."

"His favorite slogan is 'Might is always right … stupid,'" quipped Sam. "But I guess it wasn't in that case."

Paul just shrugged his shoulders as Tom continued. "When you last lived in town, you worked as muscle for the Lenzetti mob. Last known address: a boarder in Sadie Lamb's home, according to our source."

Paul and Carmine scowled at Eva.

"He also slept with his landlady, Sadie … for a fee," said Eva. "And he's a close friend of DiSipio."

Despite Lynn's increased exposure to sordid tales in the months since the investigation began, she began to blush as she recorded the conversation. After all, she had been raised in a sheltered environment at Catholic school and at home where one didn't talk of sex.

Mike put his eyes on the fidgety undertaker and began to speak. "Next up we have Carmine 'the Mouse' DeLeo, 54. You're an unemployed undertaker and also a friend of Giorgio DiSipio. It seems you also dated Eva at one time."

Eva beamed.

"Carmine's never been previously arrested," Mike continued. "Last residence: another boarder in Sadie's home." Mike shook his head and smiled at Carmine. "He also sleeps with the landlady … when he can afford it."

"Gentlemen," Tom began, after taking a deep breath, "the proposition is simple: You both burn in hell with Giorgio, or you cooperate and get life instead of the chair."

"But I'm innocent, Mr. Rossi," Carmine protested. "I'm a respected undertaker—"

Mike leaned close to Carmine's ear and said in an indignant whisper: "The only people you buried were the people you helped murder for Giorgio and his friends."

"How can you take Eva's word?" Carmine argued after a beat of silence. "The broad just wants revenge because I dumped her!"

"Who the fuck are you kiddin'?!" Mike said with a snarl. "Eva screwed you, humped Paul, fucked Giorgio and did God knows what with the rest of South Philly."

Without taking her eyes off him, Eva, free of restraints, calmly picked up Lynn's open inkbottle and baptized Carmine's head with ink.

Carmine immediately leaped to his feet as the ink ran down his face, back and torso. "This bitch is a maniac! Somebody get me a goddamn towel. Quick!"

Mike accommodated him with a dusty rag. Carmine, glad for some relief, used it as if it was made of satin, bringing his now fiery eyes to Eva's. She blew him a kiss.

Tom fired a salvo at Carmine, hoping to panic the now jittery undertaker. "Our detectives claim you and Giorgio were the ring leaders of the poison gang. In fact, we know you embalmed victims with arsenic after you used the stuff to knock them off."

"Hell, no! I didn't poison nobody. I'm only Giorgio's messenger boy."

"Don't worry, chump," Mike said. "We don't shoot messengers."

Carmine had a penitent look on his face as he started to sob. "Giorgio told us to help Robert fix the roof but I don't know nothin' 'bout murder."

"Now we're talking," Tom said. "You all were to accompany Robert to the roof, then loverboy, Howard, would push him off. But Howard chickened out. So you and Paul finished the job. Right?"

Carmine realized he had said too much. "I … I ain't sayin' anything else," he said, glancing over at Paul. "I … I … wanna call my lawyer."

The hired muscle man gave Carmine the ugly stare he usually reserved for those who were about to get their legs broken.

"Hell!" Mike exploded. "Eva told us that Sadie humped you, Howard and Paul. Then you all got together at Giorgio's direction and pushed Robert Lamb off the roof! Right?!"

"Let me talk to my lawyer first," Carmine said, whimpering and raising his hands in surrender. "If he gets me a good deal … I'll … I'll cooperate."

At this point Paul knew he was in big trouble with less of a way out than he had when he came into the room. He had already been convicted of one homicide in 1919 and had sacrificed nearly half of his 55 years doing the time. If he were to be convicted of a second homicide, a death sentence would be a given, without a thought by the judge.

But like Giorgio, Paul graduated from the old school. And in the old school, honorable men never would rat. You just didn't rat.

"Motherfucker!" Paul shouted at Carmine. "I need God to defend me from friends like you. From my enemies, I can always defend myself. I got nothin' else to say to you guys."

Tom gave Sam a nod. "Take Paul back to his cell and ask the jailor to bring in

Sadie Lamb and Howard Rice. The show's about to get interesting."

Five minutes later, Howard and Sadie were brought in, handcuffed together, and escorted by a uniformed cop. He un-cuffed them at Tom's direction and had them sit on either side of Eva.

"Now," Tom said, turning to the uniformed cop, "bring in the claims manager." The cop, in his late 20s with blonde hair and a matching moustache, shook his head at the parade of witnesses turning on each other in the D.A.'s conference room as he left.

Moments later, he returned with a tall man in his 40s who wore horn-rimmed glasses and a dark gray, three-piece suit. The man sat next to Lynn and gave Howard and Sadie a disgusted look.

"Can you tell these not-so-good citizens who you are?" Tom said.

"I'm Bob Gorn, claims manager for the Home Life Insurance Company of

Philadelphia."

"Were you the claims manager who investigated a policy issued to one Robert Lamb?"

"Yes, sir," Gorn responded.

"Are you able to identify this couple?" Tom asked, pointing to Sadie and Howard.

"Absolutely," Gorn said, nodding with a scowl. "Our company refused to pay life insurance proceeds for the death of Robert Lamb because the company doctor told me this guy"—Gorn pointed to Howard—"identified himself and posed as Robert Lamb during the physical exam he conducted for Lamb's life insurance."

Gorn then turned to Sadie. "The doctor also claimed Mrs. Lamb introduced this guy here"—again he pointed to Howard—"as her husband during the exam."

Howard and Sadie stared at the floor.

Gorn continued, "They came into my office shortly after the death of Robert Lamb in late July. I confronted them with our evidence of fraud and threatened to report them to the police if they continued to pursue the claim."

"How'd they respond to your accusation?" asked Tom.

"This joker Howard said to me, 'Excuse me, boss. We made a mistake,' then they both scurried out of my office."

"Isn't it something?" Tom said. "Thank you, Mr. Gorn. We'll call you to testify in case they don't have sense enough to plead guilty."

Eva smiled broadly at Sadie after Gorn left the office. "You little shit. This'll teach you to let Giorgio cornhole you without my permission."

Howard shook his head in bewilderment and Sadie cupped her hands over her face and sobbed.

"What the hell is goin' on in North Philly?" Mike asked Eva. "Does every landlady play musical beds with her boarders?"

Carmine began to laugh and Lynn broke out into a broad smile, as did Eva.

Sadie only sobbed louder. "How cheap," she murmured to herself. "My secrets will probably be published in the newspapers and everyone's going to know what I did."

"Sadie," Tom said, lowering his eyes to meet hers, "you'll have to fess up if you want to avoid the chair."

"I want a lawyer." Sadie was just whispering now. She shook as she spoke to Tom and tears began to stream down her face.

In the meantime, Mike pulled Howard aside and went to work. "Look, loverboy, you're about to be dipped in boiling oil. You heard the insurance guy. You and Sadie, your bashful whore, tried to pull an insurance scam and Eva and Carmine will testify you were all part of a conspiracy to murder your girlfriend's hubby." Howard looked down. "The jury won't show any pity once they hear you were humping Lamb's wife. They won't think you acted out of love, especially when they're told Sadie's 15 years older than you. They'll think Sadie's trash and you're just a horny little bastard who let his dingleberry do his thinking for him."

Howard sneered over at Carmine. "I don't know why they call you 'Mouse.' You're a crusty rat bastard!"

Howard then glared at Eva and hocked spit in her face. "You're a shit bird! Ya fouled your own damn nest, you fucking whore!"

Eva smiled at her tormentor, uncrossed her legs and rose from her chair. She walked toward Howard and Mike as she wiped Howard's spit from her dress with a handkerchief. Before Mike could react, she threw a lightning-fast punch into Howard's eye. He fell backward off his chair and slammed his head into the wall radiator behind him.

Mike rushed to Howard. His left eye had swollen shut and he had a welt on the back of his head the size of a baseball. Sadie ran across the room and threw her arms around her lover and dabbed at his shiner with a handkerchief. Eva raised her arms above her head, cupped her hands and shook them as if she'd just KO'd her opponent.

Tom had heard and seen enough. "Mike, book Romeo and Juliet as well as the rest of the boarders—Murder One."

# Chapter Thirty-Six

*October 23, 1939*

When possible, D.A. Pat Connors took Tom to lunch every Friday at the Bellevue Stratford Hotel. It gave the men a chance to discuss business, pleasure and politics.

This Friday, though, Pat wanted an update on Tom's investigation into the poisoning ring. A lot of resources had been put into the investigation and it had taken months for Tom to put his case together.

"How do the numbers look in this insurance murder case?" Pat asked.

"We've arrested fourteen wives and twelve male accomplices. Seven wives have pled guilty to date."

"Who are these male accomplices?"

"They're involved as co-conspirators," said Tom. "Some were boyfriends of the wives, insurance men or poison suppliers. One way or another, they were people who helped Giorgio and his gang commit murder and insurance fraud."

"Any fresh leads on the woman in black and her giant?" Pat was annoyed that no progress had been made in finding them.

"No, unfortunately. They've vanished. We suspect they fled town."

"How soon will Lillian's murder case be tried?"

"In two weeks, unless she can't get her withdrawal symptoms under control. We have it on good authority that her defense will be based around the idea that Giorgio threatened to kill her unless she went through with her husband's murder."

"Do you think she can sell such nonsense to the jury?"

"I've seen this broad in action. She'd make a good movie star."

Tom stood in his apartment, holding his phone, waiting for his call to be answered. But to no avail. He had been calling Hope for two weeks, but she didn't pick up. He thought about going to see her, but the last thing he wanted was to push her further away by not giving her her space.

Hope sat on the couch in her row house living room with her arms folded, smoking a cigarette and staring at the phone. *He's only making it harder.*

Tom cradled the receiver and downed another shot of Dewar's. He'd had another run-in with Bill Evans early in the day. While he and Mike were strolling down a City Hall corridor, Evans had approached from the opposite direction with his bodyguards.

"I'd like you to be the first to know I've convinced the Republican City Committee *not* to endorse you for D.A," Evans said. "Now you've got a primary fight on your hands and, as you know, no unendorsed candidate can win a major election in this town without the backing of the machine."

One of the two guards stepped toward Tom and Mike. Mike, standing three feet away, whipped out his .45 automatic and pointed it at his head. "If you want to sacrifice yourself for your fat boss then do it with dignity."

The thug stared at the barrel of the .45. "This fuckin' Jew's nuts. I've heard about him."

"You're goddamn right I'm nuts," said Mike, "and I'll blow your fat ass all over this hall if you take another step."

"You better watch your men, Tom," Evans said with a smile on his face. "You don't wanna become like the people you're trying to put away, now do you?"

Tom pulled Mike away and led him down the hall. He knew Mike would have blown them both away at the least provocation. Now, sitting in his apartment, Tom needed someone to talk to and he missed having Hope listen to him vent.

Tom hung up the phone, and put out the lamp on the end table. He didn't have time to review all the political setbacks he'd endured from this one case.

The next day, the seats in Courtroom 653 were filled to capacity with reporters from throughout the U.S. poised to take notes. *The New York Times* ran daily copy of the saga of Philadelphia's wicked wives and a crowd jammed the hallway outside the courtroom. The city of Philadelphia waited with the nation to hear about the life of society wife Lillian Stoner. She had already been in the Women's Division of Moyamensing Prison for a full year awaiting trial.

Harry Crosby, a tough, balding, Irish Catholic in his mid-50s, would preside over the trial. Crosby had taken a page from Machiavelli's book in the way he climbed to the top of his profession; his power had corrupted the Philly court system absolutely.

Mike sat in the first row behind Tom at the counsel table. He had a photographic memory as an instant, ready reference source of facts pertaining to the poison scandals and he had spent hours reviewing the evidence in the case during the days leading up to trial.

Lillian, dressed in mourning black with her blonde hair up, sat with her lawyer, Peter Martin—the same Peter Martin working for Rose Grady.

Mike leaned forward in his seat and whispered to Tom, "Lillian looks good. Those treatments have obviously helped her."

"She always looks good when the chips are down," Tom said in a grunt.

Judge Crosby had ordered the D.A.'s office to subpoena Eva Bell, Joanna Napoli and Rose Grady, along with Giorgio DiSipio, so that they could be released from prison in order to attend the trial. The judge also ordered the sheriff to seat them in the first row; jurors could easily and constantly observe the decorum of the "conspirators." All the wives wore black except Eva, who wore a low-cut, green, polka dot dress. Two uniformed sheriff's deputies stood guard in the aisle.

The jury of ten men and two women watched Tom rise to deliver his opening statement. Standing in front of them, he pointed to Lillian. "While married, defendant Lillian Stoner allowed the indicted Giorgio DiSipio," he paused to point at Giorgio, "to seduce her."

Tom pointed at Eva, Rose and Joanna. "And just like these wives, Lillian Stoner conspired with the same ladies' man, Giorgio DiSipio, to murder her husband for insurance money."

An angry Martin stood. "Objection!"

"Overruled!" snapped Judge Crosby.

Martin blinked incredulously at the judge. "Your Honor, Lillian Stoner's only charged with her husband's murder. Now, the jury's been told about a conspiracy of three more murders. I move for a mistrial."

"Sit down, Mr. Martin! You're out of order."

"But—"

"Lillian Stoner's been charged with the murder of her husband with help from others," Crosby interrupted. "Though the indictment fails to allege conspiracy, if one acts with someone, you're engaged in a conspiracy. Motion denied!"

"The Commonwealth of Pennsylvania calls Bertha Brooks," Tom announced.

Bertha took the stand. The old lady's hands shook involuntarily as a result of Parkinson's disease, but her demeanor was one of resolve. Bertha had no hesitation in appearing before the court and when she was sworn in, she gave a solid, "You're darn right I will," when asked if she would tell the truth.

"You're Bertha Brooks, Lillian Stoner's neighbor?" asked Tom.

"Yes. Lillian's conduct is a deplorable abomination."

"Please explain."

"She's always out to the wee hours. Her dates were Reardon the insurance guy, DiSipio, and God knows whom else. If you ask me, Lillian fornicated with half the men in town."

The crowd roared as Lillian raised a brow and scowled at Bertha. Joanna cried into her third hanky; she couldn't believe she was being grouped with the other conspirators. She did truly love Giorgio at one point and now she was fodder for the masses.

"Hell," Eva said, grinning in Lillian's direction. "She's an amateur compared to me."

Rose prayed with rosary beads as Giorgio folded his arms and smirked at the jurors.

Deputy Evans, sitting in the back of the courtroom, glared at Bertha.

"Objection!" shouted Martin, trying to be heard over the crowd. "This is sheer conjecture on the part of this witness."

"If the shoe fits ... Overruled!" said Judge Crosby.

"Were you awake around 11 p.m. on the night before Reggie Stoner died?" Tom asked.

"Yes. At about 11, I heard a car outside the front of my house. I got up and looked out of my bedroom window."

"Tell the jury what you saw."

"A black 1938 Plymouth parked in the Stoners' driveway. Then, a man and a woman exited the car and went into the side entrance of the house."

"Are the man and woman you saw sitting in the courtroom today?"

"Certainly. They were Lillian Stoner, sitting over there next to her lawyer"—Bertha pointed at Lillian while shaking her finger in condemnation—"and Giorgio DiSipio, sitting next to those ... those God-awful women."

The courtroom erupted in laughter; the reporters in attendance thrilled to have such a spectacular start to the trial.

"Let the record reflect the witness has identified the defendant Lillian Stoner, and Giorgio DiSipio, as being at the deceased's home the night before he died."

Martin stood to cross-examine. He peered at the witness over half-moon glasses. "Mrs. Brooks, you accused my client of ... oh, yes, I believe you testified that 'Lillian fornicated with half the men in town.' Did you actually see Lillian Stoner having sex with Giorgio DiSipio?"

"No," Bertha snapped. "But can you tell me why, on many occasions after the car stopped outside her house, her head would disappear for several minutes while he stared into space like he was having a heart attack?"

Spectators roared, but Judge Crosby didn't call for order in the court.

Martin smiled. "I'm the one asking the questions. In point of fact, you don't know if Mrs. Stoner and Giorgio were even having sex, do you?"

"Look, Mister, she didn't shine Giorgio's shoes when her head went down in his car."

Martin knew when to cease questions. "Nothing further."

Lillian covered her face with her hands, trying to hide from the crowd. Joanna sobbed at the whole sad scene. It was all too much for her. Meanwhile, Eva flirted with the young sheriff's deputy assigned to guard her.

As the jurors glanced at Giorgio, he smiled at them as though he knew the male jurors envied him and the women jurors wanted him. He straightened his tie and ran his fingers through his hair.

Evans wasn't laughing and Rose never stopped praying her rosary.

Phil Reardon, the insurance broker, took the stand once Bertha had been convinced to leave it. It seemed she was intent on airing all of Lillian's dirty laundry.

"Did Giorgio DiSipio brag to you about having sex with Lillian Stoner, Eva Bell and Joanna Napoli?" asked Tom.

"Objection! Hearsay!" Martin shouted.

"Overruled."

"Giorgio told me the happy, redheaded broad's a nymph," Reardon said, pointing at Eva. He smirked at Joanna. "The chubby broad sang opera when she did it." Then he smiled at Lillian. "The blonde, well, the blonde took it up the rear end."

Martin's objection could hardly be heard as the crowd gasped and started exchanging astounded looks.

To restore order, Judge Crosby gaveled for fifteen seconds.

Martin all but screamed, "Objection! These alleged statements by Mr. DiSipio can be construed as admissions on his part, but they cannot be attributed as an admission against Lillian Stoner."

"Objection overruled. Mrs. Stoner's been charged with the murder of her husband with help from others. Admissions may be introduced against her as a co-conspirator."

Tom resumed his questioning of Reardon. "Then I take it by your testimony, Giorgio had an intimate relationship with Lillian Stoner, Eva Bell, and Joanna Napoli?"

Reardon looked confused. "I don't know what you mean by intimate ... but he screwed the hell out of all of them!"

Spectators snickered again at the comedy unfolding in front of them.

"Who had the idea to insure Reggie Stoner?"

"Lillian ... sorta persuaded me to write secret insurance on her husband Reggie. Then she forged his signature to the policies."

"Tell us about how she persuaded you to help her."

"We went to the movies. At first we sat in the back row, where Lillian starts fiddling with me. Then, she takes me up into a dark, empty balcony and whips off her raincoat. Christ! She was ass-naked. She turns her back to me, kneels, and wiggles her cute ass at me."

"And did you accept her invitation?"

"Hell! In this type of situation? I ain't no Boy Scout."

Laughter filled the room as Lillian folded her arms and stared at Reardon. Suddenly, she jumped up and shouted at Reardon with fists clenched. "Liar!"

Spectators murmured as the judge gaveled and glared at Lillian. "Mrs. Stoner! One more outburst and you'll be gagged and tied for the duration of the trial."

Lillian sat back in her chair and sulked silently. She knew from his reputation that the judge would do it.

"The Commonwealth calls Nancy Stoner," Tom announced.

Nancy, 65, conservatively groomed with short grayish hair and dressed in a black suit, took the stand.

"Please state your name."

"Nancy Stoner. I'm the late Reggie Stoner's mother."

The crowd buzzed with murmurs and whispers.

"Did your son ever sue his wife, Lillian, for divorce?"

"Yes. I testified as a witness for my son at a deposition."

"On what grounds did your son sue?"

Nancy glared at Lillian and delayed her answer a few seconds before responding, "Adultery." The two woman jurors covered their mouths in surprise.

"What did you witness?"

"I drove to my son's house at noon one day. Reggie had given me a key to pick up a package for him because we were to have lunch at his club."

"Tell us what happened."

"When I entered the home, I smelled smoke, which led me upstairs to investigate. I called out to Lillian, but she didn't answer. I traced the smell to the bathroom and opened the door. Shocking ... just shocking."

"What did you see?"

Nancy stood and pointed at Lillian. "The infidel and one of her boyfriends were in a sleepy stupor, naked in the bathtub, having sex and sharing a lighted opium pipe."

Silence filled the room as Lillian stared at the floor.

"Did your son complete the divorce proceedings?" asked Tom.

"Regrettably, no. Over my strenuous objections, he made a horrible mistake which cost his life: He forgave her."

# Chapter Thirty-Seven

Tom felt good about Nancy Stoner's testimony in that it established Lillian as less than loyal to Reggie. He wanted to show that Lillian was capable of deception and, even though Martin had shown during cross examination that Nancy Stoner had no proof her son was killed by Lillian, Tom thought it was still productive testimony.

Following Lillian's testimony, Tom introduced his theory of the poisoning by calling the coroner's physician, Dr. Summers, to the stand. Summers explained the effects of hemlock poisoning to the jury and showed that Reggie exhibited the symptoms of the drug post-mortem. Tom was confident in Summers' testimony and he wasn't prepared for what came next.

Martin rose from his desk to cross-examine Summers. "You told the jury Stoner died of poison hemlock, correct?"

"Yes, I did," Summers agreed.

"Dr. Summers, Mr. Stoner worked with cement all his life. Is it possible that he could have died from inhaling cement dust over the years?"

Summers responded, "I'm not aware of the chemical hazards in cement."

"Doesn't cement contain zinc oxide, which can cause chemical pneumonia?" Martin asked.

"I don't believe there is enough zinc oxide in cement to cause chemical pneumonia." Summers said, looking to Tom for guidance. But Tom was blindsided by Martin's theory. He had figured on Martin bringing up an alternative cause for Reggie's death, but he hadn't planned on cement dust as the proposed cause. He shrugged his shoulders at Summers, who looked displeased at being left out in the cold.

Martin smiled. "Specifically, what percent of zinc oxide is contained in cement, Doctor?"

"I wouldn't know. I'm not a chemist," responded an agitated Summers.

"I agree. You're not a chemist." Martin said sarcastically.

Tom winced. *Damn. What's chemical pneumonia?*

Martin continued his attack. "By the way, Dr. Summers, did you identify or measure this alleged hemlock poison in Stoner's body?"

"No. Hemlock's an alkaloid. It can't be identified or measured like hard metals, such as arsenic. But it adversely affects vital organs and causes death, just like arsenic. In addition, it leaves unique ulcers in vital organs such as the liver and kidney. "

"Then, you're only giving us an educated guess that it ever existed in the body?"

Summers looked perturbed. "An educated guess? No. I'd say it's my opinion, based upon a reasonable medical certainty."

"Why did it take you six months to allege that hemlock caused the death?" Martin snapped.

Tom and Mike exchanged concerned glances.

"We ... proceeded cautiously."

"Cautiously because you had doubts about the cause of death, Dr. Summers?" Martin didn't wait for Summers to answer. "No further questions." The lawyer walked back to his seat with a satisfied look.

Tom rested his case. He was confident in what he had shown the jury, but he worried about Martin's proposed cause of death. *Will the jury buy that crap?*

He had shown that Giorgio was at the scene of the crime on the night of Reggie's death. He'd also shown that Reggie was insured without his knowledge and that the coroner's physician believed his death was caused by hemlock poison—poison from a plant like the one in Giorgio's backyard.

He hoped that would be enough.


Martin began his defense by calling Dr. Masters, the Stoner family doctor, as an expert witness. Martin went right for the weak point in Tom's case and asked, "Did Stoner die of hemlock poison?"

"No," said Masters. "Reggie Stoner died of chemical pneumonia. He inhaled cement dust over the course of many years. Cement contains zinc oxide, a hardening compound."

"Do X-rays taken of Stoner before death support your opinion?"

Dr. Masters inserted an X-ray of Stoner's lungs onto a lighted shadow box. He positioned a pointer toward each lung, and addressed the jury. "These X-rays prove Stoner died of chemical pneumonia. They were taken a week before his death at Chestnut Hill Hospital. Note the clusters on both sides of the chest." Masters placed the pointer on each side. "Proof of chemical pneumonia."

"Doctor, did you treat Stoner for several weeks before he died?"

"Yes, he had lung congestion."

"And you're certain that it was the cement dust that killed him?"

"I'm certain that Reggie Stoner died of pneumonia caused by his prolonged exposure to cement dust."

"Thank you, Doctor, I have no further questions." Martin returned to his seat by walking past the jury and pointing to the X-rays. The members of the jury were looking at each other and then at the X-rays, and the gallery was buzzing about cement dust and how Tom's case may have crumbled before his eyes.

Tom cross-examined. "Do you agree one could interpret the X-ray clusters as being caused by a poison other than zinc oxide … like hemlock?"

"Yes."

"If Stoner had been given small amounts of hemlock poison in his bourbon during the weeks before his death, then the clusters seen on the X-ray could be the result of hemlock poisoning?"

"Yes, they could be," Masters replied.

"Where in Stoner's medical history does it confirm exposure to cement dust?"

"It doesn't. I assumed that a concrete contractor like Mr. Stoner would be exposed to cement dust on a weekly basis."

"Then, obviously, Dr. Masters, your theory that Stoner died of chemical pneumonia is based on an unproved assumption. No further questions."

The spectators buzzed and the jurors stared at Lillian and shook their heads.

Now, after months of anticipation, the Philadelphia public would have a chance to hear from Lillian Stoner herself. Martin called her to the stand in her own defense.

Lillian pulled herself up off of her seat and stood up straight to face the judge. She was striking, even in the dim light of the courtroom. *Such a waste*, thought Tom.

"Tell the jury the circumstances by which Giorgio DiSipio threatened you," Martin instructed.

Lillian turned and stared into the jurors' eyes, and then began, haltingly, to tell them her story. "One night, after the three of us returned from the opera, my husband invited Giorgio into the house for drinks. Reggie got drunk and went to bed. Giorgio insisted on staying. He wanted to discuss important matters. By this time, I felt drunk and tired. It had been a long day." She took a deep breath before continuing.

"Giorgio sat on a couch and sipped wine as we listened to Caruso's opera recording of the aria *Nessum Dorma*. I entered the living room, holding a martini. I was still wearing my cocktail dress, which had a plunging neckline, and I could see him looking at me. I sat across from him. He stared at my legs when I sat down and I got nervous."

"Why were you nervous, Mrs. Stoner?" Martin asked.

"Reggie and I had borrowed money from Giorgio and we had been unable to pay him back to this point. Also, I was using opium provided to me by Giorgio and I was scared he would cut me off."

Upon hearing Lillian's confession, the crowd in the courtroom erupted with boos and cheers, and Judge Crosby was forced to gavel for several minutes until the courtroom quieted.

"Please continue, Mrs. Stoner," Martin said.

"Giorgio locked his eyes on my thighs. It made me very nervous. He said, 'It's been a month now and your husband hasn't paid me the two-thousand-buck loan or any interest.' I told him that Reggie would have the money real soon." Here, Lillian began to cry and look at the jurors.

"He said, 'Bullshit. You've been handin' me that line for weeks. I'm getting Reardon to insure your husband ... just in case.' I found the statement incredible. I said 'What do you mean you'll get Reggie insured?' and he said, 'I gotta protect my interest and you need the money. I'd be doin' both of us a big favor if Reggie got suddenly sick and ... didn't make it.' He winked and said, 'Get my drift?'"

Lillian shifted in her seat and took a sip of water from the glass sitting on the banister around the witness box. "I felt anxious," she began again, "so I gulped my drink and refilled it. I said, 'Well, you're ... you're talking ... murder. I would cancel any such insurance.' Giorgio rose and glared down at me. He towered over me. He said, 'Listen, ya stupid society bitch! My shark friends gave me the money I lent your husband. If I don't pay them soon ... they'll sorta cancel all of us. Get it?'"

"And what did you think he meant by that, Mrs. Stoner?" asked Martin.

"He meant that his friends were going to kill me and my husband if we didn't pay them back. I was terrified for my life." Lillian was shaking now and Martin offered to ask the judge for a break. It was a move they had rehearsed prior to trial and, when Martin looked at the faces of the jury, he felt like it may have worked in drumming up sympathy.

"No, I'm OK," Lillian said, and continued telling her story.

"I said to Giorgio, 'I ... I'm sorry but,' and he got visibly upset. He said, 'You take me for granted. I do you favors, I give you money, get you tickets for the fuckin' opera. I get stuff you can puff so you can go to la-la-land and forget your troubles. You don't even thank me. Instead you tease me every chance you get. You giggle when I get horny. I make a pass ... you act insulted, like I'm scum or somethin'. Well, you're playin' with the wrong stud!'"

At this point, there was an audible gasp from some of the women in attendance.

"My hands trembled and I raised my glass once more, draining it. Tears began to roll from my eyes. I said, 'I'm sorry. I didn't ... I didn't mean to lead you on, Giorgio,' and he said, 'If I tell ya to go to Reardon and get the insurance, you get it ... or else! Understand?' His eyes were icy and they stabbed me with blades of fear. For the first time in my life, I felt really terrified. I said, 'Yes, Giorgio.'"

"And what happened next, Mrs. Stoner?" prodded Martin as he surveyed the jury box.

"He said, 'Now, take off your damn clothes!' I looked at him with eyes stretched to their limits, but I didn't dare argue with him. I unzipped my dress and watched it fall to the floor. Standing before him in nothing but my bra, garter belt, stockings and panties, I could feel everything within me shaking. I must have been going into shock! He said, 'Somethin' wrong?' and I said, 'Everything.'"

Lillian told the jury that, with trembling hands, she somehow undid the remaining clothing. "Then he said to me, 'Now get on your knees, bitch!' I shivered and folded my arms across my chest to cover my bare breasts while I stared at the floor. I'd never felt that humiliated, that helpless. He pointed his thumb down toward his crotch. I unbuttoned his fly and thought to myself, 'I hope this vile bastard comes quickly ... then I won't have to think too much about it. If I don't do it, he'll take away the opium. I can't live without it.' Then I looked up at him one last time. I saw no mercy in his eyes, so I went down."

"Thank you very much, Mrs. Stoner," Martin said. "This was very brave of you. It must have been a terrible experience to be threatened by a drug-dealing pimp. I have no further questions."

"You may question the witness," Crosby said, looking at Tom.

"You used your inheritance to buy a house in Chestnut Hill. A cash purchase without a mortgage. Correct?" Tom started.

"Yes."

"You also used your inheritance to buy your husband's concrete business?"

"Yes."

"Thereafter, your husband went bankrupt so you borrowed ten thousand dollars using your house as collateral?"

"I suppose so."

"Right before Reggie died, you and your husband owed money to the bank and Giorgio DiSipio. And the both of you lacked an income with which to pay back your debt?"

Lillian squirmed in her chair. "Yes."

"Did you have an illicit affair with Giorgio?"

"No," Lillian said, vigorously shaking her head. "Totally false. He forced me to have sex with him."

"Did you seduce Reardon?"

"Absolutely not," she replied.

"You got Reardon to insure Reggie without his knowledge. Then you and Giorgio poisoned Reggie to collect the insurance money, money you desperately needed. Right?"

Lillian shook her head. "You're being absurd."

"As absurd as Bertha Brooks swearing under oath to this jury about the men who took you home and particularly your head disappearing when Giorgio parked his car?"

"Bertha has a lewd imagination. She tends to exaggerate the truth."

"Did Bertha Brooks exaggerate the truth about seeing you and Giorgio enter your house at 11 p.m. the night before you discovered your husband dead?"

"Reggie had pneumonia. I asked Giorgio to come into the house with me to help check on him."

"Oh! I take it your custom included entertaining gentlemen in your home at all hours while your husband was upstairs in bed? I see. Then the two of you poisoned Reggie."

"No!" Lillian insisted. "Giorgio went into the bedroom alone with Reggie and closed the door."

"I see … you and Giorgio conspired to poison Reggie, but Mr. DiSipio did the dirty work."

Lillian struggled for a logical explanation. "You're ... you're confusing me. I ... I don't know what Giorgio did in the bedroom with my husband. When he came out, he told me to sleep ... to sleep in the guestroom for the night, which I did. In the morning, I ... I found Reggie dead in bed."

"Didn't you think it odd when Giorgio entered the bedroom alone with your husband?"

"No! When Reggie got nasty with me, I'd call Giorgio. He came to the house a few times to talk to Reggie and calm him down."

"Were you shocked to find your husband dead?"

"Certainly."

"When you found him like that, did you suspect Giorgio had murdered him?"

"Of course not."

"Well, when did you suspect Giorgio of murdering your husband?"

"I never said I suspected Giorgio of murdering Reggie."

"On the day you were arrested, do you recall the first thing you said to three detectives when they told you you were being arrested for your husband's murder?"

"No."

"Three detectives testified that you pointed at Giorgio and said, 'The gangster did it.' Do you recall making the accusation?"

"No."

"You suspected Giorgio of using hemlock to poison Reggie because you knew he grew it in his yard, correct?"

Lillian lost it. "I ... can't remember … stop … I'm confused!"

"You allowed Giorgio to go into the bedroom and murder your husband then, just like the proverbial ostrich, you buried your head in the sand, hoping no one would discover your part in the murder plot."

"I resent that! I ... I didn't ... poison Reggie!" she shouted.

"But you did fatten the chicken, then unlock the door to the coop so the wolf could enter. No further questions, Your Honor."

For five days the jury deliberated without reaching a verdict. An exhausted Tom propped his feet on his office desk and stared at the phone. Every time it rang he jumped up in anticipation. But now, it was being stubbornly silent.

Tom was thinking of all the major events during the past year that had led up to Lillian's trial. The sudden ringing of the phone interrupted his thoughts. The jury had reached a verdict.

The solemn jurors looked straight ahead as the foreman rose to announce the verdict. Lillian shivered with anxiety as she stood with Martin, facing the jury.

The court crier spoke to the jury. "In the case of Commonwealth verses Lillian Stoner, how say you? Guilty or not guilty?"

The foreman stared at Lillian. "We find the defendant, Lillian Stoner..." Lillian stared at the foreman "... not guilty."

Lillian's eyes closed; she exhaled deeply and began to cry.

Bedlam erupted as photographers flashed and popped their box cameras at Lillian. Reporters raced out of court and spectators debated the verdict. Evans rushed to Lillian and hugged her.

The judge, obviously upset with the verdict, gaveled until he restored quiet, and then addressed the jury. "No one knows the secrets of the human heart. Lillian Stoner's been found innocent. If she had a part in her husband's death, she'll answer to a higher judge whom she'll surely meet in time."

A few people were scattered at the tables in the Venice Lounge, having a late lunch. Tom and Lynn sipped coffee at the bar and Lynn read from *The Globe*. "Wow. Listen to what a juror told a reporter after the verdict: 'We thought Giorgio and his gang used an innocent Lillian Stoner.'"

Tom laughed. "Nobody uses Lillian."

Evans entered with his bodyguards. Upon seeing Tom and Lynn, he walked up to them and in a voice loud enough for all the patrons to hear, proclaimed, "I'm glad Lillian's jury saw you for the fraud you are, Mr. Rossi."

Tom turned and faced Evans. "We have sworn statements from contractors, Bill. You accepted kickbacks. Get a good lawyer."

Lynn couldn't resist throwing oil onto the fire with a smile. "A minimum of five years. Have a nice day, Mr. Deputy."

As Tom and Lynn left, Evans could feel the cold stare from the restaurant's patrons. *It's time to fix Tom Rossi's future for good,* he thought.

# Chapter Thirty-Eight

Tom sat in Pat's office, his shoulders slumped and his expression lifeless. His failure to prosecute Lillian had left him reeling and now his battle with Evans had taken a turn for the worse.

Evans had struck again, this time managing to cause more serious political damage to Tom's aspirations of becoming D.A. Pat read the *Globe* headline to himself: "D.A. Candidate Rossi's Kin a Mafia Killer." Pat looked at Tom. "So, what's the story?"

"The media has demanded I hold a press conference to explain whether my first assistant's cousin could have been a hit man for the mob," Pat answered.

Tom shook his head in disgust. "Evans' hatchet man wrote that article and it's bullshit. Years ago, an Italian immigrant from Palermo in Sicily became a hit man for the Philly Mafia. The guy's named was Salvatore Rossi."

"Is he related to you?"

"Hell, no. My people emigrated from Abruzzi, east of Rome on the Adriatic coast. This guy is Sicilian."

"But you have the same last name."

Tom nodded. "Rossi is a common Italian name meaning 'red.' There must be a hundred people named Rossi living in our city and I've never met this guy."

"Why can't we find him and ask him to verify he's not related to you?"

"Evans knows I can't fight back; the guy is buried in Holy Cross Cemetery. He died a year ago of a heart attack."

"Tom," Pat said, giving Tom a look that a father might give to a son, "do you have the balls to fight back?"

"What do you mean?"

"What I mean is a good offense is your best defense."

"You lost me, Chief."

"Yesterday the grand jury finally indicted Evans for taking illegal kickbacks. It will be in tomorrow morning's *Globe*. At noon, you and I will attend a press conference. You tell the press the truth, exactly what you just told me. A reporter will ask you if Evans planted the Mafia article and you'll say it's obvious the deputy opposes your nomination, but you'd rather not comment since he's been indicted criminally."

"Wow! Do you think that'll work?"

"It'll work. But one way or the other, the Mafia article has done much damage. At election time in this city, people won't remember the article is false. They'll only remember you're an Italian from South Philly and somehow you've been linked to the mob."

Tom knew the bloody history of organized crime in Philadelphia and the reputation created by the gangster element in the Italian-American population.

The repeal of Prohibition in 1933 caused the lucrative illegal liquor business to cease as a major source of revenue for organized crime. Waxey Gordon, the head of Philadelphia's Jewish mob, was tried and convicted for income tax evasion in New York by Tom Dewey, the U.S. Attorney. He received a ten-year sentence for earning two million dollars in 1932 and only reporting $8,125 in income.

With the elimination of Waxey, South Philly's Lenzetti brothers initiated a surge of murders in an effort to take control of the remaining rackets from the Jewish mob and the Italian Mafia. The Lenzettis were never "made" Mafia members, but they gave the Italian Mafia a run for their money in their attempt to control illegal gambling, drugs, union busting and prostitution. The Lenzetti brothers—Ignatius, Lucien, Willie, Leo, Pius and Teo—were all named for popes. Their fates would be those of criminals.

In 1932, the Lenzettis murdered numbers kingpin Mickey Duffy, Dennis Fitzpatrick's boss. It made Dennis a rich man and brought Eva the lifestyle she'd always wanted. Thereafter, the Lenzettis targeted Duffy's uncooperative bookies. They attempted to kill Giorgio DiSipio, who was running numbers at the time, but he escaped death when machine gun bullets perforated his hat and not his head. A shaken Giorgio went to Pius Lenzetti and pled for his life. Pius decided not to kill him since Giorgio was considered a small-time punk.

Following the Duffy hit, the struggle for control of the rackets between the Mafia and the Lenzetti brothers resulted in 25 executions. Finally, an uneasy peace was secured between Teo Lenzetti and Mafia leader John "Big Nose" Avena. Pius had John Avena rubbed out in August 1936. Pius was murdered in retaliation on New Year's Eve, 1936.

Later, Lucien Lenzetti's body was discovered at the corner of 9th and Christian Streets in South Philadelphia. Twenty-seven machine gun slugs had riddled his body. Willie Lenzetti was also murdered.

By the time the article about Tom's 'cousin' came out, the Italian Mafia, led by Joe Bruno of New Brunswick, N.J., had finally stolen control of both prostitution and the numbers rackets from the Jewish and Irish mobs in South Philadelphia. The Mafia had effectively eliminated the Lenzetti brothers as a force. They were now flexing their muscles throughout the rest of the city.

Unfortunately, since the secret Mafia society consisted of Italians, anyone in Philadelphia or any other large city who had an Italian-sounding name ending in a vowel was suspected of being directly or indirectly "connected" to the mob. This was a stigma which honest and hard-working Americans of Italian descent, like Tom, were unable to shake.

Tom was glad for his chance at retribution. Evans had thrown his name in among the scum of the city, and now he'd have his day with the media.

Alone in his office two days later, Tom was preoccupied—but not with the previous day's press conference, which had gone well. The reporters from Philadelphia's dailies were much more anxious to know the facts about the indictment of Evans than they were about Tom and his supposed connection to the Mafia. They couldn't have cared less if Tom had kin connected to the mob. Evans' indictment was the hot lead story and they knew it. Tom had refused to give specifics about the indictment, but he did tell the reporters it was for accepting bribes, enough to set the reporters to salivating. It also set off a hunt of information about Evans' past that Toms was sure would lead at least some of the reporters to uncover more of the deputy mayor's dirty deeds.

Tom dialed Hope's work number. He'd been calling her at work and left several messages for her to return his calls, but to no avail. He had given up trying to phone her at home; she wouldn't answer. After four rings, a female voice answered: "Midwives center."

"May I speak to Miss Daniels?"

"Miss Daniels is out to lunch."

Tom finally lost his patience. "This is Tom Rossi!" he blurted. "Why hasn't Hope Daniels returned my calls?"

"I don't know, sir. I did give her your messages."

"Would you please ask her to call me? It's urgent."

"Certainly, sir." The nurse hung up the phone and winked at Hope, who and nodded.

It wasn't that she enjoyed torturing Tom or making him feel bad. Hope wanted to protect him from the damage she might cause him. The life she lived prior to meeting Tom was riddled with the rough men from her South Philly neighborhood and the love she felt for Tom was almost like a shock to her system. She had become so cynical in her views of love and she had come to associate it with violence and disappointment.

*Go away, Tom*, she thought. *For everyone's sake.*

Holding red roses, Tom rang the doorbell to Hope's row house located on South Street near Broad Street in South Philadelphia. From inside the house, he heard a man laughing.

The door opened and Hope appeared. Upon seeing Tom, she became somber and quickly glanced over her shoulder at someone inside the house. Then she closed the door enough so Tom couldn't see beyond her.

Tom felt uneasy. Hope had never treated him with such indifference during the time they had known each other. He groped for words. "Er ... you haven't returned my ... my calls. I hoped to persuade you to ... change your mind."

Hope stood expressionless, with arms folded as she stared at him.

"Well ... I guess my timing stinks," he volunteered.

Tom tilted his head and, through the crack in the doorway, barely glimpsed the back of a man. "You have company?"

Hope abruptly responded. "I'm busy."

"Okay. How 'bout if we get together tomorrow—"

"As far as you're concerned, I'll be busy the rest of my life. Do I have to spell it out for you?" Hope turned, entered the house, and slammed the door shut in his face.

Tom was shocked. He never imagined his Hope could be so cruel. He turned and realized that an old lady in her 70s had witnessed the scene from the sidewalk.

"Young man," she said, "there *are* other fish in God's ocean."

Tom handed her the roses and lit a cigarette. "You're right. I'll just have to accept the fact the fish who just slammed her door in my face doesn't want to be hooked ... at least not by me."

That night, Tom had trouble falling asleep. *I've been dealing with heartache and disappointment since I was 5-years-old. But this incident is one that will be damn hard to forget. I just don't understand. I treated her with respect. I loved her. How do you do everything right and still lose?* Tom's thoughts turned to his problems with Evans. *What makes such a viciously bigoted man? Hell! I know the answer.* He thought back to his childhood, the fear he felt as an immigrant, and the people who tormented him and thought little of him because he wasn't from the "right" place. He hadn't trusted too many people in his life and now the trust he gave Hope was shattered.

*There has to be something else going on*, Tom thought. *Life can't be this cruel forever.*

# Chapter Thirty-Nine

In the days following his break-up with Hope, Tom threw himself into his work. He missed his chance to convict Lillian, but he was convinced that if he went back to the beginning, to where Giorgio first started his murder-for-money ring, he would find the answers he was looking for. The Rabbi told Tom about Mary Ashten and her involvement with Giorgio, so Tom decided to start there.

Tom made his way to police headquarters and took a look through Mary Ashten's file. Her husband, John, had been a baker for 20 years by the time he reached 34-years-old. His Polish parents had "arranged" his marriage to the then 17-year-old Mary Salenza. Mary was a tall, big-boned, strong woman who stood five foot ten and weighed 180 pounds. Her blue-gray eyes were accented by long, auburn hair.

The Ashtens and Salenzas had been good friends and neighbors who belonged to St. Ladislaus Catholic Church at Germantown and Hunting Park Avenues in Philadelphia's Little Warsaw section.

After Mary and John married, they bought a three-story brick row home on Hunting Park Avenue. In 1917, Mary gave birth to a son and then to a daughter in 1920. By 1934, John had settled into a boring, daily routine. He worked like a mule, 6 days a week, 12 hours per day. Sunday, his day off, he didn't spend at home with his family. Instead, he preferred to visit his friend Arnold Adamski, who owned a chicken farm at Joshua Road and Germantown Pike in Lafayette Hills, Pennsylvania. In the evening, John would return home from the farm, located on the outskirts of the city, with a bag of freshly killed chickens.

Over the years, the Ashtens befriended the Bolskys. Both husbands were bakers and, in May 1934, Giorgio DiSipio and Boris Feldman both shared a bed with Judy Bolsky. Judy told Mary the intimate details of her affair. Mary was envious in some ways; John no longer tried to satisfy her sexual needs. His work schedule had sapped him of any spark he may have had with Mary and he was now like a zombie living in her house.

After reading the background check, Tom had decided to meet Mary. He walked down the hall to the conference room where Mike sat behind a table. Across from him sat Joe Horner, flanked by "Rabbi" Feldman and Mary Ashten. Mary and Boris were exchanging heated insults when Tom arrived.

Mary, now 39, wore a black and white, vertically striped dress and a black coat with a fur-trimmed collar. A large black fedora hid her auburn hair and her blue-gray eyes stared at Feldman.

Tom read the detectives his notes. "Mary Ashten lives on Hunting Park Avenue in North Philly's Little Warsaw. On Monday morning, January 4, 1936, at 7 a.m., police found her husband, John Ashten, unconscious near the intersection of Joshua Road and Germantown Pike. He was rushed to Germantown Hospital, but died within hours. The Montgomery County coroner ruled his death a 'hit and run.' Mary collected $10,000 as a result of her husband's life insurance. Boris here said in a statement to detectives that he and Giorgio conspired with Mary to kill her husband and divide the insurance money."

Boris smiled at Mary, who ignored him. She lifted her nose in the air and folded her arms as if unconcerned.

"The next day," Tom continued, "Detective Horner here knocked on Mary's door in an effort to question her, but she refused him entry. She claimed she had pneumonia. A day later, Joe returned with a police surgeon. After examining Mary, the police surgeon authorized her arrest."

Mike smiled. "You forgot to add she's a very close friend of Judy Bolsky, who's already confessed to poisoning her husband."

With a sigh of exasperation, Mary crossed her legs, pulled her skirt tightly below the knees, and looked away from Mike.

"She's going to burn like her boyfriend, Giorgio," Mike said with a chuckle.

Mary pressed her lips together in frustration. "I don't know any Giorgio. It hasn't been proven my husband didn't die as a result of a car accident!"

"Do you deny knowing Boris Feldman?" Joe asked.

"I've heard about this ... this man," Mary said, casting Feldman a demeaning look. "But I've never seen him before in my life!"

As usual, the Rabbi just smoked his cigarette, blowing smoke in the office air.

"Judy Bolsky claims she referred you to Boris when you were having sexual problems with your husband in early 1935," said Tom.

"It's true. Judy did recommend him," responded Mary. "But I *never* went to see him."

Mike rose from his chair and leaned across the table, close to Mary. "After exhumation two days ago, our coroner concluded death was inflicted by a blunt instrument striking your husband's head *before* he got run over."

"Unfortunately for you," Joe interrupted, "Boris likes to get drunk and brag. He claims you like to bite your man when having sex."

Mary's beet-red face lit up the room, as Boris simply smiled.

Mary looked away from Boris in exasperation. "I demand to see my lawyer now."

"I'm going to outline what we have," Tom said, ignoring her last statement, "and ask you to think about it."

Mary shot back, "You have nothing on me and you know it."

Tom came to a page in his notes and read: "On January 3, 1916, Mary Ashten, 36, married her husband John, 54, a baker. The Ashtens lived in a modest row home near their friends, Henry and Judy Bolsky." Tom stopped reading. "Boris, why don't you fill us in?"

"Be happy to," he said. "In January—maybe February—1935, Judy introduced Mary to Giorgio and me. In a few weeks we were a regular quartet. At night, while their husbands worked in the bakery, we took the wives to the movies, restaurants and nightclubs."

"Mary, I have the affidavits of four people who will corroborate Boris' story," Joe volunteered. "He and Giorgio were seen socializing with you and Judy. There's no use in denying you know both men."

Boris continued, "One night, in April 1935, after taking both Judy and Mary to a club, I dropped Judy off at her house at about 2 a.m. Mary said, 'Look, I want to talk to you. Drive to 'Lovers' Lane.' I parked the car facing the Schuykill River near Midvale Avenue on East River Drive. A block of row houses was located about 60 feet behind us. I asked her what she wanted and she said, 'Judy told me how you and Giorgio made her insure her husband then gave her poison to kill him.' I laughed and said, 'You believe everything Judy tells you?' Then she says to me, 'You guys were screwing Judy. She can't keep her mouth shut. She gave me details about the sex and she even showed me the poison you gave her to put in her husband's food.'"

At Boris' accusation, Mary stood and slapped him across the face. "How dare you say things like that? I never said those things and I would never ask a toad like you to take me to 'Lovers' Lane.'"

"Oh, don't worry, Mary. I've got a lot more to say before we're done here," said Boris, amused.

"Sit down, Mrs. Ashten," Tom ordered.

Unperturbed, Boris continued his story. "I got suspicious, so I said, 'Are you trying to blackmail us?' She says, 'No! It's just that I don't want Judy's loose lips to get you guys executed. Maybe you should think about getting rid of her ... permanently.'"

The detectives shot Mary a look.

"I said, 'Lady, you've got a hell of a way to be a friend to somebody,' but I knew she made sense. If Judy was blabbing to Mary, then who else had she told? But Mary wasn't done. She said, 'I also want to get rid of my husband. I have a five-thousand-dollar insurance policy on John's life. If he dies by accident, I'll collect ten thousand. I propose a deal by which we would split the insurance fifty-fifty. Talk it over with Giorgio and give me your answer tomorrow.'"

The Rabbi enjoyed telling his story. As Mary squirmed, he tried to impress his listeners with his sexual prowess. "Mary snuggled up to me and placed her left arm around my neck and her right hand in my lap, brushing across my cock. I got a hard-on and decided to seduce her right there in the car. Then she got real aggressive. She unbuttoned my fly and lowered my pants and shorts. She squeezed my prick till I yelped, then smothered my lips with her tongue.

"We made a comical pair. I'm five-foot-five and Mary's five-ten. It's hard to get to each other the way we wanted on the little front seat. So I turned her around onto my lap and tried to get her panties and stockings down. But she got tired of me fucking it up and took them off herself. I pulled her dress up and slid my arms around her hips and tried to clutch her stomach. But my hands got caught between the horn on the steering wheel and her huge left hip. The horn started going off and next thing I know, people in the row houses are turning on bedroom lights. Mary panicked and tried to pull up her panties and stockings but, in the process, she leaned her hip against my hand, causing me to press against the horn again. People opened their front bedroom windows to investigate.

"Before we knew it, two cops were shining their spotlight through the windshield and into our eyes. After I did some fast-talking, one of the cops said, 'You're nothing but degenerates. Get the hell out of our district before we arrest the two of you for indecent exposure and public lewdness.'"

As Boris relayed his bungled attempt to seduce Mary, everyone in the interrogation room stared at her blushing face. She looked embarrassed, humiliated, and angry. She stared defiantly at Boris, but she couldn't hide her humiliation.

Boris, happy to have evoked such an emotional response, smiled back and blew smoke at the ceiling.

"All right, Boris, let's hear about the murder of John Ashten," Tom said.

Boris grinned at Mary again, whose red face looked like a volcano about to erupt. "Mary told Giorgio and me her husband made Sunday trips to visit a chicken farmer in Lafayette Hills. She said John usually left the farm for the journey home at 6:30 p.m., carrying a bag of freshly killed chickens. She said that would be the best time to kill him. After stalking Ashten for three Sundays straight, Giorgio and I finally cornered him. He came out of his friend's farmhouse and trudged through the snow toward his car. Giorgio hid in the dark near the house. I sat in Giorgio's Plymouth, about 50 yards down the road with the motor running and the lights out.

"When he put the bag of chickens on the ground, Giorgio suddenly sprang from the darkness and cried, '*Per tutti, primo o poi, vine il giomo della fortuna!*'"

"Every dog has its day," Tom said in translation.

"I couldn't believe Giorgio was yelling," said Boris. "I thought John's friend in the house would hear him. Giorgio beat John over the head with a pipe and blood gushed from his head. He fell unconscious, 6 feet from his car."

"Stop it! Stop it!" Mary started crying and pounding the table. "You're a liar."

"Please continue, Boris," said Tom.

"I was supposed to gun the motor and run him over, but I froze up. So Giorgio had to get behind the wheel and do it. He went over him back and forth about five times out there in the snow and caused a big, red stain in the fluffy white all around John. Then we sped off and Giorgio gave me half of his cut of the ten grand."

The temperature rose in Tom's office. Mary shed her coat and hat while mopping her brow with a handkerchief. The detectives loosened their ties. Only Boris looked cool and collected.

"What do you have to say, Mary?" Tom asked.

It took all the resistance she could mount to refrain from hurling curses at Boris, but Mary didn't break. "I think your ... your Rabbi is pathetic scum," she said. "Scum with an incredible imagination."

Mary turned her head slowly to Boris and gave him a contemptuous glare. "But then again, it doesn't surprise me. This low-life needs an incredible imagination to save himself from the chair."

"We looked into your finances," Mike said to Mary. "You blew ten grand in the span of a year."

"I can spend my money any way I please."

"Yes, you have a right to spend your money," Tom said. "The problem is we know how you spent it. You gave five grand to Giorgio and, lo and behold, lady, we know you gave your young lover three grand to start a bar, which went out of business in less than a year."

Tom then turned to his colleagues. "It seems right after the death of her husband, the prim and proper Mrs. Ashten, at 35, started a two-year relationship with a 22-year-old boarder in her home."

Mary's eyes went glassy as she stared at Tom in shock. The tears began to roll soon after. She blotted them with a hanky. "It's not a capital offense to have an affair with a younger man. You'll have to get Giorgio to testify against me because no jury will buy your Rabbi's testimony without corroboration."

Boris' eyes grew wide with indignation as she continued.

"And Giorgio's Sicilian," she spat.

Tom had had enough. He stood and pointed at Mary. "Mike, book this poor excuse of a lady for Murder One."

# Chapter Forty

Judge Crosby assigned himself to preside over Mary Ashten's trial. The indictment charged her with conspiracy and murder. Tom acted as assistant D.A. and Ben Silverstein as her defense attorney.

Tom had an uneasy feeling about the State's chances of securing a guilty verdict against Mary. *Hell, the Commonwealth's case depends on Boris "Rabbi" Feldman, a self-admitted murderer and conniver.*

The courtroom had an overflow crowd and everyone was sitting on the edges of their seats, waiting to hear the details of the case, waiting to be shocked, appalled, and delighted by the sordidness of it all.

They watched as the coronor's assistant, Henry Wadsworth, a thin man with a sunken face, walked the length of the courtroom and took the stand. Although well dressed, his oily hair shined with pomade.

His voice was soft and nasal and the entire courtroom had to lean forward in their seats just to hear him.

"As a result of the second autopsy of John Ashten, I have an opinion based upon a reasonable medical certainty that he died of a cerebral hemorrhage. He'd been struck in the head with a blunt instrument, cracking his skull in three places. It's also my opinion

Ashten was unconscious when he hit the snowbank before the car rolled over him."

The courtroom temperature became oppressively hot; the hot air system had gone haywire. The stink of sweating bodies, dunked in perfume, blanketed the air as Henry Wadsworth stepped down.

Ben Silverstein didn't contest Wadsworth's testimony. Instead, he lay in wait for Tom's witnesses. Just as Tom feared that credibility would be an issue with his witnesses, Wadsworth felt it would be his best chance to win the case.

Tom called Judy Bolsky to testify. She rose from her seat at the front of the courtroom like a beached whale. Her face looked pale, her large body was covered in a drab dress and her hair hung in long strands about her face. She made her way slowly to the stand, her body oddly majestic in its sheer girth. With very little prodding, she had pleaded guilty to conspiring in the murder of her husband.

"Both my friend Mary and I had affairs with Giorgio DiSipio and Boris Feldman," she testified. "Mary confided in me she felt extremely unhappy with her marriage. But after she had her husband John killed, I told her she'd burn in hell for what she did."

"And you know for a fact that she had Giorgio DiSipio and Boris Feldman kill her husband?" asked Tom.

"Yes. We all knew."

On cross-examination, Silverstein asked, "You admitted you poisoned your husband to death. Correct?"

Judy nodded. "Yes."

"Then tell us, why did you allegedly tell Mary Ashten she would burn in hell for what she did?"

"I did my husband a favor. Due to his mental illness, I sent him on to a better life. But Judy's husband, John, didn't deserve to die. He reminded me of a saint."

"How do you know Mary Ashten had sexual relations with Giorgio DiSipio and/or Boris Feldman?"

Judy smiled. "Because we all did it together; the four of us exchanged partners."

Court spectators laughed and gasped when they heard Judy mention the sexual arrangement shared by her and her co-conspirators.

Silverstein thought to himself, *Hell, with my experience, I should know better than to ask a question when the witness' answer is uncertain.* "By the way," Silverstein asked, "where do you presently reside?"

Judy smiled. "I'm a guest at the Pennsylvania State Mental Hospital for the Criminally Insane."

Once Silverstein was done with Judy, Tom wasn't sure how the jury would take her. He hoped her honesty about killing her own husband would lend her some credibility with them, but he couldn't tell. He hoped his next witness wouldn't derail the whole trial.

When Boris "Rabbi" Feldman rose to take the stand, Tom cringed. Feldman was grinning from ear-to-ear and looked like a scruffy vaudevillian preparing to perform for a crowd. *Please don't blow this for me*, Tom thought.

Boris testified about his relationship with Mary Ashten and how he and Giorgio were more than just her acquaintances. "Giorgio and I had a steamy affair with her. Judy, Mary, Giorgio and I had quite a bit of fun together."

Boris went on to recite his version of Mary's insurance death proposal and how Giorgio murdered John Ashten on a cold, wintry January night in the snow.

On cross-examination, Silverstein asked, "Do you admit you've pled guilty to at least four murders?"

"Yes," said Rabbi, while nodding his head.

"And whether you are sentenced to life or death depends on how well you testify against Mary Ashten?"

"Objection," shouted Tom.

"Sustained," ruled the judge.

Silverstein smiled. "I withdraw the question."

Mike then testified. "As a result of our investigation, we ascertained Giorgio DiSipio had purchased a 1932 Ford roadster in December 1935. The Ford's tires left a unique footprint."

Tom then drew "oohs" and "ahs" from the crowd when he produced large blow-ups of the imprint that the tire marks had left on the caved-in chest of John Ashten. He then produced a 1935 Ford Roadster tire and showed the jury how the tire's small v-type imprints compared favorably with the imprint on the body as depicted in the photo.

On cross-examination, Silverstein asked Mike, "Do you concede approximately one thousand 1932 Ford Roadsters had been registered in Philadelphia and the surrounding five-county area in 1935?"

"Yes."

"Then there could have been 999 suspects other than Giorgio who ran John Ashten down with a 1935 Ford Roadster. No further questions."

An insurance salesman testified that John Ashten was insured with a $5,000 life insurance policy containing a double indemnity provision in the event of accidental death.

Finally, Roger Moorehead, the branch manager of the bank where Mary cashed her two checks and obtained $10,000 in cash, testified.

"I remember the incident well," he said. "We had to cash a large sum of money, so after Mary left the bank alone, I became concerned for her safety. Through the window I saw two men waiting for her. They stood beside a car parked in the street. I saw Mary Ashten's young friend, Jack Karpinski, but I didn't know the identity of the small gentleman smoking a cigar as he stood next to Jack."

Tom had deputies bring a shackled Giorgio DiSipio into court. He pointed to the smirking Giorgio. "Can you identify this man?"

"Yes," said the bank manager. "He's the same guy who stood next to Mary Ashten outside the bank. I'll never forget his face," he boasted. "A short, impeccably dressed man. He's definitely the same guy."

Prior to cross-examination, Silverstein asked Giorgio to turn his back to the witness. He then looked at the jury and instructed Moorehead over his shoulder, "If it's definitely the same guy, identify the color of Giorgio's eyes."

The banker smiled then said, "Everyone knows the color of his eyes. Like most of those 'I-talians,' he has dark brown eyes."

"Are you colorblind, sir?" asked Silverstein as he continued to stare at the jury.

"Absolutely not!"

Silverstein smiled. "Mr. Moorehead, since you're not colorblind, this must be a case of mistaken identity. Giorgio DiSipio's eyes are not Italian brown ... they're hazel."

Silverstein had Giorgio turn around and face the jury. Giorgio smirked ... through hazel eyes.

Tom felt uneasy. "The Commonwealth rests its case."

Silverstein addressed the court. "The defense will only call one witness: Mary Ashten."

The tall, proud woman took the witness stand. Mary's combed back auburn hair gave her a matronly look. Her blue-gray eyes darted from the jurors to her lawyer. She wore her usual black cloth coat with the fur-trimmed collar and a large fedora.

"Did you conspire to have your husband murdered?" asked Silverstein.

Mary looked directly into the jurors' eyes. "Absolutely not; I'm a good Catholic woman and proud mother. I loved and devoted myself to my husband, despite Judy Bolsky's testimony."

"Do you deny you had an illicit love affair with Giorgio DiSipio and Boris Feldman?"

"Absolutely!" Mary shouted. "The so-called affair which Boris Feldman described is the product of his evil and sick imagination."

"What about the testimony of Judy Bolsky? She claims the four of you had sex together."

"Poor Judy is a sick woman. She's been mentally ill for a long time." Mary looked in Judy's direction with an expression that reaked of pity and derision. It was a look one might give to an injured puppy.

Judy rose so quickly it was all the bailiffs could do to keep her mass from making it to the witness stand. The gallery yelled words of encouragement and urged Judy to attack Mary.

Judge Crosby gaveled the courtroom into silence and ordered the bailiffs to remove Judy from the courtroom before telling Silverstein to continue.

"Your banker identified Giorgio as standing outside the bank on the day you cashed the check. Is he accurate?"

"He is totally inaccurate. The man's a tiny fellow, but his name is Rudy Jenkins, Jack Karpinski's partner in the bar they had purchased. I lent Jack $3,000 to invest in the bar with Jenkins." Mary stared at Tom. "Rudy Jenkins is not Giorgio DiSipio," she sneered.

"Thank you, Mrs. Ashten," said Silverstein, before taking his seat.

The crowd buzzed as Tom rose from his seat and approached the witness stand. His approach up to this point had been to project confidence in his witnesses and hope the jury would buy into it. But he was increasingly worried that the jury wouldn't trust Boris or Judy to tell the complete truth. *Maybe this one will go a little better*, he hoped.

Tom began his cross-examination. "Is it your testimony Judy Bolsky lied when she told the jury you confided in her that you weren't in love with your husband?"

Mary's face flushed. She waited a few seconds, turned to the jury and calmly said, "Judy Bolsky is my dear friend, but she suffers from delusions. She has been treated by a psychiatrist for the last four years."

Tom felt uneasy. The jurors looked confused. "Boris Feldman descriptively outlined how the two of you had sex together and how Giorgio murdered your husband. Do you deny that?"

Mary scowled. "Boris Feldman is an admitted murderer and a loathsome conman. I hope when this jury deliberates, they'll compare my lifetime of honorable deeds with his despicable and disgraceful behavior."

Tom was exasperated. Mary wasn't budging and he wasn't sure he had anything more compelling than testimony already given. "Finally, you don't deny you were the beneficiary of a policy worth $10,000 in insurance, do you?"

"My husband and I paid for a whole life insurance policy taken out almost 15 years before his death. Because my husband met tragedy, I must be further punished? Incidentally, the result of his first autopsy indicated he died as a result of a hit and run automobile, not some alleged blunt instrument which fractured his skull!"

Tom looked at Mary. "What did you do with the $10,000 in cash?"

"I lent my friend Jack $3,000 and I stashed away the rest of the money. As a matter of fact, I had to use all the remaining money to pay for my attorney in this case."

Tom tried once again to pierce her armor. "Why in the world would you cash a check and carry the enormous sum of $10,000 in cash? Wouldn't it have been simpler to write a check and keep the money in the bank?"

"Mr. Rossi," proclaimed Mary, "we live in Philadelphia. Between 1931 and 1933, half the banks in our city had to close their doors due to bankruptcy. Does that explain why I refused to keep my money in the bank?"

The jury deliberated for three days. Finally, at 11 a.m. on the fourth day, they reached a verdict.

Mary Ashten stood and faced the jury.

"How do you find?" asked the court crier. "Is the defendant, Mary Ashten, guilty or not guilty?"

The foreman, a man in his mid-40s, stood. He turned and calmly looked at Mary Ashten. "We, the jury, find the defendant, Mary Ashten, guilty of murder in the first degree and recommend death."

Bedlam erupted in the courtroom as reporters again raced for telephones to report the news.

Mary stared into space as though she were in a trance, and then started to sob into her handkerchief. Two matrons handcuffed her and led her through the sheriff's exit to the cellblock elevator.

Tom slowly packed the file into his briefcase. A sheriff's deputy whispered to him, "Tom, Mary Ashten's waiting outside the sheriff's elevator. She asked if you would please see her for just one moment."

Tom's curiosity, more than his compassion, compelled him to see her.

Mary stood outside the elevator door. Handcuffs shackled her wrists as a sheriff's matron stood behind her. Tears started to stream from her eyes when she saw Tom.

"Mr. Rossi, over the past months you're the only person who treated me like a lady and not like a..." Mary paused. "I just wish I could tell you the real truth in this case."

Tom gave her a cold stare, his eyes blazing. "You don't want to tell me the real truth. You want absolution and I'm not your priest."

Tom turned and walked out of the room, leaving Mary staring after him. The words of Judy Bolsky kept echoing in Tom's ears. *After she had her husband John killed, I told Mary she'd burn in hell for what she did.*

# Chapter Forty-One

*June 14, 1940*

The *Philadelphia Globe* headline read: "GIORGIO DISIPIO'S MURDER TRIAL STARTS TODAY! D.A. SAYS HE'LL PROVE STONER DIED OF HEMLOCK POISONING!"

By the time of Giorgio's trial, the circumstances of the case dominated conversation in Philly. Any widow who received money as a beneficiary of her late husband's insurance was a "suspect" in a "possible" murder conspiracy.

Giorgio had spent months in jail waiting for trial and had sat through the trials of Mary Ashten and Lillian Stoner. Tom was confident in his evidence against Giorgio, but he worried that Giorgio's defense team would use the testifying wives' participation in the crimes to discredit them. Tom was also still distracted by Hope's dismissal of his attempt at reconciliation. He worried about her future and her recent behavior. She wasn't the same Hope he'd fallen in love with.

In the days before Giorgio's trial, the Philadelphia media played it up as a contest between a "good" Italian and a "bad" one, with Tom portrayed as a shining example of what Italian-Americans could be if they kept from becoming "corrupted." It wasn't what Tom wanted the focus of the trial to be. For him, it was a matter of good versus evil. Giorgio had killed people for nothing more than money and now it was time for him to pay the price.

To Giorgio, the trial was the latest in a long line of disappointments in life. His father, his wife, his mother: they'd all let him down. He wasn't going to be like them. He wasn't going to give in to anyone and he certainly wasn't going to be a weak-minded rat like his father.

Spectators packed Courtroom 453. Giorgio's trial and the poison scandals had generated national interest. *The New York Times* ran daily copy. Judge Harry Crosby was presiding once again and he scowled at the court spectators and gaveled for order. A conspicuous sign on his bench read: "HARRY CROSBY—PRESIDING JUDGE."

At a table close to the jury box, Tom sat with Mike. Across the aisle from them sat Giorgio, smirking, next to his lawyer, John McBurn.

On Judge Crosby's orders, Tom had subpoenad Eva, Joanna and Rose "to testify if needed at the trial," as the judge had put it. But, instead of sequestering the wives in a holding room, Crosby again had the sheriff seat them conspicuously in the first row during the entire trial. They were placed close to the jury box so jurors could constantly observe their demeanor as a group.

Although Giorgio's indictment confined itself to the Reggie Stoner murder, Crosby allowed Tom, over McBurn's strenuous objection, to introduce evidence in three additional murders: the husbands of Eva, Rose, and Joanna. Naturally the jury heard about Giorgio's affairs with every murdered husband's wife, the forged insurance policies and how each husband died.

Tom made sure to connect the dots between Giorgio and each of the wives and their husbands. He avoided the salicious details of the sexual affairs, preferring instead to focus on the financial conspiracy and the murders themselves.

Reardon testified, "I executed illegal insurance policies for Reggie Stoner's life at the request of his wife, Lillian. Later, Giorgio told me Marion Moore posed as Reggie for the insurance physical exam."

Tom asked, "What was the relationship between Giorgio and Lillian at the time Reggie Stoner became insured?"

"Giorgio took Lillian to restaurants and clubs in my company."

Bertha Brooks provided additional evidence. "I saw Giorgio and Lillian kissing in his car outside Lillian's house, late at night, on at least four occasions. God knows what else they were doing."

Joe Horner explained, "Giorgio owned a 1938 Plymouth. It's the same kind of vehicle seen at Reggie Stoner's house on the night of death."

Mike testified, "Upon a search of DiSipio's tailor shop, we found a poison hemlock plant growing in his backyard. We also found a pipe used for the consumption of opium, which Lillian Stoner was addicted to."

Eva also testified. "Giorgio supplied the arsenic I used to murder my husband, Michael, and he helped me get him insured."

Claude DeLuca, an insurance salesman, took the stand.

"Did Giorgio DiSipio solicit you to get insurance on the husbands of these four women?" Tom asked.

"Yeah."

"Did you succeed in doing so?"

"I got insurance for everybody but Stoner. He died on me before his policy got approved."

Laughter filled the room. Eva smiled devilishly at Giorgio, who scowled back at her. He didn't find the trial funny in the least and the evidence was piling up against him. Giorgio had no plans to talk, but he didn't want to stay in jail either. He'd hoped that McBurn could pin the murder on Lillian and convince the jury that her trial had ended wrongly and that she should have been convicted. The jury, however, didn't seem to be buying McBurn's attacks on the witnesses' credibility.

As Giorgio sat stewing, Joanna threw her arms in the air in disgust and Rose took out rosary beads and started to pray for him.

Suddenly, Giorgio exploded. With his fists clenched and veins pulsating in his forehead, he jumped from his chair over the table and rushed at DeLuca, attempting to punch him. But two bailiffs had him long before the blow even came close to connecting and

Giorgio was relegated to screaming at DeLuca as they dragged him to his seat: "Liar! Bastard! Faggot!"

"Let him rave," said Judge Crosby, who seemed to be enjoying the spectacle.

After questioning his witnesses and resting his case, Tom asked for a short recess. He made his way to one of the offices in the courthouse and tried calling Hope once more. In the past few months, with the weight of trial preparation taking most of his time, Tom had felt alone and isolated from the people he cared about. He realized what he had lost in his relationship with Hope. "No answer. Damn."

After Tom returned to the courtroom, the gallery starting buzzing immediately. The moment had finally arrived. Giorgio took the stand, smirking like a confident challenger in a boxing match, waiting for the bell to sound.

"Did you murder Reggie Stoner?" McBurn asked.

"Nah!" said Giorgio. "Albert and Lily, they was my buddies."

In the back of courtroom, Lillian Stoner sat under a veil and hat, hoping to stay hidden from the crowd and media. At Giorgio's description of his relationship to her and her late husband, Lillian raised an eyebrow and smiled to herself. They were anything but buddies.

"What were Albert's drinking habits?"

"A heavy boozer ... just like Lily!" Giorgio said with a smile aimed at his former lover. The crowd followed his stare and found Lillian with her hands over her face. They erupted in gasps and catcalls at the appearance of Giorgio's lover.

Lillian stared at the floor, regretting her decision to watch the trial.

"Did you ever observe Reggie Stoner ill?"

"He was real sick with a bad cough before he checked out. He said cement dust was killin' his lungs."

Tom thought better than to object to hearsay evidence. Dr. Masters had already testified about Albert's cough and Tom felt his explanation would be enough for the jury.

"No further questions," McBurn said.

Judge Crosby interjected and asked Giorgio, "Where'd you get the counterfeit bills police found hidden in your car?"

Giorgio scowled at the judge and shouted, "I didn't keep no funny money in the car! The cops planted it."

McBurn, shocked at Crosby's intervention, stood and said, "Your Honor, I object to the court asking these loaded questions! I move for a mistrial!"

The judge waved McBurn off with a smile and flick of his fingers. "Motion denied!"

*What the hell is going on here*, Tom wondered. *The last thing I need is for Crosby to go on one of his ego trips.*

After Crosby shot McBurn down, Tom started his cross-examination. "Did you commit adultery with Lillian Stoner before her husband's death?"

Giorgio laughed. "Sicilians ain't gonna kiss and tell, Counselor."

The crowd roared as Lillian's face turned beet red.

"Why were you growing hemlock in your backyard?"

"I didn't grow no hemlock. The cops planted it in the yard, too."

"Really? The police planted the hemlock there?"

"Yeah, that's right. I wouldn't be surprised if you did it yourself."

"Do you own a 1938 black Plymouth?"

"Yeah. So do thousands of other people in Philly."

"Did you enter the Stoner house with Lillian Stoner the night before Reggie was found dead?"

"Yeah, I was there for a few minutes. I checked on Reggie for Lily. He looked sound asleep so I let him rest."

"Bertha Brooks, the Stoners' neighbor, testified she saw you enter the house. After an hour she fell asleep, but claims you never came out of the house during that time."

"Big deal. The old broad must be blind as a bat. My lawyer told me she gave you a statement I look like Rudy Valentino. Well, anybody can see I'm better-lookin' than Rudy."

"Reardon claims you told him your old friend, Marion Moore, posed as Reggie for an insur—"

"Look," said Giorgio, his tone now serious, "Reardon, DeLuca, Eva, Detective Fine, well ... they're all damn liars tryin' to set me up, see?"

Tom smiled. "Apparently this jury must decide whether all the Commonwealth witnesses lied, or just you, Mr. DiSipio."

Following Giorgio's testimony, Tom and McBurn gave their closing arguments. Tom tried, once again, to keep away from relying on the more glossy aspects of the trial and focused instead on laying out a step-by-step explanation of how Giorgio's affairs with married women turned into a plot to kill men like Reggie Stoner.

McBurn focused on the tarnished character of witnesses like Phil Reardon, who McBurn called "a greedy insurance man looking to save his own skin."

After two weeks of testimony, the jury was ready to decide the fate of Giorgio DiSipio.

The hum of the packed courtroom stilled as the jurors returned from their two days of deliberations. They wore solemn expressions.

"Mr. DiSipio, please rise," ordered Judge Crosby.

Giorgio rose, wiped his lips, and stared at the forelady.

"Have you reached a verdict?" the crier asked.

"We find the defendant..." the forelady replied while staring at the floor, "guilty of murder in the first degree."

"With what recommendation?" the crier bellowed.

Giorgio started to sweat and his hands began to shake.

"The death penalty," the thin, middle-aged forelady replied.

"Take Mr. DiSipio away!" said Crosby, a thin smile on his lips as he stared down at Giorgio.

Two deputies handcuffed Giorgio and led him past the jury box en route to the sheriff's exit. Slipping free from the deputies, Giorgio swung at the shocked forelady with his cuffed hands and shouted, "Bitch!"

The deputies lifted him off the floor and raced him out of court through swinging doors as flashbulbs lit up the room.

# Chapter Forty-Two

*May 5, 1941*

Tom sat in his office drinking his morning coffee and contemplating whether or not to run for D.A. After his relationship with Hope was splashed across the Philadelphia papers, he questioned whether it was the kind of attention he wanted. Now, though, with his succesful prosecutions of Mary Ashten and Giorgio DiSipio, he felt his chances were getting better.

Tom's thoughts were shattered when Mike Fine rushed into his office. "Tom! You hear the news?"

"What news?"

"You're not going to believe this." Mike held *The Globe* in his hands. "The Supreme Court granted Giorgio a new trial! They said Harry Crosby prejudiced the case!" Mike showed Tom the headline: "JUDGE CROSBY GIVEN REBUKE—SUPREME COURT DECREES NEW TRIAL FOR DISIPIO, CITING JUDICIAL PREJUDICE!"

Tom yanked the newspaper from Mike's hands and read aloud: "'The Pennsylvania State Supreme Court has granted a new trial for Giorgio DiSipio, reputed leader of the notorious South Philadelphia poison murder gang. Judge Harry S. Crosby sentenced the dapper former tailor, convicted of the poison murder of Reginald Stoner, to the electric chair. The Supreme Court sharply rebuked Crosby in a decision handed down yesterday in Pittsburgh.'"

"Christ!"Tom said as he threw the paper onto his desk. "I don't believe the bastard got a new trial."

"Not only did he get a new trial," Mike said, "but the Supreme Court lowered the boom on Harry." Mike retrieved the paper. "Listen to this: 'The law confers on no judge the power of pre-judgment. A defendant is not likely to receive a fair and impartial trial if a judge, from the beginning, exhibits an attitude that conveys to the jury the impression the accused is a man guilty of an atrocious murder, but we have to go through the formality of trial before we send him tothe electric chair. It is narrated in the early days of California, a judge said to a mob intent on taking a prisoner's life, 'Well, boys, let's give 'im a trial and then lynch him.'"

"Incredible!" Tom sunk back in his chair.

Lynn rushed into the office, followed by Pat. "Tom, I can't believe it!" she blurted.

"There's no way," said Pat, "they'll let Harry sit as judge for Giorgio's next trial."

"We're not going to retry Giorgio for the murder of Reggie Stoner!" Tom stated emphatically. Pat and Mike couldn't believe what they were hearing. "We're going to try the little bastard for the drowning death of Ralph Fermi!"

"Why the Fermi case?" asked Mike in amazement.

"With this trial being overturned, I have a feeling people may call the verdict into question. I just don't think we'll get an impartial jury for a trial involving Lillian Stoner. We have airtight witnesses in the Fermi drowning and Boris claims Giorgio introduced Fermi to him by saying, 'I'm gonna make a lot of money off this guy.' Then, the insurance man, DeLuca, will testify Giorgio paid for the guy's board at a whorehouse for six weeks. Giorgio also took out a policy on Fermi's life, naming the whorehouse madam as Fermi's cousin and beneficiary. He then paid the weekly insurance premiums on the policy to DeLuca. The jury will hear the testimony of Victor Bailey, an eyewitness to the drowning. Finally, we won't introduce facts about Giorgio's other killings, which might cause a second mistrial. "Tom looked at Pat. 'This time we're going to nail the ass of the Don Juan of Passyunk

Avenue to the wall forever! Tom looked at Pat. "This time we're going to nail the ass of the Don Juan of Passyunk Avenue to the wall forever

# Chapter Forty-Three

*June 15, 1941*

Sam and Mike had investigated the drowning death of Ralph Fermi during their larger investigation into Giorgio DiSipio. The 59-year-old immigrant had arrived in the U.S. in 1934 with no family. Within three months, he had suffered a crippling foot injury, which left him with a permanent limp. Ralph stood 5-foot, 3-inches tall and weighed 130 pounds. He wasn't educated in Italy and did not speak English. That, combined with his handicap, led Ralph to become a loner. Because of his disability, Ralph could only earn three dollars a week as a dishwasher and he spent his idle time fishing along the banks of the Schuylkill River's West River Drive.

During their investigation, Mike had explained Ralph's history with Giorgio to Tom. "Giorgio befriended Ralph and took him to a whorehouse in South Philly, where he introduced Fermi to a 70-year-old madam and paid her two bucks a week to cover his room and board. Ralph didn't have a lot of friends and he became both loyal and grateful." Mike had broken into a wide grin at the thought of Ralph in a whorehouse. "Hell, the old gent loved living with all those broads running around half naked."

Sam had found that Giorgio took Ralph for treatment to South Philly's Jewish Hospital, thereby securing his loyalty even more.

When Tom had asked how Victor Bailey had been dragged into the murder, Joe explained that as Giorgio secured Ralph's friendship, he met 31-year-old Victor, a machinist being paid only six bucks a week. Giorgio had taken Bailey out frequently to socialize, but always paid for food and drinks. On two occasions, he slipped Bailey ten dollars to help him with his rent.

"Did Giorgio set Victor up as an unknowing co-conspirator?" Tom asked.

Mike nodded and chuckled at Bailey's naiveté. "Bailey didn't question Giorgio when he gave him a twenty-dollar bill and told him to meet him at 7 p.m. on April 13, 1934. Giorgio said they were going on a fishing trip under the Girard Avenue Bridge. Bailey couldn't have been more wrong."

Two months after Giorgio's verdict was overturned, Judge Harry Crosby disqualified himself as the trial judge for Giorgio's second trial. He appointed Judge Edwin O. Lewis to preside, a man with an impeccable reputation for integrity and competence. Tom breathed a sigh of relief and the news. The possibility of Giorgio obtaining a new trial for judicial misconduct or a mistake had been curtailed.

As Tom prepared for the second trial, he had his detectives look into Rose Grady's whereabouts during the deaths of Marion Moore and Alberto Sacca. Although Tom was convinced that Giorgio played a major role in the murders of Reggie Stoner and others, he was just as convinced that there were other, more influential, conspirators.

*Who the hell is the Lady in Black?* Tom couldn't stop asking himself. The involvement of the Lady and her companion was a nagging thorn in Tom's side. He was also worried about Hope. He hadn't heard from her, or of her, in several days and he'd asked one of his detectives to check her house. The detective reported no activity at her place and Tome grew concerned as he headed into battle with Giorgio for a second time. Again, Tom prosecuted the case, and John McBurn represented Giorgio.

After opening arguments, the Commonwealth called insurance salesman Claude DeLuca as its first witness. "After the coroner declared Fermi's death accidental, who collected on the double indemnity policy?" asked Tom.

"The madam running Giorgio DiSipio's cat house. He had her falsely listed as Fermi's cousin," said DeLuca, who looked at Giorgio and shook his head.

"During the next week, did you have a conversation with DiSipio concerning another proposed insurance policy?"

"Yes. He comes to the office and hands me a $50 bill and tells me to insure the madam for a grand."

Courtroom spectators gasped as Giorgio burst from his chair. "You're a goddamn liar!" he shouted as he stood pointing a finger at DeLuca. "Say the damn truth!"

Tom smiled to himself. *The little bastard's again stealing a page from the righteously indignant defendant's book of trial tactics!*

McBurn grabbed his client by the shoulders and pushed him into his chair.

Judge Lewis wisely chose not to comment on Giorgio's outburst.

Tom called Boris "Rabbi" Feldman to the stand once more. Tom knew Boris enjoyed being an egomaniac, but he also knew that Boris made a convincing witness despite his criminal background. It was his openness about his own past that made him seem believable.

The Rabbi took the stand and smiled arrogantly at his former friend, the tailor. Giorgio clenched his fists and attempted to rise from his chair, but his attorney restrained him.

"Mr. Feldman, explain to the jury your recollection of the events concerning Ralph Fermi." Tom requested.

Boris smiled, once again enjoying center stage. He folded his arms, crossed his legs and looked directly at Giorgio. "Well, in February 1934, DiSipio introduced me to the cripple, Ralph Fermi. The guy couldn't speak English. Giorgio tells me, 'I'll make a lot of money off this guy.'"

Giorgio frowned at Boris, who looked back unperturbed.

"What happened on the night of April 13, 1934?" Tom asked.

"A fellow by the name of Bailey comes to my house a little after ten o'clock at night and pounds on my door. He was excited and out of breath. 'Giorgio just gave the cripple a cold bath in the river,' he says."

The courtroom spectators stirred at the revelation of yet another of Giorgio's murders. The courtroom reporters couldn't believe their ears. They had a real-life serial killer on their hands.

"What do you mean 'a cold bath'?" asked Tom.

"He drowned the poor cripple!"

Boris and Giorgio didn't take their eyes off of each other during Boris' testimony. Boris left the stand to raucous applause from the gallery, which had to be quieted with gaveling from Judge Lewis.

Following Boris, Victor Bailey, a handsome young man with long, straight, black hair, testified.

"Tell us what happened on April 13," Tom commanded.

"Giorgio tells me, 'Tonight at seven, meet me under the Girard Avenue Bridge … you know, on West River Drive. We'll be doing some fishing together.' So about 7:30 p.m., I'm sitting on the ledge of the riverbank, waiting for Giorgio. I look at my watch. He was late and I said to myself, 'I'll give him another half hour.' After all, it wouldn't have looked right if I left and he showed up. I owed the guy a lot of dough! Finally I looked up to see Giorgio with a little old man that he called 'the cripple.' The old man walked with a limp and stumbled a few times. They were carrying fishing poles.

"Giorgio smiled and says, 'Victor, baby! Say hello to my friend, Ralphie. He don't talk much English, but he's a hell of a fisherman!' The old man grunted a hello to me, baited his hook with a worm, and cast his line in the river. The old guy stood on the ledge of the bank, looking intent.

"Giorgio backed up slowly behind him and motioned for me to do the same. He raised his finger to his lips, meaning 'Keep quiet.' He pointed to me and then jabbed a finger at the cripple and then he jerks both hands forward in a pushing motion."

"What did you do next?" asked Tom.

"I was confused and scared. It suddenly dawned on me: Giorgio wanted me to drown the sucker. I started to shake and said to myself, 'If I don't do this, this bastard is going to drown me, too!' I panicked, turned and ran toward the road as fast as my feet would let me. I heard a loud splash and when I turned around, the cripple was desperately waving his arms and gasping for air in the water. Then his head disappeared and Giorgio started pointing at him, laughing and shouting."

Giorgio's hysterical shouts once again disrupted the quiet atmosphere of the courtroom. He jumped to his feet in a rage and ran to Victor with fists clenched.

"You lying goddamn bastard!"

The jurors recoiled and gasped in amazement.

Three court criers quickly grabbed Giorgio by his arms before he could strike Bailey. They carried the screaming defendant back to his seat, where a sheriff's deputy shocked the courtroom spectators by slapping Giorgio across the face with the back of his hand. The sound resonated off the walls as Giorgio sat stunned and subdued, sinking into his chair.

"Continue, Mr. Bailey," the judge commanded, as he stared at Giorgio. Although alarmed, Lewis merely shook his head in bewilderment. He didn't want to say anything that might appear as if he prejudiced the case against Giorgio.

"I got scared. I start ... to run." Bailey appeared nervous and visibly shaken. "I run back to the Rabbi's house and tell him what happened, about 8 p.m."

"Why didn't you report the fact that you suspected Fermi had been drowned to the police?" Tom asked.

"Giorgio gave me a $100 bill and told me to keep my mouth shut."

"Thank you, Mr. Bailey," said Tom as he made his way back to his seat. He braced himself for what he knew was coming.

McBurn rose from his seat and approached Bailey as a father might approach a child that's done something wrong.

"You pled guilty to conspiracy after the fact in the Fermi drowning murder, right?"

"Yeah," Bailey said, nodding.

"And you don't deny the judges delayed your sentencing at the request of the D.A.'s office? They wanted to evaluate your testimony against Giorgio in this case before making the recommendation of life in prison or a death sentence to the judges. Right?"

"Er ... I guess so."

"Boris Feldman testified you arrived at his house a little after ten on April 13, 1934. Is that true?"

"I don't remember the exact time."

"How long did it take you to get to Rabbi's house on the night in question?"

"Maybe a half hour or so."

"So, you left the drowning scene at 9:30 at night?!"

Bailey shrugged. "It could have been 9 at night."

"Oh, it was either 9 or 9:30, not eight as you previously testified?"

"So I'm off by a couple of hours. I still saw what I saw!"

Tom's head sunk at Bailey's testimony. *How can this guy be so stupid? We talked about all this.*

"Let's talk about what you allegedly saw," continued McBurn. "How far were you from the riverbank when you saw Fermi in the water?"

"About 90 feet."

"Is 90 feet about 30 yards?"

"I don't know. I'm not good at math."

"Did you see Giorgio push Fermi into the water?"

"No. I heard a splash then turned and saw Fermi drowning."

"How do you know Fermi didn't stumble into the river? You said he looked crippled and had a tendency to stumble."

"I don't know how he got in the water. But I saw him drowning, then Giorgio laughed at him."

"Your honor," said McBurn, "I would request the Court and jurors visit the actual drowning site at nine o'clock tonight for a murder scene viewing. The conditions at the death scene could be duplicated exactly. A quarter moon existed on the night of the drowning and there will be a quarter moon tonight. I propose to show it would be impossible for Mr. Bailey to see a thing while standing in the road 90 feet from the drowning site."

"Mr. McBurn!" Lewis gaveled the courtroom spectators to order. "What do you contend is the actual visibility of the site from 90 feet away?"

"At 9 p.m. on the night of the drowning, visibility could only be 30 feet at best, Your Honor."

"OK, Mr. McBurn. The court will reconvene promptly at 8:30 p.m. at the site of the alleged drowning under the Girard Avenue Bridge," said the judge.

Later that night, court personnel and the jurors gathered around Judge Lewis on the bank of West River Drive, under the bridge. McBurn had Bailey stand 90 feet away from the drowning site, where he said he was standing the night of the murder. The jurors stood directly behind Bailey, with Tom standing to their left. Tom took a glance at the spot where Bailey stood and said to himself, *Holy Christ! You can't see more than twenty to thirty feet in front of you. Everything's pitch black at the bank ... and Bailey's full of it!*

The jurors began talking among themselves and it didn't sound good to Tom. He heard several jurors saying, "I can't see a thing." After a few minutes beside the river, the court was dismissed and the judge ordered everyone to be back at the courthouse the next morning at 8.

Giorgio took the stand in his own defense and again dismissed the testimony of every Commonwealth witness as "damn lies."

Professional courtroom spectators were impressed with Tom McBurn's closing speech given on Giorgio's behalf. They gave two-to-one odds in favor of an acquittal before taking side bets. Bailey had broken down and cried on cross-examination. He admitted he had never seen Fermi in the water because of the darkness. But he insisted he had heard Giorgio laughing and shouting to Fermi, "Too bad you can't swim!"

After two days of deliberation, the jury reached a verdict. Tom felt uneasy because the jurors entered the courtroom staring directly at Giorgio, usually a sign of acquittal.

"We find the defendant"—the foreman, a white-haired gentleman in his 60s, stared directly at the judge—"guilty of murder in the first degree. We recommend death in the electric chair!" He then looked Giorgio in the eye and smiled.

Upon hearing the verdict, Giorgio let his hands fall to his side. The muscles in his face twitched and he shook his head from side to side in disgust as he lost control of his bladder. Suddenly, Giorgio had a crazed look in his eyes. He swung around and gave Tom a defiant stare. "Don't count your chickens before they hatch,

Buster! This is going to come back to you. This is going to come back to you in ways you can't imagine."

Tom responded with a smile. "Heaven won't hear the braying of an ass!"

# Chapter Forty-Four

*October 19, 1941*

Giorgio scribbled frantically on a pad at his prison cell desk. The wall clock on death row at Rockview Prison in Bellefonte, PA, read 11:45 p.m. His head shaved, he was now dressed in prison stripes instead of the custom suits he once made for himself. A priest stood behind him, praying the rosary.

Outside Giorgio's cell, Tom, Mike and a prison sergeant stood staring at Giorgio. Behind them, four guards watched as Giorgio mumbled to himself, "They wanna fry me. They don't care nothin' about me. Got to get time ... I ain't done my letter ... to the President."

"Confess your sins, my son," the priest urged him. "Ask for God's forgiveness."

"Governor James ... gotta write to 'im, too." Giorgio ignored the priest and stared into space. "No, wait. What's the name of the President's wife?"

The sergeant whispered to Tom, "This bronco isn't going quietly."

Mike glanced at Giorgio and turned to Tom. "We're observing one of the most despicable bastards born in our lifetime."

"You got that right," said Tom. "But I've still gotta try and get some answers from him."

Tom walked closer to the bars separating Giorgio from his observers. "Giorgio, you still have time to make up for what you did. You can still help me find the Lady in Black."

Giorgio stopped writing his letter. At first he was quiet, but then he started to laugh to himself, chuckling at Tom as though he were an idiot. Soon Giorgio's laughter was a deep, guttural sound that filled the hallways of death row.

"He's really gone over the deep end, hasn't he?" asked Mike.

"Giorgio," Tom said, "tell me what I need to know. You don't have to take all of the blame for this."

Giorgio came down from his fit of laughter and rose from his chair. He walked to the bars where Tom stood and stared straight into his eyes. "Counselor, you have no idea what you're asking, or what the answer would really mean to you."

"I'm prepared for whatever you have to say, Giorgio."

"What I gotta say is … forget about the identity of the lady in black. She's too smart for you. You'll never catch her. By the time you figure out who the hell she is, she'll be long gone."

Giorgio went back to his seat and picked up his pen. Tom nodded to Mike and followed him as they left the cell hallway.

The sergeant unlocked the cell door. The guards entered and surrounded Giorgio. He stared up at the sergeant then looked back down, going back to his scribbling. "Gimme a few hours. No, wait. Maybe I gotta—"

The sergeant nodded to the guards. They lifted Giorgio out of his seat as his pen fell to the concrete floor, splattering ink. As the guards carried him from the cell, his feet dangled in the air and he looked back at his desk and shouted, "Where's the governor? I'm goddam innocent!"

As the priest led the way down the hall to the chamber, he read from a Bible. The sergeant followed the four guards carrying Giorgio by his arms and feet.

Tom and Mike sat in the first of six rows of wooden folding chairs designated for witnesses. They sat in a small room that faced a large, windowed chamber. The old wooden chair inside had clamps on its arms and legs, with electrical wires attached. A large leather mask hung from the back.

Tom and Mike saw the guards enter, carrying the hysterical Giorgio. He looked at the chair and shouted, "No! Not me!"

In a flash, the guards dropped Giorgio into the electric chair and clamped his arms and feet. As the sergeant placed a mask over his head, Giorgio looked up and screamed, "You can't do this! I'm—"

Giorgio's words were muffled as the mask slid over his face. As he squirmed in the chair, becoming more and more frantic, the crotch of his pants became wet. Giorgio closed his eyes to calm himself. Tom leaned in closer to look at Giorgio. It was as if he had escaped his tormentors by leaving his body.

Giorgio took his mind away from the chair he sat in and the captors who pinned him to it. He thought of himself as Cavaradossi, Tosca's imprisoned lover, in Giacomo Puccini's opera. He recalled Tosca agreed to police chief Scarpia's amorous demands in exchange for her lover's freedom after a mock firing squad execution. Then Tosca stabbed Scarpia to death, only to later realize Scarpia had double-crossed her: The firing squad used real bullets and Cavaradossi had died.

Before Tosca committed suicide, she sang, "Vissi D'arte"—"I gave jewels for the Madonna's mantle, and I gave my song to the stars, to Heaven, which smiled with more beauty. In this hour of grief, why, why, o lord, ah, why do you repay me thus?"

Giorgio smiled to himself. He had achieved his life's ultimate satisfaction. *A beautiful broad gave up her life for me*, he thought. *I'm ready to die.*

The sergeant nodded to a man dressed in a suit, standing outside the chamber. He had his hand on the lever that was protruding from an electrical box, attached to the outer wall of the chamber. The man pulled the lever, creating a loud click, then silence. Giorgio's body quivered violently before becoming motionless.

Tom looked at the clock. It read 12:32 a.m.

Mike lit a cigarette for Tom as they stood outside on the prison steps. A reporter approached Tom with pencil and pad. "Mr. Rossi, any comments on Giorgio's execution?"

Tom looked at the dark, cloudy sky and exhaled smoke. "In the end he met death—which he so easily dealt others—as a shameful coward."

After the reporter left, Tom shook his head at Mike. "Giorgio certainly could be described as despicable, but you know something? In a sense, he was also one of the most amusing bastards I've ever met."

On the way home, a light drizzle fell. The monotonous sound and motion of the windshield wipers mesmerized Tom as he stared out the window. "I wonder what our girl Lillian is doing now?"

Lillian sat alone on her living room couch, drinking a gin martini. She looked anxious as she heard the radio announcer's voice: "Hello, there. This is John Facenda bringing you the news at 1:00 a.m. on station WCAU. Giorgio DiSipio, the leader of Philadelphia's notorious poison gang, was pronounced dead at 12:35 this morning."

Tears filled her eyes. She turned the radio off and began to tremble as she remembered the words of Judge Harry Crosby: "No one knows the secrets of the human heart. Lillian Stoner has been found not guilty. If, in fact, she had a part in the poisoning of her husband, she will have to answer to a higher judge ... the all-seeing judge ... whom she'll surely meet in her day."

# Chapter Forty-Five

Tom and Lynn were sitting in Tom's office, reviewing Joanna's file, when Mike entered. "Tom. I have good news and bad news."

Tom winced. "Give me the bad tidings first."

"Martin, Rose's lawyer, said she finally came clean. Because of embarrassment, she didn't admit it, but at the time of the Sacca and Moore hits, she was doing time in the Atlantic County jail." Mike shook his head. "She pled guilty to corrupting the morals of a 12-year-old girl."

Tom threw his arms up in the air in disgust. "Wonderful. And the good news?"

"Do you remember when I went through Sacca's belongings and found a few New York phone numbers among his telephone bills?"

"Only vaguely."

"Well, at the time I called homicide in New York and asked their people to check them out. They finally got back to me." Mike broke out in a grin. "It seems one number belongs to an Italian immigrant named Bruno Bianchi. He lives at the Walker House in New York City, apartment 529."

Tom's mind began to race. *Rose identified the Giant as a guy named Bruno from New York.* "That's interesting, but do you have anything else?"

"He's 51, 6-foot-4, has gray hair, a mustache and," Mike paused for effect, "keeps occasional company with a brunette of about 30."

Tom couldn't conceal his excitement. He hugged Mike and gave Lynn a passionate kiss on her lips. Mike looked away. Though Tom and Lynn's relationship was an open secret in the D.A.'s office, they hadn't made a habit of public affection.

"OK, you two, we've got things to do," said Mike as he handed Tom a holstered .38 with a shoulder strap. Tom slipped it on, put on his jacket, picked up his topcoat and marched toward the door.

"Lynn, go see Pat Connors," said Tom. "Tell him we're going to New York to try to finally nail this giant bastard and his bitch. Ask him to get clearance for us from New York Homicide to make the arrests."

Lynn recovered from the shock of public intimacy after a few seconds, and a look of concern flashed on her face as she nodded to Tom. She knew he practiced firing his .38 at the police firing range once a month, but to see him actually carrying a weapon made her aware that danger might be awaiting the man she deeply loved.

A sign above the entrance of the six-story high-rise read: "WALKER HOUSE." Inside apartment 529, at 8:00 p.m. on a Friday night, Bruno and his slender brunette woman were making love on their king-sized bed. A black dress, slip, bra, panties, stockings, garter belt and veiled hat lay on a chair in the corner of the room. The Lady's black, blocked-heeled shoes were on the floor nearby.

The Lady was on her back and Bruno knelt at her belly and licked the wetness streaming down her inner thighs. He grunted as perspiration formed on his forehead; the sounds of an opera aria from the radio stimulated their lovemaking.

Suddenly, the brunette became so excited she cried out in Italian to her lover, "*Batti il ferrfinche*"—meaning, "Strike while the iron is hot."

The giant of a man quickly lay on top of her as she grasped his large, throbbing organ and slid it deep inside her. He grunted and she shrieked as they reached sexual climax together. Spent, Bruno caught his breath and then sat upright. He watched his woman pour two glasses of wine, which they clinked in a toast to their union.

"*L'unione fa la forza!*" Bruno said—meaning, "Union is strength."

Bruno drank his wine in one gulp, but the Lady in Black still had some wine remaining in her glass.

"*Se ne fa un altió*" ("The king is dead. Long live the king!"), she toasted in return.

Bruno frowned at his woman, confused by her proverb.

As the Giant lay upstairs, Tom and Mike exited a cab and rushed inside the entrance to Walker House. They scanned for Bruno as they joined a crowd waiting for an elevator. The elevator doors opened and a number of men and women spilled into the lobby.

A woman who was exiting the elevator distracted Tom. She was dressed in black and her matching veil had been pulled down. Suddenly, Tom lost sight of her as the surging crowd pushed him and Mike inside the metal box. Tom tried to push past the crowd back into the hallway, but the doors to the elevator closed before he could make his way out. The elevator lurched upward and Tom and Mike braced for a confrontation.

After stopping at each of the first four floors to discharge passengers, the elevator mercifully came to a halt on the fifth floor, and Tom and Mike poured out into the hallway. Two couples turned left, but Tom and Mike followed an arrow that read, "500-560." It led them to the right and they cautiously walked the corridor until they reached 529.

The men held their weapons at a 45-degree angle and flanked the door to the apartment. Muffled opera music waffled up from under the front door and Mike leaned in close to listen for sounds of movement or speech. He looked at Tom and shook his head, indicating he didn't hear anyone. He slowly turned the doorknob, cautious not to make any noise. The door was unlocked and, using his hands, Mike signaled Tom for the two of them to crash in on the count of three.

Tom knew once they barged into the apartment, someone could fire a weapon and kill or wound him. He hadn't been involved in many raids or arrests and his heart was pounding inside his chest. He wiped the sweat from his brow and prepared himself for a fight.

At the count of three, Mike kicked in the door and both men jumped inside the apartment with guns cocked. The first room looked clear, as were the kitchen and bathroom. But when they arrived in the bedroom, they saw a massive, naked man lying motionless across a bed draped in blue and white striped sheets. His bulging eyes were fixed on the ceiling and his hand clutched a glass containing a swallow of red wine. They crept toward the motionless body and when they reached the bed, both Mike and Tom knew Bruno was gone.

Tom twisted the glass from Bruno's hand with a hankie and sniffed. "Cyanide. Either he committed suicide or ... someone poisoned him."

"I think suicide. He knew we'd get him one day," Mike said.

Tom noticed wet spots on the sheets. "He wasn't alone. There are two glasses out and I think he just had intercourse. Just look at his dick—remnants of semen." Tom frowned and sniffed. "And I smell perfume on the sheets."

Mike bent and sniffed the sheets. "You're right. Do you think our Lady in Black executed her boyfriend?"

"I don't know, but I wouldn't be surprised. There's something very cold about that lady and it doesn't seem any man is safe around her."

"Son of a bitch!" Mike slammed his fist against the night table. "This bitch is like vapor. Why can't we find her?"

"I think we did find her," said Tom. "In fact, I think she walked right past us on our way into the building. Let's go ... there may be someone who saw which way she went."

Mike and Tom ran out of the apartment and down the stairs to the first floor, skipping the elevator this time. When Tom reached the front door he found an elderly woman standing by the stoop. "Ma'am, did you see a woman come by here dressed all in black?" he asked.

"I did. She seemed very nice. She said that if two men came by looking for her, to tell them, 'Goodbye.'"

# Chapter Forty-six

Tom sat at his desk and stared out his office window, running through the previous night over and over again in his mind. He couldn't stop thinking about the moment he almost had the Lady in Black. *So close*, he thought.

Tom spun around to face his desk again. He put his head in his hands and racked his brain, trying to find something that would lead him back to the woman who'd taunted him for months. He thought of Hope and how much he missed her ... her perfume.

"Holy shit! Holy shit! No!" Tom wouldn't accept what his mind was telling him. It didn't make sense and yet it made perfect sense. She knew Italian, she grew up around hoodlums and degenerates, and she had a deep suspicion of men. But could it have morphed into something as heinous as murder? And how did she know Giorgio?

Tom's mind leapt back to the conversations he'd had with Hope about her previous boyfriends from South Philadelphia. *She said she'd dated a wannabe gangster who traveled with his own muscle. Could that be the Giant? Oh, my God. He was the one at her house when I went to see her!*

Tom thought of Hope's words and especially what she had said about Evans' insults. "I've been called worse," she said. Then Tom remembered that her favorite philosopher was Socrates. She explained that they forced him to drink poison made from the hemlock plant.

Finally, he recalled the scene in Bruno's apartment. Tom had smelled the perfume; he just couldn't place it right away.

Mike entered the office to see Tom pounding his fist into his palm. "Damn it! I know who she is!" Tom said.

"What the hell are you talking about?"

Tom turned toward his office window and stared out over Philadelphia. "How could I be this stupid?"

"What are you talking about?" Mike asked again.

"Hope Daniels, a/k/a the Lady in Black."

"Hope Daniels!? What? Hope was your girlfriend and she was a nurse. What the hell would she do this for?" Mike paused. "Tom, are you sure? Why don't you talk me through this so I don't think you're crazy."

"The Lady in Black's description fits Hope to a tee. She's a brunette with a dark complexion. She wore the same perfume that we smelled on Bruno's sheets. She's from South Philadelphia and speaks Italian. I never really told you this but Hope was roughed up by a few of her boyfriends when she was younger and I think it really messed her up. She trusted me … sort of, but I was never really able to get out of her what exactly had happened. Plus, when I told Hope that Sacca would surrender and identify the Giant and the Lady in Black, I must have tipped her off. I'd been tipping her off the entire time! They murdered him before I could get to him, just as they knew where Marion Moore was going to be. How do you think they stayed a step ahead of us this whole time?"

"What about those threats Giorgio made on Hope's life? If he was working with her, he wouldn't have done that."

"A well-planned decoy, executed perfectly between Giorgio and Hope. After the threats, no one would ever have suspected her. Do you remember when Giorgio was in his cell and he said that it was all going to come back to me?"

"Yeah, but that doesn't mean Hope was involved in all this," said Mike. "Besides, how would she have known all of the other women?"

"She just would've had to know Giorgio."

Tom was almost frantic, but Mike wasn't entirely convinced. "Tom, let's go see Hope and clear this up. If you still think she did this then ... then I don't know what."

"She hasn't been home for more than a week. I had a detective check her place."

"We'll check again anyway."

Tom had to confront the woman he loved. With Mike at his side, he pressed hard on her doorbell and kept his finger on the button. He felt angry and betrayed. But now he knew why she had to end their relationship.

Finally, they heard Louise's voice. "Hold your horses ... I'm a'comin'." She opened the door, saw Tom, and started to sob. "Mr. Tom! Ain't it awful?"

"What's wrong, Louise?" Tom asked.

"Miss Hope! She gone! She done had a heart attack in Harlem on Friday afternoon! They took her to her aunt's house here in Philly. She died Friday night." Louise sobbed into a hanky.

"Impossible!" Tom shouted. "We saw her last night leaving an elevator in Manhattan!"

"No, Mista Tom. She done died last night and her Aunt Betsy done had her cremated here in Philly at six o'clock this mornin'."

"Cremated!?" Tom said, shocked. He realized that he had screamed at her. "I'm sorry, Louise. I didn't mean to be rude to you."

Louise curtailed her sobbing and managed a smile. "Mr. Tom, not a day went by when Miss Hope didn't mention you. She'd say, 'Miss Louise, Tom's the one in my life.'"

Tom shook his head, too numb to say anything.

Mike suggested, "Suppose you invite us in. We'd like to get the details of what happened."

Louise smiled, nodded, and beckoned them forward.


Mike and Tom scrutinized the apartment tenant nameplates. Tom rang a buzzer beside the name "THOMAS MILLER, M.D." A buzzer sounded and they walked in to see a white-haired Dr.

Miller, in his 70s, poking his head out a door. He dressed in a crumpled suit, shirt and tie and his breath smelled of alcohol.

"Dr. Miller?" asked Tom, incredulous.

"In the flesh."

"I'm Tom Rossi, D.A.'s office." He flashed his credentials. "This is Detective Fine. We have questions about a death certificate you signed."

Miller stepped aside. "Come on in."

They entered a filthy apartment. Stacks of books were piled on the living room floor beside a dusty couch and a coffee table. Tom noticed cobwebs hanging from the ceiling and a nearby lamp as Miller opened a desk drawer and pulled out snifter glasses and a bottle of brandy. The glasses looked like they hadn't been washed in a year. Tom and Mike scowled at one another as Miller poured himself a drink. He asked, "Would you like to join me?"

Mike shook his head and smiled. "No thanks."

"So, what is it you'd like to know about my certificate?"

Tom handed it to him. Miller clicked on the desk lamp, read the piece of paper over half-moon glasses then nodded and drained his glass. "Hope Daniels. I remember her. A thin, colored girl." He giggled. "She had a tattoo on her belly which read, 'Hot Mamma.'" Tom knew Hope didn't have such a tattoo on her belly. "Are you sure you have the right corpse?" Tom asked. "Hope looked white."

The doctor seemed annoyed. "I may be 78, but I'm not senile. Her hair looked bleached blonde and cut real short, like a boy. Now ain't that unusual for a colored girl?"

"Uh ... where did you examine the body?" asked Tom.

"At her aunt's house," Miller said, glancing at the certificate. "Here it is ... Betsy Daniels. Told me her niece went to an afternoon jam session ... got pains in her chest. They took her back to the aunt's house ... she sat in a chair and died."

Tom took the certificate back and nodded with approval. "Thanks, Doc. I guess the aunt can supply details."

Betsy Daniels' row house was also situated on South Street, barely a block from Hope's home. With Mike beside him, Tom rang yet another doorbell. He didn't know of the existence of the tall, smiling colored woman in her 60s who appeared.

"Good morning, gentlemen."

"Hello. My name's Tom Rossi. This is detective Fine. We're here to pay our respects to Hope. She was a close friend and—"

The woman looked at Tom with a cold stare. "It's a little late for sympathy!" she said with more than a little hostility. "I'm Betsy Daniels, Hope's aunt. We cremated her this morning!"

Tom was surprised at her belligerent attitude. "Well, we—"

Betsy attempted to slam the door, but Tom wedged his foot in the doorway.

"You have two choices. Talk to us here or at Homicide, maybe even from a cell in the city jail."

Betsy backed away from the door and reluctantly showed them in.

Tom and Mike noted the expensive rug and furnishings as they took seats in the two chairs across from the couch where she'd positioned herself.

"Why did you call an old physician like Dr. Miller?"

"He's my family doctor. I didn't know my niece's doctor, or if she even had one."

"According to Miller, the woman he pronounced dead was blonde with short cropped hair and a tattoo on her stomach. We know it's not Hope."

"Dr. Miller's getting senile. Drinks too much."

"Why did you cremate Hope immediately?"

"If you were her *friend*, you'd know the answer. According to her beliefs, she had to be cremated."

Mike and Tom quickly glanced at each other.

Mike glared at Betsy. "How convenient," he smirked. "Do you own a car?"

"I sold it."

"Let me guess," said Mike, "a black 1936 Buick?"

"Everyone knows it."

Tom asked, checking some notes, "It says Jelks, the undertaker, verified Hope was cremated. Is he a senile drunk, too?"

"He knew who he cremated. He and Hope were distant cousins."

"Where was Hope when she had this alleged heart attack?" Mike asked.

"The Cotton Club in New York. Two people drove her to my house from there. Check it out."

"It's logical," Mike said with a sneer. "You wouldn't take a heart attack victim immediately to a hospital emergency room or a doctor. You'd drive her 90 miles from New York to Philly."

Tom had the final say as he rose. "I can't say it's been a pleasure. But the next time I see you, it'll be in jail for conspiracy to defraud and as an accessory."

Betsy stared anxiously at the two men until they were out of sight.

Mike and Tom stopped their car short. "What are you thinking?" asked Mike.

"It's complete bullshit," said Tom. "I'm just not sure why her family is going along with all this. Hope never told me about an aunt and this family doctor is a complete quack. He'd sign anything for some booze. And how did Aunt Betsy afford the furnishings in her house? There's no way a black woman is earning that kind of money in Philly. It had to be from Hope

"So what now?"

"Now we keep going."


Tom and Mike sat across the desk from Jelks, a well-dressed colored man in his 40s. Behind him a wall sign read: "JELKS' MORTUARY."

"Yeah, I'm positive we cremated Hope," he said in a hostile tone. "I've known her all my life. We were cousins."

"Why didn't Dr. Miller order an autopsy?" Tom asked.

Jelks laughed. "Shouldn't you be asking him these questions? Besides, you know how things are done in Philly. The city don't waste money ordering autopsies on niggers."

"Mr. Jelks, I know you're lying," Tom said. "Hope Daniels didn't look anything like the description given to us by Dr. Miller. She was in New York after the time she supposedly had a heart attack and now you're putting yourself in my line of fire because you're hampering an investigation. Now, do you want to go to jail?"

Jelks leaned forward in his chair. "Mr. Rossi, I don't know what your problem is but Hope Daniels was cremated right here this morning."

Tom tried one more time to bait Jelks into folding. "Mike, get a warrant for this man's office when we get back to City Hall."

Jelks didn't flinch and Mike and Tom rose from their seats and left the funeral home with nothing more than they had at the start of the day.

After leaving the mortuary, Mike and Tom stopped by the pub down the street and called Joe, who told Tom that Hope had closed out her bank account the week before, as had Bruno.

"Now I know why Hope refused to see me the last time I went to her house," Tom said, puffing on a cigarette as Mike drove him home. "Bruno's the man I heard laughing inside. At the time she must have been preparing to fake her own death. Hell! She deeded her house to Betsy and closed out a $20,000 bank account. It all fits. Bruno closed out a $15,000 bank account the day before being murdered."

"She probably conned Bruno into thinking they would flee together," Mike suggested, "but murdered him instead and then stole his cut of the money: thirty-five grand. I could go to Miami and live in a mansion like Al Capone did with that money."

"Yep. It all makes sense now," said Tom. "Hope and Bruno were pretty clever. They set Giorgio up to do all the dirty work, knowing he'd never squeal, even if he got caught. Remember, Giorgio had eighteen grand in the bank when arrested. If he didn't get caught, Hope would have cleaned him out and then murdered him, just like Bruno."

Tom went silent. His prosecutor's mind stopped moving and his heart ached at what he didn't want to believe was happening. *How did I not see this?* But he knew that Hope had hidden her secret life well. When he thought back on their time together, he realized how much he didn't know about her. So busy with his job, Tom didn't have time to really pay attention to Hope's life outside of their relationship.

"You know, Mike, there were days when I couldn't get a hold of her and I didn't think twice about it because I was so busy. She must have been meeting with the other wives or Giorgio. I guess he really did get the last laugh."

"Why don't we demand an inquest to prove Hope didn't die?"

"We'd look like fools. Miller's a senile old drunk and we couldn't prove Jelks didn't cremate her unless we had her alive and well in cuffs."

Tom leaned his head back against the seat and took it all in. He closed his eyes and let go of the idea of Hope that he'd held onto for so long. *She really is gone.*

# Chapter Forty-Seven

*December 2, 1941*

Lynn entered Tom's office and handed him a large envelope before leaving again. The envelope read: "To: Thomas Rossi, Esquire, District Attorney's Office, City Hall, Room 600, Philadelphia, PA, 03. <u>Personal and Confidential</u>."

Tom opened it and shook its contents onto the desk. A newspaper clipping and the necklace he had given to Hope Daniels fell out. The envelope also contained an article about witchcraft. "PHILADELPHIA PUBLIC LEDGER—MAY 5, 1902. CATHERINE DEMEDICI: AN EVIL WITCH FROM EVIL TIMES, 1300 A.D."

Tom sniffed the bouquet emanating from the newspaper and smiled. He recognized the perfume.

His eyes traveled to the handwriting at the bottom of the article. "Tom, I never meant to hurt you or even get involved with you. I didn't choose to fall in love with you. It just happened and I'm glad it did. You're a good man and I hope one day you'll understand.

"This is an old article about an Italian witch named Catherine DeMedici, an expert on poison concoctions, their potency and symptoms. She formed a wives' club in Florence. Soon, her club consisted of young, wealthy widows. Her scheme was not discovered until after her death. I thought you'd find it interesting. But, remember, if you take love from life, you take away all its pleasures."

Tom opened the locket, studied Hope's picture, shook his head and smiled.

# EPILOGUE

Seventeen wives were arrested and charged with murdering their husbands in Philadelphia between 1938 and 1940. Sixteen were indicted but two were freed for lack of autopsy evidence.

Twelve wives were found guilty or pleaded guilty to murder. None were executed.

Two wives were found not guilty after jury trials.

In addition to the wives, a total of twelve male and female conspirators were convicted of murder and conspiracy to murder. Two were executed, six were sentenced to life in prison, and four were given lesser terms.

Lawyer John McBurn became a Justice of the Pennsylvania Supreme Court.

Peter Martin became Philadelphia's first colored judge of the Court of Common Pleas.

After the Pennsylvania Supreme Court decision, Harry Crosby became known as "the hanging judge."

Phil Reardon and Claude DeLuca were granted immunity for agreeing to testify as Commonwealth witnesses, but their insurance licenses were revoked by the Insurance Department of the State of Pennsylvania.

Victor Bailey paid a terrible price for accepting $100 from Giorgio to buy his silence in the drowning of Ralph Fermi. He spent years in prison before his life sentence was commuted in 1958 when he was 57-years-old.

The 70-year-old madam who collected Fermi's insurance check for Giorgio served one year in Moco.

Physician Lawrence Goldberg was sentenced to ten-to-twenty years after pleading guilty to second-degree murder. Authorities paroled him on December 8, 1949, after he served almost ten years. In 1953, while dying, he petitioned the Pennsylvania Pardon Board for a pardon, hoping, "I may meet my Maker with a free conscience." The board rejected his petition, explaining: "It would seem it's something between him and his Maker."

Dr. Goldberg's co-conspirator, Mike Gold, got lucky. Another judge only sentenced him to two-to-twenty years for conspiracy and not murder. After serving two years of the sentence, the parole board granted him parole.

Sadie Lamb served four years of a three-to-twenty-year sentence for agreeing to betray her lover Howard Rice and implicate Paul Squilla and Carmine DeLeo for the murder of her husband. In March 1943, at the age of 50, she won her freedom.

The price Howard paid for his love for Sadie proved costly. He served nineteen years of a life sentence and made parole in April 1958 at age 48.

In October 1940, Paul "The Cat" Squilla and Carmine "The Mouse" DeLeo were sentenced to life imprisonment for the murder of Robert Lamb. On October 18, 1941, the day of Giorgio's execution, Paul viciously cut out Carmine's eye. Two hundred prisoners and guards in the yard at Philadelphia's Eastern State Penitentiary witnessed the heinous act. Paul received an additional three years for committing mayhem. He died in prison in 1953 at age 70.

The one-eyed Carmine got transferred to Western State Penitentiary in Pittsburgh to finish his life sentence. He also died in 1953 at age 69.

Boris "Rabbi" Feldman received a life sentence on January 7, 1942, after pleading guilty to murder. He died in prison on February 9, 1954, at age 67.

Deputy Mayor Bill Evans pleaded guilty to bribery. In return for promising to never again engage in politics, his two-year sentence was suspended.

Giorgio DiSipio's wife refused to claim his body. The Commonwealth of Pennsylvania paid for his burial.

Mary Ashten served 17 years of a life sentence. She returned to her neighborhood, but neighbors and friends shunned her. Her application to become a Catholic nun was rejected. She died as a hermit at 70.

Joanna Napoli changed her plea to innocent at trial. She blamed her husband's murder solely on Giorgio DiSipio. Her defense was that she was so in love with Giorgio, she became temporarily insane at the time of her husband's murder. The jury didn't believe her. They found her guilty of murder and recommended she be sentenced to death. One day before her scheduled execution, the governor commuted her death sentence. Joanna had a heart attack the same day but survived to serve 17 years before being paroled.

Eva Bell died in prison while serving 14 years of a life sentence at age 58, the only convicted wife who refused to petition the governor for clemency. Prison matrons claim she slowly died of a broken heart after Giorgio's execution.

Incredibly, a jury found Rose Grady not guilty of murdering her third husband, old man Conte. Her first husband was embalmed with arsenic, making prosecution impossible. No corpse was available to be examined after a drowning killed Rose's second husband. She moved back to her hometown in New Jersey after the verdict.

Lillian Stoner also chose to move out of Philadelphia. No one heard from her again. She died in Bucks County, Pennsylvania, of natural causes.

In December 1942, a lady wearing sunglasses and resembling Hope Daniels appeared at an outdoor café in Buenos Aires. She sipped Napoleon brandy as she sat with a young gentleman.

Tom Rossi decided not to run for D.A. Instead, he founded one of Philadelphia's most successful and prestigious law firms. He also married his longtime secretary, Lynn Sullivan, in September of 1943. They had a baby boy and twin girls.

Fini

# ABOUT
# THE
# AUTHOR

Gus Pelagatti is a practicing trial lawyer with over forty-three years of experience trying civil and criminal cases, including homicide. He is a member of the Million Dollar Advocates Forum, limited to attorneys who have been recognized as achieving a standard of excellence as a trial lawyer. He spent years researching the murder scandals and interviewed judges, lawyers, police and neighbors involved in the trials. He was born and raised within blocks of the main conspirator's tailor shop and the homes of many wives convicted of murdering their husbands.

Gus lives with his wife, Rita, in Gladwyne, Pa. and is still an active trial attorney in Philadelphia.

Printed in the United States
116451LV00003B/14/P